THE

Bachelor's
GUIDE TO
Post-Apocalyptic
Success

*Join the mailing list at **palmcirclepress.net** to receive advanced notice of new releases and for the chance to receive FREE books.*

THE
Bachelor's
GUIDE TO
Post-Apocalyptic
Success

RORY PENLAND

PALM CIRCLE
——PRESS——

Printed in the United States of America

ISBN: 978-1-7359325-3-8

Book Design by Oladimeji Alaka

Interior Layout by Rachel Greene for elfinpen designs

Published by Palm Circle Press
www.palmcirclepress.net

This book is dedicated to you – the reader.
For only you (and you alone)
can make a difference.

Foreword

Having been a writer for over twenty-five years and having only sold a single manuscript in that time (the original script for the Artisan Films 2002 release *Deadly Species)*, I have done what most writers would not allow themselves to do. I found a manuscript (of sorts) and decided to market it with my name on it.

I should not say I found it by myself. My older brother Raymond and I found it while visiting him at his home in Florida. Though we found it together, he agreed to let me have it and the rights to it are solely mine. With that said, I will quickly relate to you how the discovery came about.

My brother and I were walking along the beach near his house in Key Largo. Floating in plastic Tupperware-style containers were several journals. The containers were fastened together with plastic wire and it was a miracle we were the first to find them as they were large and quite visible.

This manuscript was the first of those journals written by a man who called himself "Brandon Hoffner." He was supposedly a man living many years in the future. He claimed the world as we knew it would come to an end on February 17, 2034. This was obviously the work of a crazed lunatic, but the journals were, in this humble writer's opinion, fascinating and an incredible study of an insane and delusional mind. The details of what he wrote about his world and the choices he made, right and wrong, were quite amazing.

In the first journal (and in later manuscripts) he mentioned placing his pages into plastic containers and sending them afloat in the Bermuda Triangle in the hopes of warning mankind of their evident and impending doom. This was deliciously unrealistic and typical of the childish workings of an unhinged soul. Whoever wrote these original works had thought out every last infinitesimal detail to pull the reader into his mad alter reality. His prose was carefully thought out and at times very amusing. The writer obviously did research on cloning, cryobiology, and a variety of other subjects to be able to explain many situations he wrote about here. I even found myself at times wondering if it were all possible.

I remembered stories about the mysterious "Devil's Triangle" from my childhood, but those theories of time portals, UFO abductions, and strange magnetic fields were all satisfactorily disproved by scientists decades ago. The Bermuda Triangle off the coast of Florida was no more a portal to another time than my bedroom wardrobe. One thing was certain, at least in my mind. The subtle (and often times not so subtle) underlying messages and tones in these pages I felt were important, regardless of whom their author truly was. In this age of ozone depletion and global warming we didn't need to be careful and take care of what we had, so there was a tomorrow. This was another reason why I decided to try and have this manuscript published.

I did not have experts or scientists inspect the original journals to find out how old they were, but they did appear fairly weathered. I myself found it an enjoyable, albeit bizarre, read.

I hope you will enjoy it too. If the release of these notes proves fruitful, I intend to release more of this author's journals to the world at later dates.

Rory Penland, 2018

THE

Bachelor's

GUIDE TO

Post-Apocalyptic

Success

First Day: Reorient Yourself.

I was somewhat stunned when I awoke suddenly to an empty world. By empty, I do not mean it was devoid of material things such as cars, clothes, corning ware, and currency. It was merely lacking any other living thing. This was immediately apparent to me, Brandon Hoffner, forty-something (okay, pushing fifty) ex-baseball star, and ex-entrepreneur. Though the skies were very blue, and the air was very clear, no birds flew through it. Though the grass and trees grew high and green, no butterflies or other insects made their way about. Though the sun shined brightly, and the temperature was almost a perfect 76 degrees Fahrenheit, no one walked the streets. It was eerily quiet. A world without sound.

Now, history withstanding, I am an average guy about six-feet tall and of steady build, and I was beginning to think I was experiencing a form of mass hallucination. A mental mirage, if you will, brought on by a combination of malnourishment and oversleep. Oversleep being *cryo-sleep.*

As I slowly arose from my frozen chamber of slumber, I tried to make a sound, but nothing came out. "My larynx might be paralyzed," I remember thinking to myself. "I hope it works itself out soon."

Standing was another problem. I hadn't done it for a long time, so I collapsed immediately (and repeatedly) upon trying until I finally used my hand to steady myself by grabbing onto the side of my cryotube. It would be several hours before I could actually take steps and walk. I even used an intravenous bag holder as a cane to steady myself.

"Shit!" I thought. "I wonder how long I have been out?"

The room was dark and musty. I checked the status of my cryochamber. The panel blinked, gray digital letters on a semi-luminescent, green background. The following words appeared, moving gently from right to left in the panel window: "BATTERY POWER LEVEL – CRITICAL."

"Figures," I thought to myself. Then I tried to harken back. "What was it the doctor had said? Even if everything comes to a halt, the backup battery system will keep you alive for another sixty years." The statement was made for my comfort's sake as well as to finalize the sale, no doubt. I was pretty sure those were his exact words.

I continued to stumble about until I found a gurney with a green cotton sheet on it. I quickly yanked the cloth off the gurney and wrapped it around my naked body like a toga because my ass was getting cold. I practiced walking around the medicinal hallways until I found my way to an elevator. There was no power anywhere, it seemed. No water either. Not a drop. Nothing worked. Getting down four flights of stairs took me quite a while. I actually faltered twice, nearly landing face-first onto the hard, concrete steps.

In the front lobby, there were no doctors, no security staff, absolutely no one in sight. The building was completely deserted, yet it was daylight. The outside grounds, which I could see clearly through what were once the glass windows functioned as the front wall of the building's front lobby, were also completely empty. A strange thought hit me. It felt like 4:30am when you are on your way home after a bender and there is no one else on the road, but I knew it was not 4:30am because the sun was just going down.

As I was barefoot and there was glass all over the floor, I had to go out through a side door. When I made my way back out to the front, I noticed the only sound was the light rustling of the trees and bushes as the slight wind blew through them. To a nature lover, it would have been pleasant, but at this moment in time, it was somewhat unnerving to me. I looked up and read the sign over the door, and true to my expectations, it read: "THE ATLANTA INSTITUTE OF CRYOGENICS."

"I wonder how many others are frozen in there?" I shook off the thought. "First things first! I need to find something to eat." I walked slowly and purposefully up Jefferson Davis Avenue, looking around for a grocery store or supermarket. When I found a Piggly Wiggly, the doors were open, but shelves were empty. I continued until I found a Circle K convenient store. Though the store stood soundly, the shelves again contained nothing. No food and nothing to drink. I found the same thing in every food store I went to. Whatever happened had caused everyone to loot the stores. I envisioned crazed people smashing glass storefronts and taking whatever they could get their hands on in a mad frenzy.

"What the hell happened?" I remember saying to myself. It was a question that still haunts the recesses of my mind, even as I write this. "Did the bombs go off? Did an asteroid hit the planet? Did a deadly plague wipe out all life?"

After depressing myself for several moments with these thoughts, I went off on my next venture—to find a department store where I could search for clothes. What little was left, was dusty, musty, mildewed and totally unappealing.

After looking through the entire establishment, I managed to find some usable clothes stored in plastic in some boxes which had been tucked away in a back stockroom. Luckily for me, the looters didn't get as far as the back stockroom at this particular store. I packed a rolling collapsible suitcase bag thing with whatever fashionable garments fit me, mostly t-shirts and jeans (my favorite outfit) and found a few pairs of some suitable shoes in my size. As pickings were slim, the shoes were all high-top basketball sneakers in bright-neon colors, but I figured you don't stand out when no one else is around. I needed protection for my feet, especially with the broken glass around. One problem solved but so many more to deal with. I needed to find food and lights of some sort. It was dark now and though my eyes were adjusted, I had no flashlight, or even candles to light my way. I tripped and slipped on things left and right.

Realizing it was late in the evening, I decided to go to sleep and continue my quest for useful items the next morning. I was so terribly hungry. I remembered simple things that pleased me, like warm fresh baked bread dripping with butter (not that fat-free margarine shit), fried chicken and ice-cold beer. Hell, even a cold cola would hit the spot, but it was not to happen this day.

I slept on collapsed cardboard boxes and clothes in the stockroom. During the early morn, I woke up only once, just before the sun came up, to relieve my body of some water. I decided to urinate in the corner of where I was as there was no one around to chastise me for it.

Though I could not remember any dreams from my many years in cryogenic slumber, I dreamed that night of playing with little children in a park. I also had a nightmare about walking outside into a world full of snakes. There were snakes all over the ground and in the trees. They were different shapes and sizes and they were everywhere. Just for the record, I really hate snakes. I lost my mind when I was around them. It was a definite phobia.

Second Day: Forage for Food and Water.

I wish I could say the previous five pages of banter was a nightmare and I was home in Kansas again with Auntie Em. I wish I could say I woke up to the sound of roosters crowing. Unfortunately for me, the world was just as empty, if not more so, than when I'd left it a few hours before.

Top of the list of activities for the day was finding food. That was paramount to my survival and my stomach telling me to find something edible fast. Last night's exploration proved fruitless, so I decided to go to the edge of the city and see if I could find anything growing in the nearby fields. The fastest way to get there would be to find some wheels of some kind.

As most cars would be locked, I hunted for a motorcycle. After a two-hour search, I found one parked in a garage and it did not take me much longer to find the keys on a nearby key rack on the wall.

I checked the engine, and everything looked surprisingly in order. A search for a gas can with anything in it but dust was a joke, and I ended up walking the Harley to a gas station about three blocks away.

The windows were already broken so it was easy to get into the station. The pumps were dry as I expected, but I had an alternate plan. When I was a kid, we used to watch the gas man come in his big tanker truck and fill up the large tanks at the edge of the station. If there was any gas in those tanks, I would find it. I figured out how to open the tanks and I almost laughed out loud (still having trouble with the larynx thing) when I couldn't smell petrol fumes. I abandoned the Harley and found a bicycle with a large basket on the front. It would have to do the job. It was way past time for me to eat.

I peddled my un-Harley-like ten-speed with what little energy I had. I smiled from ear-to-ear at my ridiculous situation because no one was here to see it or criticize me. I clumsily navigated onto the empty highway that took me out of town. An hour later, I found a field with some corn in it. Hallelujah! Lunch was served. I found a citrus orchard too, growing wild and uneven, no longer growing in uniform rows as they were not planted by farmers. The last treasure of the day stumbled across a pear tree as I returned to the city. I was saved. I could sustain myself if I was smart and careful. I could plant my own gardens in town.

As I rode back, a dilapidated sign caught my eye about twenty minutes out of town. It read: "TAGGART SPRINGS" with a big blue arrow pointing. I took a ride down a sideroad next to the sign until I found the cleanest-looking, then kicked myself in the ass for not bringing a container for water. After standing there, looking at the peaceful, quiet stream, I finally dipped my hands in and drank. My God, it was so good. My body screamed for it. I took off my new stolen clothes and swam in them until my fingers were suitably wrinkled. There were no birds, no bugs, no animal sounds to speak of. In retrospect, that was a little disheartening, but the water felt so good I just enjoyed that fact for a moment. Still, for some unknown reason, the hair on the back of my neck stood up and I decided to exit the small paradise.

When I returned to town, the sun was on its way down again. I am not sure why, but I returned to the house where I had found the Harley. It was a nice house, not too fancy, and a sense of honor or maybe guilt made me feel it was where I should stake my claim. I found a window unlocked and got in. I unlocked the doors and opened all of the windows. I found no evidence of anybody in the house. It had been deserted. I went and gathered my food.

Inside, my fears were confirmed. No power and no water from any faucet. I ate a dinner of oranges and pears, leaving the rest of the food items on the counter in the kitchen. I had to remove an eighth of an inch layer of dust from the table and counter, but the kitchen itself was still relatively functional. I found a pack of matches and lit a candle after the sun went down.

I looked about the house for anything of interest and found a newspaper with the date "February 14, 2034." That was about five years after I had been put into my cryogenic state. There was nothing seriously unusual in the paper's headlines aside from the obligatory tension and impending war between super countries. The problems in the Middle East were escalating. Again, no surprise there.

I decided to walk around the neighborhood to gather more input. It was not easy to navigate through the town at night. There were no streetlights working and even though the moon was out, and my eyes had plenty of time to adjust, the whole city was pitch black. You didn't realize how useful and necessary things like streetlights were until you didn't have them.

Amazingly, I found a small library a few blocks from my new dwelling. I broke in and lit my candle. I looked around. The magazines and newspapers were dated "February 2034," so I figured whatever happened occurred around that time. As was the case with the paper at the house, there was no clue as to what caused this once bustling metropolis to become a ghost town.

I pondered well into the night about what books would do me the most good in my current situation. A book on wilderness survival was my first find, followed by a book on first-aid. I grabbed a few books on cooking, including a fine vegetarian cookbook published by Betty Crocker. Though I am a fan of scary fiction, I bypassed King's, Koontz's, and Rice's novels on this trip, only grabbing the essentials. At the front desk, I found a small ledger with only a few notes written on the first few pages (which I promptly tore out). I decided to make a diary of my survival on the off chance that if there were someone else out there and I didn't make it, the book might prove valuable to them. "Hell," I thought to myself, "it will help keep me sane as well."

I placed my books in a sack and carried them back to the homestead. I made a mental note as I walked that I would try to find a working generator the next day. I would also look for other gas stations in this neighborhood.

When I got back to the house, I was tired. I ate another orange and went to the upstairs master bedroom. By the light of my candle, I put new (old) sheets on the bed. I wrote about the last two days' adventures and promptly fell asleep. I had dreams about atomic zombies: The kind of flesh-eating walking dead you saw in old George Romero films. This was a common nightmare for me when I was younger, and it was no wonder why they cropped into my sleep time now. Like clockwork, I awoke just once before dawn to whiz. I slept soundly after that, having no dreams until I woke up somewhere around mid-morning the next day.

Third Day: Establish Your Home Base Camp.

After a breakfast of diced pears, I decided to walk about the neighborhood, getting used to the layout of the land around me. As I did so, I made mental notes about gas stations and broke into a few houses near my home base camp.

I found more candles in various homes and a back-up generator with a solar panel on it at a house close to mine, which I wheeled over to my residence. I followed the instruction manual and was able to get limited power going in my house by midafternoon. I decided I would only use it for showering and occasionally to cook with. I had an ample supply of candles for light, which I liked anyway.

As I was not sure what the gas situation was, I used my confiscated ten-speed bicycle for tooling around outside the neighborhood. I also nabbed a shopping cart for wheeling heavy things to and from my house. I was a homeless person with a home.

In my neighbor's homes I saw computers, digital movie players, and other frivolous electronic sundries, but I bypassed them all at this point. I did grab a few wind-up clocks and a winding watch from a neighbor's antique display case. I guessed the time pretty closely and I set my time pieces accordingly. Time was strangely elusive

to me, but I would nail it down slowly and surely through very careful reasoning.

I was not exactly sure what time of the year it was, but it was early spring or late autumn. It was neither hot nor cold and in a few weeks the temperature would tell me the time of the year. If it started getting hotter, it would be summer. If it got colder, I would be coming into winter. Simple enough.

With my generator now hooked up, I tried to get the water going next. What came out of the pipes in the early stages was not pleasant, but I did succeed in getting running water in my home. Another search of neighboring garages secured me a large tank water purifier, which cleaned up the water and eased my conscience quite a bit about the safety of bathing in it. I even found a mini purifying pitcher I could use for drinking water. Happy days!

In a dozen homes I'd checked, I found no sign of people. Not a body... not a soul. My pervading thought: "Where was everyone?" Should I check more houses? I brushed off the thought. If there was anyone around, they would find me eventually. I had more important survival-type shit to do.

I ventured out once again and happened upon a barber shop that apparently had not been looted. It stood to reason: Who would loot a hair salon, right? Inside, I found a nice set of scissors and clippers that were not rusted along with a shaving straight-razor also miraculously in good condition. Both looked like stainless steel and they were packed in a salon case. I was just happy to find them. The cans of shaving cream yielded nothing, so I would have to find something else to lubricate my puss, when it came time to groom myself. I decided I would just give my hair and beard a trim, for now.

When I returned home, it had donned on me that the best thing for me to do would be to clean my dwelling completely. If this was my home, I should keep it clean, despite my lack of visitors. Hygiene was important to my health and I wanted to continue to live as long as I could.

I started with the bedroom and bathroom upstairs and then worked my way down to the living area and kitchen. Soap and cleansers in plastic containers seemed okay. I swept and mopped the floors, as well as wiping the shelves, countertops, and tables.

I made the bed and hung mosquito netting around it. I cleaned the stove and oven inside and out. Many thoughts raced through my mind as I cleaned house. It finally dawned on me that I could have anything I wanted for free if I put my mind to it. I could break into a Lamborghini dealership (and I might yet) and ride around in style if I wished. Wait…no gas. Anyway, the point being, all of this thievery without any repercussion, but I didn't want to waste too much precious time on tomfoolery. Plus, I still hadn't established how prevalent or short gas was. Still, I realized now: "This post-apocalyptic Georgia is a pretty sweet deal." I nodded to myself with a satisfied smirk, thinking I had already nabbed quite a few precious items this last couple of days.

Actually, I was quite pleased with myself because in three days I had secured the basic necessities of life I needed: food, water, sensible transportation, a suitable shelter with power, toiletries, and reading material for entertaining myself. Not bad for someone who had been frozen like a T.V. dinner for God-only-knew how long.

I had always been a solitary sort, never relying much on others. This was one of the reasons why my relationships in my previous life had failed miserably. It was also the reason why I had no children to speak of… at least none I ever knew about. That was not to say I wasn't going to apply myself and not try to procreate for the benefit of mankind. Of course, I realized it was my duty to try. So not to worry yourself, dear reader. I would certainly get to that task when the time was right.

In my mind, judging from the condition of things around me, I had been thawed some fifteen to twenty years after my icy slumber had begun. This was corroborated by the fact that not much had changed in the way of cars, architecture, and fashion. The city didn't look like a vision from an Asimov story or The Jetsons. Buildings still looked like buildings and cars, although a bit sleeker, were still grounded on four wheels. Men still wore suits and women dresses on giant billboards all around. It still looked as I remembered it. Men still wore neckties and women still wore high heels.

My curiosity still nagged at me to get answers. I would ride a little farther out tomorrow. Perhaps that would give me more pieces to the puzzle.

That night, I took a semi-warm shower and washed my hair with a fossilized bar of soap. Even in my frozen state, my nails, hair, and beard had grown rampant, albeit very slowly. I took my scissors and trimmed my hair and beard to a comfortable length. I carefully clipped my toenails with a set of slightly rusty nail clippers, being ever so careful not to nick myself. Bolt cutters would have done a better job, but apocalyptic beggars could not be choosers. I picked up the sizable nail clippings and took them to the back porch. I threw them out on the back lawn. I looked out over eerie, black Atlanta. No lights of any kind, other than the beautiful stars and a half moon lighting the tops of the houses. Again, there was no sound of crickets chirping or mosquitoes buzzing, just a gentle, ever-so-quiet breeze. I waited for a long time, soaking in the silence, then I went back inside.

After my grooming, I put on a new robe. (Yes, I had been standing on the back porch scratching my ass in my underwear. No one complained.) I had approved of my new look in the bathroom mirror and that was all that mattered. I went to my room and jotted down notes about my first three days.

I continued to wonder about the fate of my peers. Atlanta was the biggest city in the south of the United States. It was kind of like the New York of the south. Did a plague wipe everything out? I had been up and about for three days now with no ill effects. Granted I had felt better, but I probably would have noticed symptoms of a deadly viral disease or plague by this time. Did someone push the button and start Armageddon? Did aliens take everyone away? Maybe tomorrow I would get my answer.

Then I went to bed very late and slept soundly. If I had dreams that night, there was no evidence of them in the recesses of my mind the next day. Sometimes it was like that. You could not, for the life of you, remember if you dreamed or not. Unfortunately, this usually meant you had a good dream. We rarely remembered the good ones, but we remembered the nightmares. Those came back to us vividly. The important thing was that you dreamed. I could not remember where I had heard or read it, but psychological experts said crazy people did not dream. As long as you dreamed, you were still one of the sane ones…

Fourth Day: Find and Secure More Suitable Transport to Expand Your Horizons.

I woke up the next day in the middle of the morning with a start. It was not due to a nightmare or a large noise: Quite the opposite — it was eerie quiet. My body clock was letting me know I'd slept longer than usual and was getting me up as quick as it could.

I would have killed for an egg or a donut with some fresh coffee, but I was satisfied with the large grapefruit I ate. It was another beautiful even-temperature, sunny day outside.

Having been in hibernation for so long, I was rather pale skinned at this time and surprised the sun had not burned me much, though I had been running around a lot outside lately. I guessed (and this was mere conjecture, mind you) without man being active on the planet for so long, the atmosphere and ozone were possibly back to normal as there appeared to be more UV protection now than there had been in the early twenty-first century. Another unexpected perk of my situation.

Today was a search for gas in the morning. The search for fossil fuel was futile. Seven stations, all dry. My mind swam. "How long would it take for gas to separate and evaporate?"

As an alternative, I found and raided an electric bike shop that afternoon. As expected, no scooters were on the floor, but after careful inspection around back, I found a locked loading gate that wasn't breached. Efforts to break it open were fruitless to my attacks. In a moment of clarity, I went back into the shop and found a locked door to the back-storage area. That was easier to break open. There were a handful of e-bikes there.

I spent the rest of the day trying to get one of the batteries charged with the solar generator I had found. A search of some of the area toolsheds gave me the battery tester I needed for the task. Of the five batteries tested, only one worked. Thankfully, it was the largest one. I would charge the one good battery, venture down to Macon about 100 miles south and maybe on down to Florida the next day. I'd strap the solar generator onto the back of the bike to give me more charge when I needed it.

My last task of the day was to find a map. I went back to the library that evening and stole the maps I needed for my journey. I had a big map of the USA, a map of Georgia, and a map of Florida. As an afterthought, I even grabbed a globe of the world on my way out. I saved myself that extra trip as I knew it would inevitably come in handy later. If I could eventually find the means and the inclination to go international, I would do it, but first thing was first. The next few days were devoted to nearby territories. "Baby steps," I told myself.

Fifth Day: Expand Your Horizons.

I made a kind of a duct tape saddlebag with sacks and jugs, which I threw over the rear end of the seat of my new black and blue scooter. I secured the moderately-sized generator to the flat rack on the back. I headed out of town going south at around 11:00 am. True to my timekeeping, the sun was directly over my head at 12 noon. I gathered more fruit and vegetables on my way to Macon, Georgia down Interstate 75.

I found beans, peas, more citrus, pecan trees, and bananas. I even stumbled across some peanuts, though they were kind of a pain in the ass to dig up.

As I moved farther south from Macon, I suddenly, very suddenly became aware of the fact there were bushes and grass but absolutely no tall trees, just small trees and bushes. The remnants of signs and billboards which were very prevalent on this stretch of highway, were suddenly gone as well. A chill went up my spine and the hair on the back of my neck stood up prickly. I noticed there were shapes that looked like vehicles on the highway in the far distance. I stopped the scooter and stood there on that one spot on the highway for several minutes contemplating my next move. Did I really want to see what was up ahead? The answers would invariably lay elsewhere. A horrible dread built in me. I realized it was the same fear that had built inside of me when I checked in people's homes back in Atlanta.

I finally screwed up enough courage and moved forward slowly and steadily. "Where am I?" I thought to myself. "Valdosta?" The shapes were charred cars and trucks splayed all over and around the highway. There were hundreds of them, some on their sides, some even upside down, each of them immobile. Inside were old, dusty, rotted skeletons of drivers, couples, families. My worst fear was at last confirmed. This part of the world had gone out with a bang. I remembered that just a few miles southeast of here was a prominent naval base in Jacksonville, Florida. Atlanta had somehow been miraculously spared, but most of America probably resembled what I was staring at now. I wondered what had finally caused the nuclear holocaust to happen. Who struck first? At this point, It really didn't matter. The result was this empty world.

There was no point in me going any further south. I turned the scooter around and headed back toward Atlanta. Now I would not go as far as to say I was an overly sensitive guy, but I would admit I cried that day. So much so, I had to stop a couple of times on the highway, going back to catch my breath and get my wits back. I looked back on my life and had many sobering moments, but realizing at this time how stupid the human race was that it would let its pride and patriotism destroy every last fellow being, the innocent masses along with the guilty few, and I might add, obliterate every other defenseless creature on the planet without thought or care. I looked up at the sky and yelled. It was the first sound I had made in decades. It was primal and guttural. My weak throat was rubbed raw by the sheer force of it, but what else could I do? I was enraged as I believe anyone in my colorful shoes would have been.

The battery drained not shortly after, and I was emotionally drained. I set up the generator, hooked up the battery, and found a shady spot off the highway to park myself and ponder. And that I did for hours.

When I returned home in the evening, I barged into the house without unloading my cargo and went right to the shower. With my t-shirt, jeans, and high-top shoes still on, I turned on the water and crouched down in the stall, letting the water cleanse me. I wept again for mankind and what might have been. I bawled, fearing for my own sanity. Over and over I said to myself, "Why?" I actually said it aloud, though it was weak, and my utterances cracked like a person just getting their voice back after a bad case of laryngitis.

Thoughts were rampant and fleeting: "Is there anyone else? Which cities and countries were spared? Am I in danger of radiation poisoning? The radiation goes away after fifty years, right? Why do I remember that?"

Suddenly I stood. "The cryo-center!" I ran out the open door and all the way to the Center where I had awoken just a couple of days prior. There had to be more people there, frozen like myself. "My cryo-unit was still functional," I thought to myself. "I may be able to get it to show me a date."

I went inside and bounded up the stairs back to the room where I had been sleeping. I slipped and slid along the way (like an idiot). It was dark but my eyes were adjusting. My chest heaved as I breathed heavily from running. Water still dripped from my wet clothes as I checked the cryo-panel again. I tapped it and pushed buttons, but it was dead. The battery was used up. It did say "critical" when I woke up four days ago. "Damn!" I said to myself. "Damn the fuckin' luck!" I decided to stop whining and to move on, undaunted.

In other rooms, I found cryo-units with dead bodies in them. I was sure the rich socialites who had invested so much of their fortune on their future would have been aghast to know that. At least they were spared the slow, painful death by radiation poisoning.

In another room, I found empty cryo-tubes with no power. Then I found a truly disgusting section where people had only had their heads frozen. Most of the heads were decomposed to mere skulls and only a couple of them were still operational.

It was here I actually found what I was looking for. I tapped the display on one of the working units and watched it light up. I waited for it – Eureka! The date on the panel was 10-03-2092. If the holocaust had happened around 2034, then it had been about fifty-eight years since then and the radiation would have been gone for some time. I sighed to myself, feeling very lucky.

I went out of the room and down the hall. It seemed darker now and I had difficulty seeing where I was going. I stumbled past a door that said: "PET CRYOGENICS."

"No way!" I thought to myself, and I entered eagerly. True to the sign out front, there were several cryo-chambers containing cats. As I am not a cat person (I am allergic to their dandruff. It makes my eyes burn), I looked for a dog to thaw out. I found only one still in suspended animation. He was a golden retriever named "Beau." I croaked his name aloud to myself and smiled.

I looked all over for a manual on how to operate the cryo-chamber, but it was too dark, and I could not find one. "I will be back tomorrow, Beau." I whispered inaudibly as I exited the room.

I made my way downstairs and returned to my house and changed into some dry clothes. I shelled and ate some pecans. I went to sleep and dreamed I was a superhero. The people I helped and saved had no faces at all.

17

Sixth Day: Get Yourself A Companion.

October 4, 2092

7:35 am

I woke up early this morning at about seven-thirty. I was excited about the prospect of having a dog for a companion. I would go back to the cryo-center right after breakfast and see if I could unfreeze Beau.

I had another banana and another grapefruit for breakfast. I also ate some peanuts for protein. The forecast was sunny and beautiful again for the fifth day in a row. I found that rather odd, but I was by no means complaining.

8:15 am

I returned to the Atlanta Cryogenics Center and went straight to where Beau was. I had brought candles this time and a pen to jot down the model number of his cryo-chamber (IB-7077C), and I spend most of the morning looking for an instruction manual on how to reanimate my new companion.

A customer log told me Beau was perfectly healthy, but his master, a one Theodore Binder was suffering from advanced prostate cancer. Evidently, the rich shipping magnate did not have long to live and his closest ally was his pampered pooch. He decided both would be frozen until the day when cancer would be cured. Obviously, that day never came. Beau has been a dog-sickle for over 70 years according to the center's records. That was 490 dog years to you and me. This did not include the years before he was frozen.

11:45 am

After three hours of searching and finding nothing on the IB 7077C, I decided to experiment by attempting to thaw a cat. My first subject was an epileptic Tabby named "Cyril." The log showed his master, Ms. Constance Giles, had him frozen back in May of 1997. Ms. Giles had herself frozen on the same date at the age of seventy-four when she had complications during triple by-pass heart surgery. Evidently, she had a stroke which incapacitated her ability to eat solid foods. Her living will stated cryo-suspension in this event. I was happy to find her cryo-chamber was still functioning and she seemed to be resting peacefully, though she was the only other living human in here.

I pushed some buttons on Cyril's chamber and carefully monitored the read-out. On the screen I saw an option for "OPEN CHAMBER," and I chose that option. After a hiss of gas and a hydraulic hum, the door to the cat's chamber opened. The room became very cold as the gases from inside the chamber escaped. I returned to the control pad and found an option for "TURN OFF NITROGEN." I pushed that.

I extracted a breathing tube from the frozen cat and removed him from his chamber. I placed him on a table and wrapped him in a sheet. I waited. He did not appear to be breathing.

1:10 pm

I had made a grave error. I should have left Cyril in his chamber to revive. Removing his life support tube too soon was another big mistake. Cyril was thawing but showing no signs of life. He was still not breathing and there was no heartbeat. When I woke up, I did not remember having a respiration tube. I must have pulled it out myself in my groggy state, without realizing it. Checking my chamber, a similar tube lay to the side of where I was positioned in the pod. "Whoops! Too bad for Cyril."

2:00 pm

There were two other Siamese cats, Max and Myra, belonging to Herbert Moore, whose final remains occupied another chamber. Mr. Moore was one of the unfortunate souls whose chamber malfunctioned on him a few years back. His feline friends would be my next Guinea Pigs and if I failed to revive them successfully, well, then I had no one to answer to. I chuckled to myself at my own cryptic joke as I began to carefully inspect their life support systems. They appeared to be healthy, freeze-dried little cats.

It appeared a proper revival would be accomplished if I left the cryo-chamber closed before choosing "RESUSCITATE" (an option I had previously not seen before). I marveled as the chamber slowly defrosted and life functions to the two felines were slowly but surely restored. The cats began to convulse in their chamber. I opened it when prompted to do so, after the gooey liquid (whatever the hell it was) emptied out of the chamber. I then removed the breathing tubes from the disoriented cats. One of the cats scratched me as I did so, the ungrateful little bastard.

7:40 pm

I released Max and Myra, who seemed as normal as two cats could be after being frozen for over half a century, then reanimated. I was hungry so I went home for supper and to get more candles. I would attempt to re-animate Beau tonight.

9:15 pm

I returned to the center and I repeated the process that worked with the two Siamese cats. I pushed the "RESUSCITATE" command button and I stood by, closely monitoring to make sure Beau made it safely through his reanimation process. I felt a little like Dr. Victor Frankenstein (actually more like Mr. Colin Clive — Henry Frankenstein from the old Karloff monster movies). Beau's cryogenic revival went smoother than the previous ones. My heart leapt as I saw his body begin to breath. Yes, his ribs were slowly heaving. Man's best friend moved. I was elated more than I wanted to admit. "He's alive! He's alive!"

October 5, 2092
3:05 am

I almost lost Beau. He began to convulse during his thawing out and he stopped breathing at one point. I opened his chamber and removed his breathing tube. I pulled him out of the pod and shook him. I held him tightly, contemplating performing cardiopulmonary resuscitation on him when he finally let out a glorious yet pitiful little yelp. The poor, dumb animal was extremely confused and whimpered quite a bit, not realizing his situation, and I was pretty sure he was blind by the way he moved his head around. His motor skills were not there yet, so I wrapped him in a blanket and carried him home. I remembered how unsteady I was on my first day back. It would probably be doubly so for him. He would adjust in due time. I smiled to myself as I carried him home in my arms. I had successfully secured a living companion. Hell, I had even brought back the species of dog and cat to the planet. That thought gave me great self-satisfaction.

3:55 am

I placed Beau in a bed I'd constructed on the floor in the kitchen, utilizing some clean, soft blankets I pulled in from the store. Again, these were in pretty good shape because they were stored on the shelf in airtight plastic bags.

I watched my new dog for a while to make sure he was going to be okay. I smiled to myself, realizing I was no longer alone. I now had a canine companion. He was still dazed and disoriented but he seemed to understand I meant him no harm. His eyes remained open. He had slept a long time, so he probably wanted to stay awake now, even if it was dark and probably a bit puzzling.

I left papers on the kitchen floor near him in the hopes that when he had to relieve himself, he would know what to do. I wouldn't scold him if he did poop or piss on the floor. He had been out of the loop for a long while. If he wasn't paper trained, then we would work up a routine for letting him in and out of the house. The back yard was fenced, but I really wanted him to be an indoor dog. I wanted him to be close to me.

I was exhausted. It had been a long day filled with life and death surprises. I was going to bed without showering. I just said, "Good night, Beau," and he looked up when I said his name. He remembered. That was good.

Seventh Day: Find Answers.

October 5, 2092
10:20 am

I was up. Beau still lay in the bed I'd made for him out of several thick comforters. When I looked at him, his head came up attentively. Whatever problems he had with eyesight last night must have worked itself out somewhat. He still struggled with getting onto his legs, but he seemed strong and healthy. The motor skills would return soon. I pulled up my handy journal and wrote about yesterday. Soon I showered and made breakfast.

I tried grinding up some of the wheat I had in a bowl. I looked for a recipe for bread and found one. I cursed the fact I had no eggs and no butter.

I hadn't found him dogfood yet (That was a joke). I was posed with the problem of what to feed Beau. I mixed some wheat with some cooked bean paste. I let it cool to warm and put it before him. He lapped it up hungrily. I probably could have put anything in front of him and he would have eaten it. He had been without food for several decades. Not surprisingly he also drank a lot of water.

I contemplated what I would focus my attention on today. I weighed my options on what I should do first. I could go back to the library, hunt for a solar or magnetic-electric generator, get more items from the back stockrooms of the department stores, visit a local hospital for medical supplies, or security stores to make my home safe for the unlikely event of intruders showing up. I opted for the hospital visit first as it was a new adventure for me, and the other things were kind of a rehashing of previous jobs.

11:55 am

I found ST. MARY'S HOSPITAL OF ATLANTA and entered through the Emergency Room doorway. The door was slightly open as there was no power and it was probably automatic, the kind that opened via a motion sensor. It had probably been pried open by someone long ago, wanting to get in (or out). The ER was empty as expected but every bed inside contained skeletal remains. The charts contained doctor's notes about the patients who had mostly succumbed to radiation poisoning and hypothermia. Another disheartening confirmation of my worst fear.

12:20 pm

I found boxes of bandages that might come in handy later but, all pills and medicines were obviously useless at this point, being way past their expiration dates. Most had oxidized into powder. I found residue of marijuana, including some dry seeds in a carton. I pocketed the prize, hoping that if and when I planted it, I would miraculously produce five-leafed friends for the benefit of my relaxation.

It was amazing just how much was unusable after a nuclear holocaust. I had

been lucky in many respects but faced an equal amount of disappointments. Nature had provided me with much sustenance but most anything man-made was useless to me unless stored away in plastic. Plastic seemed the one resource that (with very few exceptions) survived the apocalypse.

12:40 pm

I located the doctor's offices and rummaged about. I found a laptop with a power supply as well as a micro-digital recorder with

23

charger in a Dr. Richard Swales' office. I put them in my sack with the other sundries, hoping to glean more information from them later. I realized in my searches, money was everywhere around me, in every nook and cranny, but utterly useless now. There was no bartering in a single-soul society.

12:55 pm

I returned home for lunch. Beau was on his feet now, moving about, occasionally bumping into things sideways. He still had not come to really know me yet, so he came into the rooms I inhabited but didn't get close yet. He was wary. At least he defecated on the papers I'd set down for him. "Good boy!"

I pan fried some beans for myself, all the while, wishing I had some pork, brown sugar, and/or tomato sauce to mix with them. Even something as simple as regular table salt and black pepper would make things a little bit more palatable. You never missed these things until you didn't have them readily available to you. It was always the way – and to the umpteenth degree for me now.

5:10 pm

I dozed off after I ate. I must've been tired from the stress of the last few days. The seventh day was supposed to be a day of rest. Maybe I owed myself that.

5:30 pm

I grabbed a couple of candles and went to the library. I found a Farmer's Almanacs, which contained articles on making salt and sugar from raw minerals. I started making notes on things I should gather.

A pepper mill and black pepper corns
A clay bowl and pestle for grinding
A coffee mill and fresh coffee beans
A garlic press and cloves of garlic

As I wheeled some books back to my home with my shopping cart, like a bag lady, I chortled to myself, harkening back to the Australian "Road Warrior" pictures of the late twentieth century. I was a far cry from those rough and ruthless scavengers.

Beau came out to greet me, squeezing out of the outer screen door, but continued to keep his distance.

At that moment, I thought to myself, "If I wanted meat and meat by-products such as milk and eggs, the one solution that comes to my mind is cloning." I had to read up on cloning research. But if necessary, I could survive as a vegetarian. If worse came to worse, I could also raise human clones to repopulate the earth if a suitable female candidate could not be reanimated from cryogenic sleep to be Eve to my Adam. This would be an absolute last resort though. The thought of the entire planet starting over with clones just did not seem right to me. I was not usually prejudiced, but clones? I remembered an analogy way back in the day. It was a schoolmate of mine named Katie Bradley who said, "Clones would be like a Xerox copy of ourselves. They would never be as good as the original."

Regardless of my personal feelings, it was evident I was going to have to venture out of Atlanta to make things happen. I made up my mind to find a suitable boat and sail out of Savannah to check other countries for survivors and supplies. I could sail down to Cuba for coffee, then through the Panama Canal and up into the Pacific where I could check the Asian sector. To my knowledge, we had never cloned animals or people cells in America, but I had read somewhere that serious cloning had been done in Korea. But I was getting ahead of myself. I still had to do some research before I went off half-cocked.

9:20 pm

I had a late dinner with Beau and connected the generator to the doctor's equipment in an attempt to recharge it and the digital recorder. I was eager to read his notes and hear another human voice. I checked my connections and the breaker switches in the breaker box, then I turned on the lights in the house. It was bright. I admitted to myself I really liked the soft light of the candles better. I turned the lights off.

10:05 pm

I was back at the library. I could not find any good books on cloning research but there were many articles in science magazines and medical journals I had found and brought home with me. I thumbed through some of the magazines and a story in *Science Monthly* caught my eye. Several men in Tokyo, Japan had married robot wives in a giant ceremony. The pictures accompanying the story showed the robot wives indeed looked like young Japanese girls and, though their skin was obviously of a synthetic rubbery texture, they still did look amazingly realistic and lifelike. I remembered reading a similar story like this, just before I was frozen. I laughed to myself then and I laughed aloud now. A guy would have to be extremely desperate or a total loser to be forced into a union like that.

My jovial moment was short-lived. The reality of the situation was I should not "poo-poo" the idea so quickly, being the last living human on Earth. If I could not find anyone else to communicate with, a robot sidekick would at least help me to keep my sanity.

Another article about stem cell research at a facility in Pusan, South Korea also got my attention. Seoul was a military target and would undoubtedly be gone, but Pusan being on the southernmost coast might have been spared like Atlanta and Savannah, Georgia. It would be worth checking out. The name of the facility was The Pusan Center for Genetic Research and evidently, a doctor there named Ms. Wi Hua Soong was not only cloning human organs for transplant without permission, she had been cloning animals there illegally as well. Ms. Soong had discussed her work with her colleagues and, though they had not seen the results, she had convinced them she could in fact control the sexes of her clones. She stated she had cracked the genetic code and could manipulate X and Y chromosomes in sheep and dogs to create a boy clone from a girl animal, and visa-versa. Though Dr. Soong's research was shut down for bad publicity from religious groups, many other scientists in the field of genetic research respected her, some even calling her a genius. I was certainly amazed and impressed at the content of the article. Wi Hua Soong and her advancements in clone research had gotten my attention.

11:50 pm

I tried to start the laptop computer, but it would not come on at all. I knew the generator was working so I was disappointed. I turned on the lights a few hours before. Using a multi-line power adaptor, I tried the cassette recorder. It worked, but I was ill prepared for what I was about to hear: A series of recorded messages which I have transcribed for you here, dear reader:

Dr. Richard Swales, February 17th, 2034. A routine check on Mrs. Carlson shows that she has basically recovered from the plural effusion in her left lung. Her breathing seems to be back to normal and she is showing progress in her recovery from last week's surgery. I am taking the rest of the day off, but as always will remain on call. Dr. Nadir will fill in for me if any serious emergency arises.

(Recorder click.)

February 18th, 2034. Doctor Richard Swales. We were not hit directly by the nuclear strike that destroyed most of America this morning at around seven o'clock. All communication with the outside world has been shut down. Not much works anymore. The electromagnetic pulse from the nuclear bombs going off has destroyed the inner circuitry of most electronic devices. The microchips have been destroyed. I don't know how, but this recording device still works. The skies are filled with thick, black smoke and the temperature has dropped to subzero temperatures in just a few hours. With no sun and no power, everything will die in a few days.

(Recorder click.)

27

This is Dr. Swales again. It is February 19th, 2034. I was told that it's about 10:30am, but you cannot tell night from day anymore. People are lighting fires in the garbage cans around the hospital in an effort to keep warm, but it is colder here than it has ever been in Atlanta. My guess is 50 degrees below zero. People are bundling up, but we are filled to overflowing with not enough blankets to go around. There is not much food here and to go outside for more than a few minutes means freezing to death. Many people here are suffering from severe hypothermia, radiation burns, and now most of us here are having respiratory problems. Most are coughing and spitting up blood. I am noticing skin lesions that I have never seen before. My diagnosis is radiation poisoning from fallout. I don't know how much longer we can hold on.

(Recorder click.)

(Wheezing:) Dr. Richard Swales... I think its February 20th now. I am not sure...We lost a lot of people in the last eight hours. There was a mass suicide downstairs in the chapel...I am amazed that I have been able to hang on as long as I have...It is very difficult to breathe...This will undoubtedly be my last entry...I tried to go outside a little while ago. It's like the North Pole out there. I know that my wife and son must be dead by now. (Long pause.) In my whole life...nothing has ever...I...I...Jeese...(Sobbing:) What happened? What happened?

(Recorder click.)

(Severe wheezing:) All dead...All dead...why am I...not dead...want to die...skin burning... lungs burning...(Coughs.)...bleeding...No hope for any...one...(At this point, respectable Doctor Richard Swales, with degrees hanging on his wall, began laughing a very creepy insane kind of laughter. I could never really describe it accurately, but I would never forget it until my dying day. He coughed

and spit one last time, then said his final words: No one…will hear this…

(Recorder click.)
(Recorder static hiss.)

I was stunned by the recording. I realized these writings, my writings, may never be read by another living soul. Would I be another Dr. Swales? How horrible it must have been for the survivors in their last few days. Tomorrow was my eighth day. I had rest today. I would not sit idle. If I was alive today to hear the last words of Dr. Richard Swales, then someone else may be found. If I failed, there was still a chance my efforts would benefit someone else later. I could not lose hope. I had done some amazing things already, and I was proud of my accomplishments this first week back on the planet. I was determined to live actively regardless of what happened next.

Day Eight: No Time to Rest.

October 6th, 2092

7:30 am

I was up. Beau actually came up to me for a morning pet when he saw I was awake. He was getting comfortable around his new master. I fixed a breakfast of bananas and fresh crushed peanut butter, saving the excess oil from the peanut crushing for cooking. I also filtered some water.

8:15 am

I took the scooter out and gathered several sacks of food from some of the fields I previously raided. I returned home with the goods and prepared lunch for myself and Beau. He was definitely livelier today. This pleased me as we were about to embark on a long journey together. After some frisky play we set out together to find better transportation. The scooter was nice, but I couldn't load it up with everything I wanted to bring with me on this trip.

11:25 am

After several tries, I found an electric car at a dealership with an actual working battery. I hooked up the generator and scooted back to my place to pack provisions. I prepared my water purifier and several jugs of water along with all the food I had into bags. I packed up my candles, clothes, knives, including a machete I found in the neighbor's garage and some books. Then, I put them on the scooter. I folded up my ten speed and strapped it to the back of the scooter. It looked cumbersome, but it should have made the short journey to the car. I had never been a light packer. "Everything but the kitchen sink!" was my motto. I rode out to where the car was charging several blocks from my house.

3:30 pm

I packed up the car, ditched the scooter, though I put the battery in the trunk (you never know), and picked up Beau. We were on our way to the coast. Beau seemed to enjoy the ride and we made good time heading down to Macon, where we switched over to Interstate 16. The BYD hatchback had an iTunes player in it, and I enjoyed listening to music for the first time since my revival. It was classic rock from the late twentieth century, including Robert Palmer, Peter Gabriel, and Sting. I had to rig up one of these in the boat we found. Music lifted the spirits.

7:20 pm

We stopped to recharge somewhere around Warner Robins or Dublin. As it was night, we would have to sleep here and recharge the charger at dawn. As usual, it was quiet and peaceful. Beau enjoyed being outside as most dogs did. It was nice.

He did not run off as there were no birds, rabbits or squirrels to bark at. The night was creepy quiet without the sounds of crickets or cicadas.

There were no gnats to irritate us, no ants to bite us, no mosquitos to suck our precious, undernourished blood. This was what I liked about my fresh new world. The cold silence of the night was something I would eventually get used to. I did like the gentle sound of the wind blowing through the trees.

I went to the passenger side, hopped into that seat, but kept the door open. As if reading my mind, Beau lay on the ground by the open door. I reclined the seat back and didn't remember anything else after that. I must have been tired because I conked out immediately. I slept deeply, not getting up in the night to urinate or inspect my surroundings. There was nothing out there to hurt me, so there was nothing to worry about. The rising sun would wake me as nature had intended it.

Day Nine: Get to Savannah.

October 7th, 2092
6:10 am

I woke up at dawn. I set-up the solar panels on the generator. It would have enough charge in it to charge the car battery at lunch. With luck, we would be in Savannah at dinner time. A trip that would normally take a person four hours would take us two days.

1:00 pm

Beau and I played all morning in the woods. We didn't have to worry about snakes, chiggers, spiders, ticks, scorpions. We had lunch together and now we wait for the juice to go from the generator to the car battery.

4:15 pm

I couldn't wait any longer. We packed up the generator and headed to Savannah. The battery should've had enough juice in it to get us there.

6:40 pm

We made it to Savannah, but it was dark now. I had a little battery left so I was going to try and find a boatyard to park. We'd find us a nice boat and head out first thing tomorrow morning.

I scoped out the empty city of Savannah, looking for a suitable boat to take me to all parts of the world. Again, I didn't have to worry about paying for it, or being caught stealing it. As I got closer to the harbor, I began to see boat retailers in my dim headlights. Then I spotted her. The craft was a huge sheltered monster of a seacraft. I stopped the BYD, lit a candle, made it through the fence and got to her, marveling at her in the moonlight. And Sweet Mother of Pearl, she had two big, magnetic-electric engines.

At first, the word magnetic did not register with me. I just saw electric engines. They were experimenting with magnetic electricity just before I was freezer framed. They had perfected it between that time and the day of the nuke parade.

I easily broke into the sales office by smashing the front door window and began grabbing keys from a pegboard right behind the front desk. I finally found the set of keys that went to my cruiser. I saw a big poster on the wall advertising: "MAGNETIC ELECTRIC ENGINES: THE ENERGY OF THE FUTURE!" I grabbed some rack literature about my cruiser and magnetic electricity.

Magnetic electric engines contained a series of magnets that moved turbines when they were spun by a single large anti-magnet. No solar or wind power needed. The engines never required recharging and parts were supposed to last for decades. Though they were very expensive, I was sold. You only lived once, right?

I went back to my craft and looked inside. The cabin was massive. It had all the comforts of home: a nice, big bed, a dining table, a bathroom with a sink, toilet, and a shower, but I was hooked the minute I laid eyes on her. I pulled the car around and hitched up the beast. It was mine and nobody would stop me. Beau and I would sleep here in comfort tonight.

10 pm

Beau and I loved our new boat. Despite having sat here for 60 years, the engines started right up and purred like a kitten compared to old fossil fuel engines of yester-century. This was proof that covering your boats did extend their life.

In retrospect, I should have searched longer at the car lot. They probably had cars with magnetic electric engines and that would mean no more pain-in-the-ass battery charging. This was a welcome trial-and-error revelation. I would recheck Atlanta for this better, more advanced transportation when we got back.

I grabbed the provisions and even brought the iPlayer from the car since it was so hard to find electronics that hadn't been wrecked by EMP. Tomorrow, we sail.

Day Ten: Out to Sea.

October 8th, 2092
7:40 am

After searching for about forty minutes, we found a suitable ramp alongside a dock for lowering the boat into the water. I positioned the car with trailer, backed the boat into the water, and un-winched it from the trailer. My little electric hatchback was almost submerged by the time I got the cruiser loose. I threw a line hanging off the front of the boat to the dock and hurried around to secure the rope before it slid into the drink. I then pulled the car back up the ramp and hopped aboard my large sea craft with Beau. He seemed almost as excited about the trip as I was.

I didn't bother to lock the car, feeling it would be alright until we returned, whenever that might be. Beau went to the front bow of the boat and actually barked for the first time since I had known him. We moved slowly out of the marina without a care in the world. I set up the generator to charge the cabin lights for later. We drifted out to open waters.

5:50 pm

I had found my Nirvana. The salty sea smell and light breeze were intoxicating. The sun was going down, turning the sky orange, pink, and purple. It was great to be alive and be living this moment now. Beau was curled up on the carpet of the cabin floor. He seemed equally content with only his eyes moving to me from time to time in that way large dogs do when they look like they are thinking deep thoughts about something. As I noticed him, I thought he almost looked like he was smiling at me and this thought struck me funny. I was so glad I could share this with him. As I piloted southward down the Georgia coast, heading for Florida, I relished the sound of the small waves lapping at the front of the boat. This was the life.

9:00 pm

I stopped the engines to let them rest and listen to the ocean around us. The wind blew southward and I checked my compass to make sure south was where we headed. Beau and I enjoyed a dinner of beans and fresh fruit. I had found some nice grapes and strawberries and more citrus yesterday before we got to the border. Surprisingly, Beau liked fruit. He ate several grapes and even a couple of sections of orange I gave to him (though he spit out the hulls and slices after he had removed the juice from them). I checked the digital player in the cabin, and it did not work. Those who got nothing are those who didn't try. I would use the player in the car sparingly during our voyage. I would whistle and hum songs to myself as well.

10: 15 pm

We were back to candle power now. I read a book entitled "The Pros and Cons of Cloning." Though well-written, it was philosophical and had little real technical information to offer me. I was about to abandon it at page forty, as I was tired, when a fact caught my eye. For cloning to occur, you needed a host to carry the cloned embryo. My heart sank. How could I have forgotten that key point? If I had a female host, I would insert my own baby. I should have done more research before embarking on this wild goose chase of a trip.

At this point, I made a snap decision. I was still going to Asia to see what had happened to that side of the world and still seek out the research of Dr. Wi Hua Soong because it may have still held a key to man's survival. Beau and I would do it together. We had come this far. The engines could easily go a hundred miles an hour and that would take us far and fast. Who knew what rare treasures the orient might hold for us? Oh man, I was giddy from fatigue.

It had been a grueling few days. The sea was so relaxing. It was hypnotic and sleep-inducing to me. I put a couple of blankets on the carpet for a bed for Beau and put papers down next to the cabin doorway, which I left open. I dropped anchor to make sure we didn't drift into the Bermuda Triangle while we slept. According to our instruments we were probably somewhere near Daytona or St Augustine, Florida. I wrote that day's events down and fell asleep doing so.

Day Eleven: Navigating South Carefully.

October 9th, 2092

8:30 am

I woke up and stepped out onto the deck of the boat. It was another beautiful sunny day. I scratched my ass for a bit, got my bearings, and moved to the top section of the sea craft (where you pilot it from), and worked the winch. The anchor drew back into the bow of the boat and we began moving southward again. Beau kept to the back of the boat. I could not have asked for a better first mate. He was always chipper and never complained.

We ate breakfast and I scanned the coastline, which was flat and dreary, completely free of trees. From time to time, I caught a glimpse at rubble that was once Canaveral, Stuart, Melbourne, Boca Raton, Palm Beach, Broward, and Miami, Florida. Most was overgrown with grass and small shrubbery now, but the whole state appeared to have been leveled.

5:30 pm

Down below the remnants of the seven-mile bridge, I was elated to see parked cars, houses, and coconut palm trees in the lower Keys. I would go ashore at Key West and search for provisions tonight and tomorrow and maybe pick up a few coconuts.

7:40 pm

We docked. The moon was bright tonight, but Key West was dark. After dinner, I ventured ashore. I brought the ten-speed on the boat, but I figure there were plenty of bikes on land I could use. I would take some bags ashore and try to find other useful items. Beau would stay and guard the boat.

10:15 pm

After going ashore, I grabbed a few coconuts, but it was too dark to find anything at this point. Scavenging would commence early tomorrow. Beau was happy to have me back. We played aboard the boat. I needed to find him a ball or something to play with. Actually, I brought a baby coconut on board which was perfect for our game of catch. Beau was beside himself with joy. But even good masters couldn't help themselves and "fake the throw." We both had a good time. He was a good dog.

11:30 pm

Did some more reading on cloning and stem cell research. I knew I hadn't left anything important back in Atlanta, but I still had that feeling deep down inside there was something important I had forgotten. I guessed if it was really important, I would not have forgotten it. I must sleep.

Day Twelve: Navigating South Carefully.

October 10th, 2092
8:00 am

Key West looked exactly the way it did when I visited it in my teen years. It was amazing to me: like I was stepping back in time. Duval Street, though empty, had not changed at all. Even Sloppy Joe's was still there. I found a nice bike, dusted it off, and I was on wheels again. I checked a few houses and found a snorkel & swim mask set, a nice set of binoculars, and a wine cellar. Now there was a resource that got better with age. I spent a good portion of the day moving the bottles from the cellar to my boat.

3:30 pm

Strangely enough, I was drawn to the Ernest Hemmingway House at the center of the Key. I decided to bring Beau with me this time and we walk in and delve around. The place was dusty, but you would never know that hundreds of six-toed cats had once lived here.

I broke through the flimsy barrier into the room, which was supposed to be his study, where he wrote. I enjoyed invading this space. I rummaged through his bookcase and sat at his writing table. I liked the feel of sitting in front of it. I knew it would be a big pain in my ass to move it, but I decided to borrow Mr. Hemmingway's writing desk and put it on my boat. I was not particularly a huge fan of Hemmingway's writing, but... I was master of the world now and if anything pleased me, then it was mine. I also found and confiscated a khaki floppy safari hat and hunting knife with leather sheath that supposedly belonged to Hemmingway as well. I was truly ready for action now.

8:00 pm

Beau and I were back on the boat. As expected, moving the writing desk to the boat was a monster of a task. I found a loading cart to help me and it looked great in my cabin and I was going to love using it to write my diary/memoirs. According to the southern-most-point marker, Cuba was only 90 miles away. We pulled up anchor and bid farewell to our second world haven, Key West.

11:40 pm

I saw a dark mass far in the distance that I was sure was Cuba. My ship's compass confirmed I must be right. I dropped anchor and enjoyed a few bottles of vintage pre-nuclear-holocaust wine. I drank to Poppa Hemmingway—an inspiration to me—not as a writer, but as an adventurer and a liver of life. I would strive to live each day to its fullest and not waste any time by being unproductive. I laughed to myself as I drank to Hemmingway "The Liver" and to "Hemmingway's liver." I had a nice buzz going on, so I decided to retire and start a new adventure tomorrow. What a great day full of wonderful surprises.

Day Thirteen: Cuba and the Great Discovery.

October 11th, 2092
8:50 am

Beau and I were up. I'd forgotten to put papers down for him last night, so I had to "swab the deck." Cuba resembled the other devastated areas. I debated whether I should go ashore, and my love of coffee won over my fear of what else I might find. After feeding Beau and myself, I raised anchor and slowly motored to the desolate country, searching the coast for a place to go ashore. I found a nice beach and prepared to jump ship. I cursed myself for not grabbing a proper swimsuit while in Key West. I cut off the legs of one of my pairs of heavy cotton trousers, tied a few sacks together with some rope (so I could sling them around my neck), and grabbed my machete along with my new hunting knife. I carefully placed the sheath on my belt, placed the knife in it carefully, snapping it in safely and jumped ship.

10:05 am

While wading to shore I noticed something astounding. There were little fish in the water. Oh, my merciful God in heaven! There were actually fish.

"Beau!" I yelled back to the boat. "There are fish in the water! We can eat fish, boy!"

I cursed myself again for not getting proper fishing gear when I was in Key West, but how was I to know fish would survive the radioactive winter? It stood to reason though. As deep as the oceans were, the aquatic life could have gone to the darkest depths to avoid the radiation. I tried to remember the name of the prehistoric fish that survived the Ice Age and I would read news stories in my youth that they would catch one from time to time around Madagascar — The Coelacanth. That was it. Again, it stood to reason. Life on this planet had begun in the sea and the amazing proof was certainly swimming about me. I was overjoyed beyond belief at the sight of them. I was never a huge fan of seafood, but you could bet I would be from now on.

On shore, I looked about searching for plants that might yield fruit or coffee. I moved inland and after an hour of searching and hacking shrubs with my machete, I founnd bushes with coffee beans. Two great finds in one day.

12:45 pm

I lugged the bags of fresh picked coffee beans to the beach and I went back to check a pile of burnt wood and sticks looking like they might have once been someone's beach hut. My instincts were correct but the only thing I could find there of use to me was a couple of sticks of old bamboo. I returned to the beach and waded out to the boat with the sacks of coffee, desperately trying not to get them wet. Beau was happy to see me and barked during my return. I threw the bags, the machete, and the bamboo into the boat, then hopped in myself. I grabbed a long piece of bamboo and tied my pocketknife to it, making a spear for fishing.

3:00 pm

I tried my hand at spear fishing and came to the conclusion that at this point in time, I was just not good at it. I would need to practice... a lot.

I made a quick decision to return to Key West in order for me to find fishing gear. The thought of fresh seafood for Beau and me was just too exciting. The boat had a range-top stove for cooking. The prospect of coffee was also fueling my turnabout. I would try and procure a coffee bean grinder as well.

6:10 pm

Beau and I docked at Key West at sunset and I wasted no time in going ashore. I found several nice fiberglass fishing rods with reels at a bait and tackle shop. I loaded a large tackle box with strong fishing line, sinkers, hooks, lures, and bobbers. The bobbers and lures would come in handy if and when we decided to go freshwater fishing anywhere inland on our travels. I found several flashlights with rechargeable batteries in the bait and tackle shop. I would check them on my boat tonight, hoping to find one that had a battery still working. It took me a bit longer, but I also managed to find a coffee mill in a little gift shop after dark. Life was getting better and better. I was happy there wasn't much looting in the end at Key West.

8:35 pm

I went back over the day in my mind and made my notes. The rudder was set for Cuba and we cruised back that way. We would drop anchor when we saw Cuba and sleep as we did before. I was excited about going further south into the Caribbean. As we were in no real hurry, I only ratcheted up the engines to a mild 30 miles per hour. With luck we would be able to use the some of the flashlights and grind some coffee for blessed caffeine consumption.

11:00 pm

I checked the flashlight batteries and not one of them worked. Now I had a bag full of useless batteries. After the great discoveries of the past two days, there was no way I was going to let this one disappointment like this to get me down. Beau and I had been extremely lucky. We had also worked hard in gathering all we had and we would continue to gather our sundries with triumphant hearts.

As we were coming back to Key West and I knew there was life in the sea, I kept my eye out for big fish. I did spot dark shapes in the water and I was even convinced at one point I saw a stingray. I had been smiling a stupid "shit-eating grin" all day today, though I could never understand that phrase. Why would anyone smile if they had a mouth full of shit? It made no sense and yet my father and his father loved using that expression.

Day Fourteen: The Caribbean.

October 12th, 2092
7:00 am

We were up early today. Looking at my map, my guess was it would be two days or so before we reached Panama. I decided to drop trail a line and fish for my lunch. It wasn't long before I hooked and landed a nice, fat Bonita. He was a playful bastard too. When I finally got him in the boat, he flopped around, and Beau had a time barking at him.

When he calmed down, I scooted Beau away, cut the fish open, gutted it and fried the filets up. Bonita were not the best tasting fish in the world, but Beau and I were content.

12:15 pm

Havana was to our left, as we steered around the West side of Cuba to save time. I ground up some of my Cuban beans and made coffee the old-fashioned way, in my antique grinder with its crank handle and little drawer at the bottom. I usually took it with cream and sugar, but it felt so good just to drink coffee again. I didn't really care it was strong and black and that I was spitting little coffee grounds. I made a mental note I should try and find tobacco plants tomorrow, so I could have an after-dinner smoke. As rolling papers had not recently been manufactured anywhere in the world, I would have to settle for pipe smoking, and I could make one of those easy enough. I promised myself I would not do it regularly, just occasionally.

I was never a regular smoker, just an occasional cigar tooter, every now and again. It just would not do to speed up the demise of the last savior of mankind on Earth. "Smoking." The word rang a bell in my mind but after some thought—nothing. I shook it off.

9:45 pm

I dropped anchor again. Time to read. One of the books I brought was about the Caribbean and it had a section on Panama and the Canal, which I reread to myself. Luckily for me, my eyesight had always been good. I didn't need glasses to read, even in a dark candlelit cabin. I'd been told by an optometrist I had a cataract in my left eye, but it was to the far left, so it did not really affect my vision.

The Panama Canal was 80 kilometers (50 miles) and took most ships about 8 hours to navigate from one end to the other. But most ships that went through there were huge and had to move very slowly, so I could do it in my boat in a lot less time, especially with my magnetic electric engine power. There were three sets of gateways called "locks" I had to steer through. The first one was at Gatun near the Atlantic entrance. The second one was called Pedro Miguel and the third one Mira Flores were on both ends of the Mira Flores Lake near the Pacific entrance. If I could get through those, I would soon see the Bridge of the Americas, then the Pacific Ocean.

My worry was I did not know if these locks would be open or closed when I got there. If they were closed, and I was just guessing here, they would be damned near impossible to open. There was a good possibility Beau and I would have to turn back and return to Atlanta with our proverbial tails between our legs, and though these last few days would not have been a total waste, having to cancel on Asia would've definitely sucked at this point in time. However, I was still hopeful. At times like this when so much was at stake, my father would once say, *"Son, you rolls yer dice and you takes yer chances. That's*

43

life in the fast lane." Well, Dad, and whoever else might be paying attention—I was rolling the dice and taking the chance.

10:40 pm

I dropped anchor when we reached the bottom Western end of Cuba. We took it slow and easy today. I would save the full power of my engines for the Pacific. That would be the real long hall. Beau and I were on the bow of the boat. His head was down in my lap and I slowly petted his cranial tuft. I could not remember a time more serene. The boat rocked ever so gently and the only sound we heard was the little waves of water as they lapped up against the boat. All I could think to say was: "This is really nice." When I was young, I used to go camping and fishing to find this kind of quiet peacefulness. I thought we would sleep here tonight, and I would write my notes about it tomorrow when I got up. Yeah, as my father used to say: "That is a real Jim Dandy of an idea."

Day Fifteen: On the Open Water.

October 13th, 2092
7:10 am

Beau and I fell asleep early last night, so we were up early. I pulled up anchor immediately and we headed southward toward Honduras, then followed the coast past Costa Rica until eventually we saw the Panama Canal. That was the plan anyway. I was careful to go due south from the West end of Cuba because if I followed the Mexican coastline, I would waste precious time getting to Cozumel, then going too far westward toward Belize.

I was not that hungry, so I decide to skip breakfast. I fed Beau some of the fresh wheat and bean paste he liked. I worried a bit about feeding him a predominantly vegetarian diet, but with luck he would get a good dose of fish later today.

7:45 am

I checked through my box of fishing items and dropped a round bobber onto the deck. It rolled to the back of the boat and Beau scuttled after it like it was a baby coconut. We spent a good twenty minutes playing fetch with the plastic bauble. It would be just blue sea for most of today anyway. My thoughts drifted back to yesterday, when we had passed what I thought was Havana. The map said it was on the coast and as we drifted closer, it appeared to be a sizable city – or what was left of one. I saw small pieces of building foundations, mostly corners and some steel rebar. It was creepy to see a city blown apart and overgrown with greenery. There was a large docking area but there was no sense getting out there. There was clearly nothing there to salvage.

9:30 am

The engines ran steady and we traveled at about forty miles an hour. I caught another fish though it was smaller than the Bonita and I was not sure what it was. How could I have known to bring a book on various fish and fishing with me on this trip?

4:30 pm

We passed some small islands which were probably the Swan islands. I saw tiny specs, remnants of civilization but again, I opted to stay in the boat. There would not be much there we could use.

8:45 pm

We finally reached the coast again, so I dropped anchor. Judging from the map, my feeling was we were somewhere off the coast of Nicaragua, because the coast on our right had us heading south. I played Solitaire with a deck of cards but went to bed early again.

Day 16: Trying to Find the Panama Canal.

October 14th
6:00 am

I was woken by the sunrise. It was magnificent and I had an overall feeling of warmth and pride as I wiped the crust from my eyes. Beau came skittering up to me. greeting his master happily. Today was the day we should find the Panama Canal. Breakfast was more ground wheat with some crushed peanut. The coast to the right of us was wild and uneven. There was absolutely no sign of habitation. It was like I had gone back in a time machine to the Stone Age.

11:00 am

We veered to the East to follow the coastline. That meant we were at Costa Rica. Good. We should've been at Panama by that afternoon.

6:30 pm

Son-of-a-bitch! The sun was going down and we were still heading east along Panama. I dropped anchor and prepared dinner. This was turning into a much longer trip than I imagined, and yet I opted to take it slow and easy. At least I was smart in that I charged the cabin lights with the generator in the afternoons now to save on matches and candles.

Day 17: Still in Search of The Panama Canal.

October 15th
7:00 am

Headed out early this morning, the coastline turned southward right after we started. We would see the canal in a few hours.

9:25 am

I saw what I felt was the opening to the Panama Canal. The land on either side was destitute as the U.S. East Coast and Cuba. There were no large trees, just grass and shrubs. No manmade structures at all. According to my compass and map, this should've been the place. I turned the wheel to the right and set our course to go up the canal.

9:55 am

We came to the Gatun lock. I was sure it was the place described in the book. There was a tiled pathway I should've moved through that was about 100 feet wide (about 33 meters). It was wide open. Nothing stood in our way at this point. I was overjoyed.

10:20 am

I had to be careful. Lake Gatun was very big – not really canal-like at all. I had to keep my vessel pointed due west according to the map. I was already seeing differences in the geography of how the Canal was originally designed. This was expected as the Canal would surely be one of the targets of a nuclear aggressor. My compass and rudder were pointed in the direction we needed to go.

11:45 am

We stopped to eat some lunch and because I was a bit disoriented. What should've been the section of the canal between Rio Chagres and Culebra Cut was just a big lake now, like Lake Michigan. This spot in the dead center of the waterway must have been hit directly by a nuclear warhead.

After chowing-down on some disappointing grunt fish, I kept a watch on my compass and kept my eyes vigilant from side to side, hoping I would see something familiar soon. I had changed my direction to northwest per my calculations, and I would head that way for a bit. I moved forward faster now as I was in a very wide-open space.

12:40 pm

I found my way to what I thought was the lock at Pedro Miguel. The path had become a narrow channel again. It was no longer an open lake. Unfortunately, the twisted metal wreckage of a huge tanker was in the way. My heart sank at the thought of turning back after coming so far. How many days had it been? The book said many ships came through the canal daily and we had not seen one today until now. Our luck was good at first, but it just didn't hold out. We rolled the dice. We took the chance and we lost this time.

1:00 pm

After having a severe tantrum aboard my boat, I decided to inspect the massive tanker in an effort to see if I could find a way to move it. I also wanted to get a better view, to see if there were more obstructions in front of it. I steered to a place where I could tie off the boat, climb a high staircase to level ground and march over to where the tanker was situated. It listed to the right and touched the side of the canal, but the top of it was still a good twenty-five feet over my head, maybe more. I walked further down in front of where the ship was situated. I heard Beau barking in the distance behind me.

From my new vantage point, I saw the passage looked clear ahead, as far as the eye can see. I also noticed what looked like a small

48

coastguard boat moored just a few hundred feet ahead of the Tanker. I could move everything from my boat to it and use it to search the Pacific. It would take time, but it was a viable option. I would need to inspect it. One thing was certain in my mind: the tanker was going nowhere without the aid of heavy explosives, which I did not have… not yet.

1:30 pm

I made my way down to the Coastguard boat. It was empty and weather-beaten but appeared seaworthy. My heart sank… It had a gas engine. I would have to find another way.

2:15 pm

I returned to my boat. I packed up my survival gear and got Beau ashore. We would have to hike to the West coast and see what we saw.

8:10 pm

What a day. I was so tired. We hiked for miles before we reached the Pacific coast. We were having to sleep on the hard ground. As I harkened back to my comfortable luxury cruiser with its Ernest Hemmingway desk, Beau looked up at me as if to say, "We're really fucked, aren't we?" I could not remember ever being in a worse situation. But we had come this far and we had rolled with the punches as they had come. Tomorrow was another day.

11:50 pm

The breeze was nice and the sound of the Ocean waves below were relaxing. I decided we would hike by moonlight.

Day 18: Finding a New Mode of Transport.

October 16th

8:10 am

Walking up the West Coast, we saw signs of civilization. We found a small house and broke in, finding a family of skeletons huddled together in one room, wrapped in tattered blankets. There wasn't much here. There was a gas engine motorcycle out back. We moved on.

11:45 am

We finally found what I thought was the Port of Balboa (though I thought we would've found it a lot sooner). It was once a prosperous city. There were many streets and shops. I found a motorbike shop and, after breaking in and inspecting the small collection of bikes, I found a scooter with a magnetic electric engine. The problem now was what to do with Beau? The platform at the bottom was large enough for him to ride between my legs, but I was so worried he would jump off and hurt himself. I would just have to chance it, but I didn't like it as he was the only other living thing on the planet. I found a rain cover to attach to the scooter to keep the sun off of our skulls.

We spent a little time breaking into houses to find more candles and matches, but little else of use to us. Even though the sun was high in the sky, we had to go further north.

2:10 pm

We rode up the Panama Coast looking for our new Pacific Ocean craft. Just beyond the city we discovered some seaside properties of the wealthy variety. Finally, a break.

2:50 pm

Life by the ocean could be nice. I was tempted to give up my quest and just settle down in a mansion by the sea here. After passing several affluent homes, I found a large boathouse and docked, and I almost orgasmed when I saw the yacht housed inside. It was easily twice the size of my cruiser on the canal and the engines were humongous magnetic-electric behemoths. I almost got down on my knees on the dock in grateful elation. It paid to search in this day and time – and search carefully.

4:15 pm

I loaded the scooter and Beau onto our yacht and, after breaking the lock to the boathouse front door, we were finally out on the water and heading back to the Panama Canal to get the rest of our food and gear. This baby handled like a dream, and when the engines had you doing a hundred, it was like it wouldn't no thang! I couldn't have asked the Gods for a better vessel to get us to the Orient. Providence or dumb luck, I didn't care. As many setbacks as we had those last two days, I thought we were destined for a win.

7:20 pm

I transferred everything to our yacht. I used a loading plank that was a feature aboard the vessel. Beau was excited about the change,. He had even more room to move about. Dogs liked that. Of course, he was happy, just because I had included him in what I was doing. We would get out of this canal and be out in the Pacific even though it was after nightfall. We now knew there were no more obstacles. I just hoped there were no more setbacks.

9:30 pm

We passed back through what I believed used to be the bridge of the Americas. There was a lot of twisted metal that looked like it might have been a bridge at one time. I was able to steer around it. The sun was going down again. The pink and orange hews of the sky were mesmerizing. After such a tough day with getting that engine around the downed tanker, I needed to see this. Again, nature's beauty came through for me, keeping my spirits uplifted.

10:15 pm

We were in the Pacific. I dropped anchor but decided to make a simple dinner of bean paste for Beau with apples, bananas, and peanuts for myself. We both ate with gusto and I repeated my coffee ritual from before.

11:00 pm

I wrote my notes for yesterday and today, using my map to help me with the particulars as to where I had sailed our ships.

I cracked open a bottle of red wine. I corked it because it was not easy to open a bottle of wine with a hunting knife but enjoyed it just the same. I just spat the cork bits out. It was cooler tonight and the wine warmed my blood.

Midnight

I decided to play Solitaire again as I need the practice, but it was just as exciting as it was before, so I abandon it after just a few games.

I found an old newspaper on board our new yacht and the girls from the lingerie ads were quite lovely. It had been several decades since I'd indulged in carnal delights, so I was ashamed to admit it, but I pleasured myself off the side of the boat while Beau slept. My mind went back to previous girls I had been intimate with. Some were attractive and some were just naughty. Some I had impressed with my technique and others with my endurance. It was funny how we only remembered the best sexual escapades at a moment like this.

It felt phenomenal as it would after such a long hiatus. I chummed the waters suitably. As was often times the case, I needed sleep now: long, hibernative rest. Was that an actual word? Hibernative? If it wasn't, it should've been. I hereby declared as the last man standing – a new word for mankind. *"Hibernative"* (H – long

- I - ber - with the accent on NA ending with a tive) – the act of hibernating. Being in a deep sleep.

Day Nineteen: Moving Up the Pacific to the Orient.

October 17th, 2092
8:30 am

I awakened by the sound of thunder. For the first time since I'd been defrosted, I stared at a dark-gray sky full of ominous clouds. This looked like a bad storm, too.

9:15 am

Today was horrible. I could not begin to tell you how harrowing it was. We got caught in a nasty typhoon and everything pitched from side to side. I dared not run the engines at high speed. Every minute I feared the boat would capsize. I wanted to move forward though and try to navigate out of the storm. I went onto the deck and secured anything I had not lashed down. I did not want to lose any of my precious provisions.

Beau came out to see what I was doing, and he immediately fell overboard. With rope still in hand, I grabbed a life preserver and jumped off the side to save him. Though I was able to wade out to him and grab him, he was scared, and he snapped at me. However, I calmed him down and pull him closer to the boat. Unfortunately, the storm was so bad I couldn't drag us both onto the boat quickly, so we spent a good portion of the afternoon tied to the side of the boat, bobbing helplessly in a cruel sea. I got sick several times and I thought I was going to pass out. It almost came to an end for Beau and me, but I just couldn't lose him. He was the only companion I had.

The sea was still a bit choppy tonight, but I felt we had coasted through the worst of the storm. I hoped it was behind us and not following. I didn't think I would sleep that night, just headed up north and then west towards Asia.

As I had never navigated across the Pacific in any type of boat before, I had no idea how long it would take. We would just have to wait and see. I wrote down how many miles it was from place to place, so I made a rough guess. My plan was to head up the coast to Guadalajara, then go due west to Hawaii. I could then go around the Hawaiian Islands and head due west toward Asia.

Beau was asleep. The poor animal had had a rough day. He shook violently when I got him aboard. I wanted to sleep myself, but, honestly, the storm scared the living shit out of me too. It was ironic how I realized my own mortality in a world such as this. I could die so easily, then what would happen to the future of mankind? If fish survived the apocalypse, then sea predators probably existed too. Beau and I could have easily been a snack for a shark or some other unknown beast.

My mind harkened back to the science fiction movies of my childhood. Could nuclear radiation have created any mutated monsters in these oceans? Were there giant octopuses, eels, or stingrays in the briny deep? Without human intervention, would sea life thrive and grow to gigantic proportions? I laughed at the thought. "Nonsense!" I said aloud to myself. If I were British, I would have said "Rubbish!" This was the real world: Not science fiction.

11:15 pm

I didn't eat much tonight. I drank a lot of water. Probably more than I should have. I could hear the sea water lapping up on the bow of the boat. I could also hear the boat's engine, which was a whisper, even though we were going sixty miles an hour.

I couldn't help but wonder to myself, what we might come across on the Pacific and what part of Asia we would see first. The prospect should've excited me, but if there were no people about, then the trip was just a logistical one: gather supplies and head for home.

I nodded off and had a dream where I was with a young female clone of myself. She was almost of childbearing age. The situation was emotionally difficult for both us, because I had raised the child myself, so she was like a daughter. Then, when it was time to make a clone baby with my clone daughter, we heard a loud boom. We both went outside to see a giant mushroom cloud not far in the distance. I woke up just as the shock wave hit us.

I finished writing this section to stay at the wheel and keep an eye on my compass to ensure we stayed north and didn't meet the storm again. I still saw faint flash lightning in the clouds behind us in the far distance. I would try and grab a couple of hours of sleep before dawn.

4:45 am

I shut down the engine and dropped anchor. I was nodding at the wheel again, so I figured it was time to call it a twenty-hour day. I could make out the coast to our right again, so we would most likely see something interesting tomorrow.

I had been saving the citrus fruit from my stash for this portion of our trip. The Pacific stretch we crossed was much larger than the Caribbean Straight we navigated down, so I wanted to save "the good stuff" for the longer haul. I didn't want Beau and I to get scurvy and have every sort of medical maladies associated with it. I'd read a short article on it back around Cuba a couple of nights ago and it sounded quite nasty.

I was not sure if dogs suffered from it or not. If I had Wi-Fi or the internet, I could check that information on my laptop or touch pad, but…*C'est la vie*, as the French said. It stood to reason that any living creature was subject to it on an ocean voyage, so I did my best to keep myself and my canine companion as healthy as possible. When we did see land, we would certainly go ashore and restock our provisions. Miraculously, I didn't lose much during the storm. I had kept most of my stuff in the cabin.

Day 20: I am through with the fancy titles.

October 18th
11:30 am

"Ugh!" I went to bed before dawn and overslept. If Beau hadn't woken me up, I probably would have slept well into the afternoon. The sun shone bright and the sea seemed calmer, but I was "whipped" from yesterday's unfortunate adventure and the yacht's king-sized bed was super comfortable.

I fed my ravenous first mate and tended to my own growling stomach. I was getting a little burned-out on fish but at this point it was a necessity. I had to ration my supplies until we got to our next port of call here in the Pacific. I hadn't had to use the water purifier yet but if we didn't go ashore soon, I would probably have to get it out and set it up. My jugged water was almost gone.

2:15 pm

I was on shore in Dominical Beach. I saw the name on a resort sign while looking around. Absolutely nothing for me here, but I had a bearing on where I was. Puerto Vallarta was where I need to go to head west toward Hawaii, according to my maps. If I followed the coast and saw land on both sides, then we had gone too far.

7:00 pm

A lackluster and disheartening day. I had better get used to it here on the Pacific. I had to clean up Beau's shit with my own hands and throw it. I spent most of the afternoon following the lifeless coast, kind of half-asleep. The sun was cruel on the cabin today. My guess was over 100 degrees, probably closer to 110. I had fish for dinner. Again.

My rudder was set, and I checked my compass to make sure we were heading north by northwest. By all intents and purposes we should've been hit Puerto Vallarta soon. The question remained...*when?*

I told myself I should be happy I had a nice, comfortable yacht. I was not in a sailboat covering twenty-five miles a day or worse yet— adrift in a rubber raft. I had a covered cabin which protected me from the hot sun and cold night air. I didn't have much fresh water, but I did have a filter purifier and the meant to get food to sustain me. I had plenty to read and if I kept my eye on my navigational instruments, I could successfully cover up to a thousand nautical miles per day in my pleasure craft. So, things were not bleak for Beau and I. Just had to be patient. I decided I was done writing cute chapter headings. I was over it. This is a journal -- a diary. Get used to it.

Day 21 - October 19th

10:30 am

It was another hot, sweltering day on the open water. But my barge moving at eighty miles an hour created a nice wind. I felt content piloting with my compass still pointing northwest. I had fed Beau already and rigged up my two fishing poles at the back of the boat, but I didn't save any fish to cut up for lures, so I used pieces of orange rind as bait. I hoped it worked. Next time, I went on a long sea jaunt, I had to remember to bring a shrimp net or cage.

2:30 pm

One of my fishing lines went haywire after a whole day of nothing. I resigned to the fact my orange-rind bait wasn't cutting it when *bam!* I got a huge hit and my reel spun wildly. Excited, I cut the engines, ran out, and grabbed the pole. I spent half an hour reeling in a twenty-pound black tuna. God, it was just the type of fun adrenaline rush I needed to break up the monotony of following the empty coastline.

5:45 pm

I saw something on the shore that attracted me, and I pulled up closer to the shore. As I had hoped, it was another resort community, and there was a dock. I tied off the yacht and hopped over to the closest resort. The front door was not locked, and it was completely empty. A check of the registration desk showed me letterhead for a resort in Puerto Vallarta. Eureka! We could head West to Asia.

I returned to the yacht and cooked dinner. I saved some strips of tuna and put them in the yacht's fridge for later. The solar generator would keep the fridge cool overnight. I would cook the fish quickly and not use the lights in the cabin tonight. The fish was good. Beau ate some of it and seemed to like it. That was good as what I had to feed him was limited. For that reason, I should've done a provision run tomorrow morning before we headed west. I didn't know exactly how long it would take us to get to Hawaii. My calculations said about 3,400 miles, which meant it could take about three and a half days to get there.

Day 22 – October 20th

7:30 am

Beau and I had some left-over smoked fish for breakfast. We were fed and had watered up. Now we spent the morning foraging for food and clean water. This trip had been tedious since we passed through the Panama Canal, but we did have an electric scooter and a nice yacht to show for our efforts.

What had we learned from all of this?

- When traveling by sea in a post-apocalyptic world, find magnetic electric engines because sailing would take too long.
- Bring plenty of fresh water and filters for your water recycler.
- Bring plenty of food for yourself and your pet.
- Bring fishing gear to catch more food.
- Bring good tools like axes and hammers.
- Chart your courses on maps. Always know where you're going.

11:25 am

Went ashore. Found beans, mangoes, some avocados, and some melons with a dark-orange fruit pulp inside and a giant, dark-brown nut. Not my favorites but edible food.

1:00 pm

Decided to make an inventory of my assets before heading out for our quest for The Hawaiian Islands. My objective was not just survival, but also to find a mate: Someone to help me repopulate this planet. I had to achieve my goal at all costs. If I failed, it would take millions of years for things to crawl out of the sea and evolve into beings, then there was no guarantee that those beings would be monkeylike humanoids that would eventually become intelligent. So I had to be smart. I had to be prepared.

I completed my inventory and here was what I had...

- ✓ a roll of duct tape
- ✓ over 3 boxes of wax candles (63 candles)
- ✓ several books (mostly about Asia and cloning)
- ✓ 1 bamboo pocket-knife spear
- ✓ 1 fully equipped yacht
- ✓ 7 life preservers (should be eight, but one was lost)
- ✓ 4 pillows
- ✓ a comforter blanket (needed at night to keep warm)
- ✓ a water filter pitcher with five filters

- ✓ 1 folding bicycle
- ✓ 1 scooter
- ✓ 1 hunting knife that once belonged to writer Ernest Hemmingway
- ✓ 3 fishing rods with reels
- ✓ 1 tackle box containing mostly freshwater tackle
- ✓ 1 snorkel and mask set
- ✓ 1 duffle bag with a couple of changes of clothes
- ✓ 5 empty potato sack-carrying bags
- ✓ 1 pair of hiking boots
- ✓ 1 backpack (empty now)
- ✓ 2 box of matches (seventy-four matches left)
- ✓ 8 gallon water jugs (filled with spring water)
- ✓ 1 ship compass
- ✓ various dried citrus fruit peels
- ✓ 1 bag of avocados
- ✓ 1 bag of mangoes
- ✓ 1 bag of raw beans
- ✓ ½ bag of coffee beans
- ✓ 1 coffee bean grinder
- ✓ the clothes I had on: trousers, t-shirt, hat, shoes

Again, with all these provisions on board, I was doing better than your average seafarer.

1:30 pm

We headed west on the Pacific Ocean at 100 nautical miles per hour.

I didn't know what Beau and I would find in Hawaii or Asia, but I hoped it would be worth it. When all was said and done, I would need to come back this way on my way back to Atlanta. I had another great boat waiting for me at the Canal Tanker point.

Beau had been a good dog. He was the epitome of man's best friend: Loyal to the end and always good-natured. With every problem, he had been by my side keeping my spirits up but never really getting in my way. My boon companion didn't eat much today. Come to think of it, neither did I. We hadn't caught any fish. They just weren't nibbling at the smoked tuna bits I had been putting on the hooks. I had better luck with the goddamn orange rinds.

Though we had an ample supply of water, a strange fact came into my head. They said some men had gone up to a week without water, but I knew it could be dangerous to not drink water for more than three days. Sea water might've kept us alive, but it would make us very sick. I hoped it didn't come to that. Perhaps, I was worried we wouldn't find fresh water in Hawaii. The stretch between there and China was twice as far.

I had never been overly religious, but I put up a prayer to the heavens now. Please give a poor sinner and an innocent dog a smooth voyage from here on out.

Day 23 – October 21st

10:30 am

I was up very late last night. I kept a close eye on my compass to make sure we stayed on course.

With my bamboo spear as a handle, I rigged up a small net with a ripped open pillowcase. I was able to catch one small fish which looked foreign to me. I could not identify it. I filleted it and cooked it up, but it tasted awful to me. Whatever it was, I gave most of it to Beau. He scarfed it up quickly, looking right up at me as if to say: "Please, sir. I want some more."

3:00 pm

I spotted land directly ahead. I asked God for good luck and damned if he did not deliver. Let me take this moment to give a shout out to the man upstairs.

It was surely not Hawaii. It would probably take us another hour to get there, but it was a joyous sight for me and my boon companion.

4:15 pm

I went ashore. It looked like an island and I was not sure which one. Would report more later.

8:00 pm

We had fresh jugs of water and a few coconuts again but little else. I was disheartened because we slowed down and wasted half a day and had very little to show for it.

I found a watering hole with fresh water and refill my jugs. I also grabbed a small stalk of bananas from a tree. They were not regular-sized bananas, but the little, half-sized ones. Bananas were rich in potassium and I needed that now. I made two trips from boat to land to do this.

God. Don't think I was ungrateful here, but I hoped I would get better luck for my shout out next time?

Day 24 – October 22nd

6:20 am

I went to bed early last night, so I got up just after sunrise this morning and did a little snorkeling near the shore here. I used my net here to grab some small fish for bait which I put in a bowl I found. So I had a better chance to catch fish. We would shove off soon, despite the island being safe. If we stopped at every one of them, it would take us forever to get to Asia.

My hope was that we would find good fruit in Hawaii. I was not crazy about our melons with the giant nuts in them. I did search this island quite a bit, but only turned up mini-bananas. It stood to reason these tropical islands should be abundant with citrus fruit but... well... there you had it. Maybe I should've looked harder and I would in Hawaii.

10:30 am

Not much to report from today. Um,…ocean…and more ocean…Oh, and ocean.

Day 25 – October 23rd

9:30 am

The sun was dreadfully hot today. I kept my rudder and compass stationed at west. I drank just enough water today, though I was tempted many times to drink more. I gave Beau plenty of water. A dog needed his water. I did my best to stay out of the sun, piloting in cabin up top. Now, I threw cards in the floppy hat.

My body ached a lot today. I hadn't really been overexerting myself beyond walking and swimming at the island yesterday morning, so I could not chalk it up to general fatigue. My body was just getting old. How depressing.

I caught a nice yellowtail today and we cooked it up and ate it for lunch. I ate fried baby bananas for dinner, because we didn't have many beans or peanuts left, so I

saved those for Beau's meals. The fried nanners were not my favorite, but again…were edible. I hoped we hit Hawaii soon. This idea kept me going forward.

Day 26 – October 24th

5:30 pm

After another boring day of sea all around us, I used my machete to hack off the top of some coconuts so Beau and I could enjoy fresh coconut milk. It tasted good and he really liked it too which made me laugh. I chipped out some actual coconut meat for us to eat. The white part was called "meat," right? I seemed to remember that, though I could not for the life of me remember where I learned that little tropical tidbit. The juice was called "milk" because of its white color.

8:00 pm

Just before sundown, I spotted land which I was certain must've been the Hawaiian Islands. According to my calculations from the map, it could not be anything else. It was beautiful with white sand beaches and tall palm trees.

I was like a kid going to bed early on Christmas Eve, anticipating the presents of the next morning. Early tomorrow I would scout it out and take my time this time. I was absolutely giddy about the prospect of what I might find in this paradise.

Day 27 – October 25th

12:30 pm

I got up with the sun this morning and quickly piloted us over to our new jungle paradise. As the trees were tall, my guess was that Hawaii was not hit directly by a nuclear blast. Then again, on an isolated island such as this, maybe things just grew quickly. Hawaii was a strategic military location. I did not see any huts, houses, or other man-made structures as I strolled around gathering items.

I found what I had hoped for: lots and lots of citrus. We now had an ample supply of pineapples, oranges, lemons and grapefruits. I also grabbed a stalk of man-sized bananas and lots of Macadamia nuts. I was elated about my latest procurements. My "shout out" finally did make it to the heavens as I was the only Earthling praying now.

6:45 pm

What a great fucking day! I loaded the passenger cabin up top with lots of fruit and coconuts. We had a lot to sustain us now. I couldn't have been happier.

I took Beau for a swim and a run on the beach too. The poor guy had been cooped up on the yacht for over a week. He was in heaven. It warmed my heart to see my best friend so happy.

7:35 pm

I thought about this island paradise and its inhabitants being incinerated in a split second. A bright light and a giant wave of intense heat. Did the innocent tourists and their children feel any pain? Earlier today, as I scanned the beach that was once Waikiki, I felt a huge lump in my throat again. It was the same lump I felt when I first took my electric scooter down I-75 in Georgia and saw the carnage of nuclear war for the first time near the Florida border.

10:00 pm

I went ashore again about an hour ago and set fire to the trees around Waikiki beach. I did not know why I did it. I was just angry, crazy or maybe both at the same time. Call it a personal statement only I would witness. I watched it burn now from the yacht. The fire was glorious, and it roared all along the Oahu coast. We moved slowly away now as I distanced myself and Beau from my manmade disaster. I continued to watch it burn yellow on the horizon like a moth wanting to go back and bury myself in it. Sorry if that sounded a bit insane. It was no more insane than causing the violent deaths of billions of innocent people with one swift push of a button.

I would pilot the boat due west now, directly to Hong Kong as my maps dictated. I didn't know how long it would take, but my guess was about six or seven days.

Day 28 – October 26th

12:00 noon

We headed out early this morning. God, I wanted to stay. It was such a beautiful place, but I got shit ta' do. Had to keep movin' forward. Plus, I set fire to the place.

I fished for lunch and thought I would make a quick log entry. As expected, just open water this morning and that was okay. Beau and I had our rest and relax yesterday.

Keeping on a direct western course our next port of call would be Hong Kong or South China. If we traveled ten to twelve hours a day, at approximately 70 to 80 nautical miles an hour, we would be there in roughly six and a half days. Anyway, that was what I'd calculated.

11:00 pm

I caught an ugly parrotfish today. It had a beak mouth like a parrot. It was good eating though. I also caught a long and thin fish that looked like a rainbow. Again – good eatin.' Fishing was the best part of the day.

Beau relaxed most of the day, soaking up the sun. He only perked up when I brought the fish on board. Not much else to report.

Day 31 – October 29th

8:00 pm

I didn't write anything in three days because I didn't want to bore you with the same shit/different day scenario. The last two days had us cruising west during daylight hours. I'd been fishing and Beau had been fairly inactive. Piloting this stretch, even at top speed, was incredibly dull. My body ached a lot again today.

Day 32 – October 30th

10:10 pm

We saw some whales today. Yes...*whales*. I wasn't sure what kind they were, but they were greyish with spots and there were several of them and they seemed curious as to what our yacht was. Some came very close to us, which was a little scary, but very exciting.

Day 33 – October 31st

9:30 pm (roughly)

I forgot to recharge the cabin for tonight, so we were dark tonight this Halloween. I hoped we found land tomorrow as I calculated. I was going stir crazy on the sea here. I needed to get my feet on dry land again.

Day 34 – November 1st

9:45 am

I practiced cutting pineapple today. That may sound strange, but try it… anyway you cut it, it had little green barbs in it. I had to cut it then pit out the green plugs like potato eyes. What a pain in the ass. Beau and I loved the fresh pineapple juice. What a treat after all the oranges and lemons we'd been eating. Have you ever eaten a lemon straight up? Man, it bit like whiskey – so sour.

It was actually a little nippy this morning, even in the tropics. My body was sore again, mostly my joints today. It was just a deep-down soreness. I was just getting old. Ironically, it was the "Day of the Dead" today in far off Mexico where we passed some days back.

8:00 pm

I caught a nice-sized dolphin. Not the kind you saw doing tricks at sea parks, I was talking about the flat-faced-fish kind of dolphin. I made a little Mahi-Mahi for Beau and myself with some white wine from our private stock. We both scarfed it up. For once, the lemon juice came in handy.

No sign of land today. Poop!

Day 35 – November 2nd

7:10 am

I was awoken by the sound of Beau barking. There was something on the horizon, straight ahead. It was small and black, so it wasn't land. I think it was a boat.

8:30 pm

Beau and I intercepted a Chinese boat (I think they call them "junks") early this morning and we spent the day onboard her. We went aboard at about eleven, though it was old and weather beaten, it was a very impressive seacraft. Of course, I found the remnants of the previous owners – a family of three. After a proper burial at sea, Beau and I made our way from stem to stern. Obviously, there was no edible food aboard. There was a gas cooker, but no gas in the tank. It had a gas motor, but again, dry as a pie crust. All in all, we found little in the way of tools or items that could aid us on our journey, but it was a big ship with a big sail and a dingy. Finding it here meant we were close to China. My heart lifted again.

After careful consideration, I decided to tow her back to Asia. I would just go slow and easy, so as not to put undo stress on my yacht. I just loved the character of the junk. I knew we would find China tomorrow. I just knew it.

Day 36 – November 3rd

6:30 am

I was up early. We moved at about forty miles an hour. I did find two lanterns for my candles, reminding me I needed to learn how to make candles. I was not using them as much lately, but I would be careful and have backups, just in case. I wouldn't have my generator with me always and it could break down.

2:30 pm

I caught another unidentifiable fish and, when I brought it into the boat, Beau guarded it, barking loudly and happily until I could club it dead. I then took it to the kitchen (galley?) and cooked it on our electric stove with some mango juice. It was good, probably because we were both so hungry from our exciting day. It had been a good day and I felt blessed to have my large, incredibly well-equipped ocean craft.

There was a comfortable-looking rope hammock on the junk's main cabin but even though I tried it out and liked it, the yacht's king-sized bed was just much superior. I unhooked it and brought it to the yacht. I would set it up in the back yard when Beau and I got back home.

My sleep was just so-so when I first started sleeping on the yacht. I used to have the same problem when I'd sleep in hotel beds or visit relatives and sleep in their homes. No matter how comfortable the bed was, I just needed time to get used to the new bunk. I was very used to the yacht's bed now.

4:40 pm

We still waited for Asia to come into view. Should've been any time now. Maybe I miscalculated the distance to Hong Kong. I was understandably eager to get to the Orient. We had traveled so long and so far. Beau was just happy to be with me.

I discovered Beau had suitably marked his territory here. He had pissed at every nook and cranny on our vessel. Even though I ran out of newspaper days ago, I didn't mind cleaning up after him. He was a dog and that was what dogs did.

7:00 pm

I spotted land straight ahead. It stretched all the way across the western horizon from left to right. It had to be China.

10:45 pm

We anchored just off the coast. We were so close we could smell it. It was too dark now to determine where we were, but we would find out tomorrow morning.

Day 37 – November 4th

12:40 pm

I went ashore this morning and my best guess was South China. The land looked like Florida, Cuba, and the islands we visited. Whatever place this was, the bombs had leveled it. I didn't think there was much in the way of buildings or houses here at this particular spot, but the lack of thick trees, taller than twenty feet, pretty much confirmed it'd been nuked.

I found some yellow star fruit here but little else. I remembered reading about them before in my Asian travel books.

6:30 pm

We piloted our yacht and junk dingy up the coastline and I knew where we were now. The topography was unmistakable. We were now moored in Hong Kong Harbor. Much of the area was overgrown rubble, but I could still make it out from photographs in my books on Asia.

There was a concrete dock where I tied the boat off. Tomorrow, I would ride up into the mountains with some plastic jugs and look for a spring. If I found any more fruit or food that Beau and I might enjoy, I would grab it as well. I would take the saddle bags as well.

Day 38 – November 5th

7:00 am

Early to bed and early to rise made a man healthy wealthy and wise. I got the folding bicycle off the yacht and onto the dock with little trouble. I spent most of last night reading about Hong Kong. It was a bustling city – a shopper and diner's paradise. Under British rule for over a hundred and fifty years, it was given back to the People's Republic of China in 1997. Due to the large British population and influence on culture in that region, the people of Hong Kong enjoyed liberties that mainland Chinese didn't have (freedom of assembly, freedom of press, freedom of speech, etc.), but now… just ruins. It had probably been on the outer fringes of a big blast. It looked like Mainland China was the target of a nuclear strike and Hong Kong, being on the southernmost tip, was toppled by the shockwave but not completely incinerated by the blast. Also, the mountains between mainland China and Hong Kong probably helped to shield it from total disaster.

I would do my best to navigate around the wreckage on the bike and find food and fresh water. I ate the star fruit for breakfast today although I had to say, the bitter sour taste was not to my liking. Beau didn't seem to like the taste of it either. Hopefully, we would both eat better tonight. We found shrimp cages on board the junk. Now that we were finally here, I could put them down in the water.

8: 45 pm

It was a busy but enjoyable day. I enjoyed being a pirate. *Arrr!* I found very little in the city, and it was very hard for me to navigate around the fallen wreckage, but there were several houses on the mountains facing Hong Kong still standing. I found some coffee filters in plastic I thought might work in my water pitcher and a few paperback books in English still in pretty good condition. After several hours of searching I finally found a freshwater mountain stream and I filled all of my jugs. I cleaned myself in the cool water. It was heavenly.

In the late afternoon, I found some Litchi (pronounced Lee-Chee) fruit trees and loaded up a bag with them. I had seen pictures of these in one of my books, so I knew they were safe to eat. I also found small tangerine-like oranges that were delicious. I made a special trip back just to fill two of my sacks to the top with them. I cursed this world without fuel or electricity. I got a serious workout peddling around the mountains today.

I finally got back to the boat the second time at about 7:30. Beau was happy to see me and jumped around playfully at my return as dog's usually do. I fed him some of the tangerines. He absolutely loved them. I kept telling myself that citrus on a sea voyage would only do us both good.

I checked my shrimp traps but nothing in them. I decided to use one of my freshwater lures to see if I could get a saltwater fish to bite. After flyfishing off the side of the yacht for about forty-five minutes, I finally caught a nice-sized fish. Didn't recognize what kind of fish it was, but no matter.

After dinner, I checked the new filters to see if they could function in my filter-pitcher. Not a perfect fit. I tested it with seawater and I still tasted a little salt. It probably wouldn't upset Beau's stomach as much as mine, drinking filtered seawater, so I used it for his water to see how he reacted to it. We could always return here and get fresh water before we returned, if need be. I reminded myself to keep on the lookout for more water jugs.

It was still eerie to go on land with no other people, animals and insects. I was not complaining – Malaria used to be very common around this region. It was silent and peaceful, but a very creepy quiet, like the calm before a catastrophe... actually the calm after the disaster.

11:45 pm

I settled down to read one of the books I'd found by candlelight tonight. The Junko-lantern (as I called it) gave off a much better light from the candle. It was a bit of a pain to clean it out. I still had over two boxes of candles, so we were still good to go in that department. We may find more along the way. One can only hope as I do like candlelight.

The book was an interesting and based on a true story. Titled "The Injustice," it was about an English businessman whose young daughter was kidnapped by a ruthless Chinese gangster. The businessman went to the police and they apprehended the criminal. The gangster, who had killed the innocent girl, only caring about collecting his money, was tried and convicted. He was given the death sentence, but the father of the slain girl was allowed to visit him in prison which he did regularly.

At first, he just stared at the prisoner, making the man uncomfortable. The gangster pleaded with the authorities to stop the visits, but the police continued to allow it. The father brought pictures of his daughter and showed them to the prisoner, again not saying a word. The prisoner cussed at him, insulted him, but was kept back by the guards.

The next week, the prisoner was paraded out again and the father, not saying a word, forced him to watch a DVD of home movies of his daughter. The criminal committed suicide in his cell the next week on the night before the father's next scheduled visit. Just two weeks before his scheduled execution.

The story was short (about 190 pages – ah, a novella) but it was fascinating, and I read through it quickly, but now I had to finish my notes and go to sleep.

Tomorrow, Beau and I would try and make our way to South Korea, passing up the east coast of China. I wanted to search for the Pusan Institute for Genetic Research. I wanted to find out more about

Dr. Soong's work. It was the main reason why I'd come over here. Looking at my map, it wouldn't take me long to get there. I would just go up the Chinese East Coast past Shanghai and Dalian. With luck, I would be there by tomorrow night. I suspected Korea and Japan would both be completely demolished: wiped out, as it were, but today's journey through Hong Kong was encouraging.

Beau waited for me to go to sleep. He lay on a blanket on the floor near my bed, totally content, but his eyes were still opening and surveying the room.

As I sat there writing and examining the room myself, I wondered what life aboard this junk was like before the holocaust...a fisherman and his loyal wife with a beautiful son or daughter running about the big boat. A simple but poor life, I imagined, but they'd been probably happy together until the end, more faceless and nameless innocent victims of this global tragedy unfolding before me.

China once had over 2 billion people. It was so overpopulated that each family could only have one child. It was called "The One Baby Rule." You had to pay a huge fine to the government to have a second offspring. Little did they know, very soon, none of that would matter.

Day 39 – November 6th

8:00 pm

I felt crappy and lethargic today, so Beau and I just stayed on the boat and ate fresh fruit. Korea could wait.

I read more books about Chinese culture. The Chinese had different feelings about the afterlife. Many believed in reincarnation. They thought when you die your spirit would find its way into the next baby born. Of course, you would have no recollection of your old life (or lives), though a visit to a medium or spiritualist might get you a backstory.

Many Chinese people also believed there was a place like Heaven where your ancestors dwelled. If you burned specially crafted and blessed paper products with the ancestor's name on it, then it would appear to them and they could use it on the other side. So many people burned specially made money and paper clothes, paper watches, even paper houses for long dead relatives, so that their afterlife was rich.

Now, you had to wonder if this was a slick marketing campaign making unreligious conmen small fortunes. Greeting card companies in the West certainly changed the holidays of Valentine's Day, Easter, Halloween, and Christmas. Where had the Easter Bunny come from? How did Santa Claus become more popular than Jesus on his birthday? A paper car was a paper car, was I right?

Day 40 – November 7th

5:45 pm

Another day of just lazing about. I knew I should get my ass in gear, but after finally being here after the long sea voyage, I just felt drained and unmotivated. I enjoyed just reading and relaxing aboard my yacht.

Day 41 – November 8th

10:10 pm

I was still recharging my batteries. I promised myself I would make the trip to Korea tomorrow. I was ready for it now. Vacation time was over.

Day 42 – November 9th

12:30 pm

I was up early again this morning, my body clock totally in tune to rising at seven-ish, China time. That was twelve hours difference with the American East Coast, meaning we were twelve hours ahead of Atlanta. I felt rejuvenated today and finally excited about our journey.

The first thing I did was check my cages. Only a couple of shrimp but two nice, olive-green colored crabs were hanging on. I used the shrimp for bait and caught a nice- sized fish shortly after we started up the coast. I dropped anchor to prepare the crabs and fish for lunch. Delicious.

After we ate, we let lose the junk leaving her behind us. I had every intention of leaving the junk in Hong Kong, but whether it was sentimentality or laziness, I hadn't untied her from the back of our yacht until now. She belonged here.

4:00 pm(ish)

We were just off the coast of Shanghai now. The city of Shanghai used to have one of the most distinct and interesting skylines on this side of the world. I remembered seeing it often on T.V. and in the movies…but it no longer existed in my world. It had been totally leveled. I'd seen very few buildings along the coast this morning.

6:45 pm

It was getting dark early now, so I dropped anchor at what I thought was close to North China's beach city of Dalian now, but it was hard to tell when all the land topography looked so similar. Beau and I ate leftover fish and some of our tangerines. Man, I could've eaten those little juicy fruits all day. Beau could've too. I hoped we saw something (anything) tomorrow.

Day 43 – November 10th

4:15 pm

Today was eventful. Beau and I got up early and headed up the coast again. At about 8:30am, we passed an actual Japanese battleship. The son-of-a-bitch was huge and silent, just sitting there…a giant reminder of a long-ago civilization. I would have liked to have boarded her, but I couldn't see any way to.

"Ahoy!" I said aloud, laughing to myself. "Can you drop a ladder?" I cupped my ear mockingly and waited for an answer. After a moment of silence, I looked at Beau and said. "Oh shit, man. They don't speak English." My companion only looked back at the massive structure as we passed. It was impressive.

At about ten I started to see trees and small houses on the shore, albeit some of the houses were collapsed, but it was a positive sign. Had we reached Korean territory?

The peninsula I had been searching for since late yesterday was evidently no longer there. As it jutted out from China near where Beijing would have been close to, it was obviously scuttled by a direct hit, just like the Panama Canal. The detonation of nuclear weapons had dramatically changed the geography of the planet. My compass said we were going southeast now, so my feeling was we were making our way back down the South Korea coastline.

8:00 pm

I pulled up to a concrete dock and went ashore at about 4:30pm, and we were definitely on the South Korean coastline. I saw a sign I could not read, but the language was Korean. The letters had little circles in them. To the best of my knowledge, no other Asian language had that. I found some carrots and cabbages and greens growing wild in what I believed used to be someone's personal backyard garden.

I was back on the boat by 5:30 and we made our way farther down the coast. An hour later, as the sun started going down, we found Pusan. As there was only one big city on the southernmost coast of Korea, I figured this had to be it. It took us almost a month to get here because of all the problems along the way, but we were here. As expected, it was a mess but, like Hong Kong, many structures still stood. I was elated beyond description. My big gamble had so far paid off.

I would look through my books and magazines again tonight to try and find any clue about the whereabouts of The Pusan Center for Genetic Research and/or Dr. Wi Hua Soong. Maybe there was something that I overlooked: some small detail that could make a difference in our quest for a better life in this vast but desolate world. Tomorrow we could sift through the rubble to find some answers.

Day 44 – November 11th

6:00 am

Beau and I were up earlier than usual today. I was already packed and ready to go. Beau had been fed. I'd packed some fruit, but I was too excited to eat at the moment.

Last night, I reread the magazine articles and clippings about Dr. Wi Hua Soong. Two pieces of information jumped out at me and I couldn't believe I'd missed them before. The first one was a clue to the whereabouts of The Pusan Center for Genetic Research which one article stated was in the CENTER of downtown Pusan. Hallelujah! A direct point to head to.

The next piece of information I discovered was equally surprising in that it was so obvious and so completely overlooked it. It stated that after Dr. Soong was forced out of the center because of the bad press, she retired to her MOUNTAIN home just outside of Pusan. Not as direct a marker but again, it would narrow down my search quite a bit.

With my new directional tidbits, I was more than ready to start tracking down what I wanted and needed. Hopefully, my next entry would be a juicy one with lots of good news. Be patient, dear reader.

10:30 pm

Well, it was an interesting day. After writing this morning's entry, I slipped and almost dropped the bike into the sea. Luckily, I caught it before it totally fell off the gangplank, but in doing so, I pulled a muscle in my left shoulder. It hurt like a bitch all day.

I searched around the center of Pusan most of the day, trying to find the Genetic Research Center. I found a few dilapidated street maps and signs, but none mentioned it. All the signs had English on them underneath the Korean. That was an unexpected convenience, but alas… I was not getting any closer to finding what I wanted. What had happened to the research center? Had it closed down before the holocaust? Why couldn't I find it?

I did find a three-wheeled bicyclecart in front of a shop and it was surprisingly functional, so I parked my smaller ride against a building and spun around town on the trike during the afternoon.

At about 3:45 pm I found the research center. The sign had been destroyed partially by the shockwave of a blast, so it took me a second of looking right at it for me to re-puzzle it in my mind. I went inside and looked all around. The place was a disaster area upstairs. No visible remains of people, but dust, dirt, paper remnants, etc. everywhere.

I candled up my lantern and made my way down a staircase. The laboratories would be downstairs, right? As I crept along slowly, I had no fear because there was nothing left in this world to attack me. The worst thing that could happen was I fell down the stairs, or the building fell apart and came down me with me still in it. That would have been a truly ironic ending after coming this far.

I found several labs underground. I had no trouble getting in because the electronic doors no longer had power. They were all open. I brought my big military bag with me and loaded it with tools, beakers that I wrapped in paper or cloth, anything I thought would be useful. I found a room that had large glass jars which once contained embryos. They were probably clones, but the solutions keeping them preserved had long dried up, ergo, *they'd* dried up.

I searched every desk at this level and grabbed any handwritten notes and books I'd found. There was a French scientist here by the name of Claude Tourneau. He'd written everything in English (though his handwriting was fucking lousy).

I didn't know why, but I noticed a laptop computer in the drawer of his desk. Though it probably wouldn't work, I decided to grab it anyway. I remembered the few things that had surprised me by working. Maybe I could get something out of it. I decided to take everything on the trike cart back to the boat.

It was not easy for me to peddle the trike-cart through the rubble back to the boat, especially as it was weighted down with my booty (my treasures, not my ass). But I liked the idea of having Beau come and ride around with me. He could sit in the back and we could adventure together again.

Beau was happy to see me when I rolled up. He jumped around again and barked with excitement. I thought to myself as I slung my bog bag over my shoulder and walked up the plank that I was truly happy to see him, too. Man's best apocalyptic friend. I quickly made my way to our cabin and unloaded my cargo. I carefully sifted the items into groups on the floor – papers in one pile, electronics in another, tools and other useful shit in yet another.

By that time, the sky was turning orange and pink as the sun was starting to go down, so I went out again and checked my traps finding a couple of "bait shrimp." Good! I could do a little sunset fishing. By the last light of the sun as it dipped below the purple horizon, I hooked a nice-sized "grunt fish." It wasn't long before it was cooked, and my dog and I enjoyed dinner.

As I wrote, I was anxious to try the laptop computer I'd found. Maybe tomorrow, I could charge the generator on the boat when I woke up. I would look for other useful items in Pusan as well. I was tired, so I would go to bed early tonight. I could also read Tourneau's notes in the morning.

Day 45 – November 12th

8:15 am

It was colder than usual today. I'd logged it being colder in the early mornings this past week or so, but this morning was especially chilly. I put on an extra-long sleeve shirt I'd packed.

Tourneau's notes were not easy to read. It was like breaking a secret military code. From what I could gather, this guy was working closely with Dr. Soong and helped a Dr. Rara Li who took over Soong's work when she'd left the center. There was a lot of technical mumbo jumbo about cloning sheep and cats, but nothing about human cloning experiments and no clues to the mountain location of Dr. Soong's home.

I crushed up some Litchi fruit for Beau and myself. I sprinkled it with tangerine juice. We had almost eaten all of the little tangerines, but we hadn't eaten a lot of the Litchis. Beau looked up at me as if to say, "What's this crap?" Feeling like a parent with a finicky child, I said to him, "Eat it. It's good for you." He sniffed it, then began to nibble but it was obviously not his favorite breakfast.

I grabbed up Beau in my arms and took him ashore. When I put him down, he frolicked about excitedly and it was hard for me to get him into the back of the trike. Finally, I got him into it where he was comfortable. When I started to peddle around, it scared him a bit, but when I started to move forward more quickly, he seemed to like it better, as most frisky dogs did when they got a ride.

12:15 pm

This morning I brought my journal with me. We searched some of the roads not taken yesterday. I found there was a lot less scattered crap to peddle around as I took us around the edge of the city. The highways still left were smoother and I could cover more ground.

2:00 pm

We found a hardware store. I broke into the back stockroom and grabbed some tools for the boat, an electric lantern I was pretty sure would hook up to the generator. There were a lot of useful tools here and I was like an unsupervised kid in a candy shop.

7:30 pm

Beau and I scouted a mountain west of Pusan. This would be harder than I'd thought. All signs out here were written in Korean. It was like looking for a needle in a haystack and I had to walk up the mountain road because peddling sucked. We would sleep in someone's house tonight.

8:30 pm

Beau and I had some of the vegetables I'd grabbed from the garden a few days back. The carrots and cabbage were good. I boiled them by making a wood fire out by the back porch of the house. The fire lit up the backyard and Beau enjoyed running around for a while.

I didn't find much in this house that would be useful to us. I couldn't find any books or magazines in English. Everything was Korean here. We would turn in early. The saddest part was that there were no beds in this house. Koreans ate and slept on the floor. I would have to sleep on the floor with Beau.

1:45 am

I awoke to the sound of Beau yelping. At the moment I woke up, I felt little pins sticking in my fingers and toes. At first, I thought it was because I'd just woken up and my circulation was just catching up. Diabetics often woke up with tingling toes and fingers, but Beau yelped again and I heard him scratching about. Something was wrong here.

I lit a candle and there they were... dozens of them. Big cockroaches! They were actually biting my toes and they were biting Beau. He jumped around and I began lashing out at the cockroaches, trying to squash them. These roaches were aggressive. They didn't scamper away when attacked. They only backed up minimally, then moved forward again. Only when I got a direct hit could I squash them. I was pretty sure I said "Shit!" and made my way out of the room with Beau and bag in tow. Cockroaches had survived the nuclear Armageddon. If the fish had made it, it stood to reason cockroaches would have survived as well. Vermin were scavengers—survivors. I would have to watch out for rats too, I was betting.

In the living room I heard their chirping-clicking. There were more roaches in the other rooms of the house. They were slightly large, but nothing overly menacing about them. They were just more aggressive than the roaches in America and they did bite, albeit very tiny bites, like an ant bite. They were more a big bunch of pests to us than anything else, but their biting had certainly put "the fear of God in me."

Beau and I huffed it back down the mountain to the tricycle again, rode back to the yacht, and slept there. We would have to come back to the boat every night for our safety. Now that I knew some undesirable creatures had survived the nuclear annihilation, and we had no idea which other critters had also and how dangerous they were, we would had to be more careful. Rats, spiders, mosquitoes, centipedes, snakes. They could've all caused huge problems for Beau and I in a world such as this. We couldn't make a grave mistake by being careless. These varmints could be poisonous or be carrying diseases.

Day 46 – November 13th

8:00 am

I was still a little rattled by last night's encounter with the cockroaches. In my mind now, the roaches did seem larger than your standard palmetto bug-style cucaracha. was this my imagination running wild? No. They were not huge, but they were bigger. Bugs did not have a long-life expectancy, so these buggers were evolving. Living off the fat of the land and growing. When they sensed Beau and me, it must have been pretty mouthwatering to them. I checked my hands and toes. No marks that I could see on my fingers, but I did have a couple of small ant-like welts on my feet and under my toes. Little red bumps no bigger than a pinhead. But it was not really the roaches I was afraid of. It was the chance something else was out there lurking about. Some other dangerous insect or predator.

I'd seen photos of green, gnarly, deadly centipedes which had grown as long as three and a half feet in Thailand. The black ones with the red heads could kill a small man with their bite. I was not a small man, but I did not want to face an agonizing venom purging

85

sickness that might last as long as a week. Beau would've been a goner, for sure. We needed to "keep our eyes peeled" and always stay on the alert for such nuisances.

Beau and I would check out the next mountain at the north end of Pusan today. If we were lucky, we would find Dr. Soong's place there before nightfall.

1:15 pm

We made good time. We still hadn't found the Soong residence, but we had covered a good portion of the mountain. Luckily, the Korean government had only allowed a few elites to build on the mountains. There were very few houses here. I'd resigned myself to the fact I might never find Dr. Soong's domicile, but Beau and I did have time and I felt we must keep trying.

We found some eggplant growing in a field. I was not a huge fan of eggplant, mostly due to its soft squishy interior. I had the same problem eating raw tomatoes, but it would be tasty enough if we barbecued or stir-fried it.

5:30 pm

We canvassed the northern mountain near Pusan. There was only one highway around it and very few homes. I took Beau back to the boat. I powered up the solar generator when we were back on board.

11:30 pm

I stir-fried the eggplant and, though it would have been better barbecued, it was actually very good. Beau seemed to like it. We were both tired of our fruit-filled meals. My thoughts drifted and took me back to Atlanta. Life for Beau and I was pretty good there. I was getting a little homesick.

About an hour ago, I tried the laptop computer. The screen had gotten weird- looking green lines running up and down it, but it appeared to be working to some extent. Though not easy to read, I could make things out better when I moved them to the right side of the small screen.

I could not see all of the icons on the desktop screen clearly but I could open things with the toolbar on the bottom left corner. I looked for anything with Dr. Soong's name attached to it. She was mentioned in several documents, but there appeared to be nothing written by her in this laptop.

I had read some of Tourneau's journals. His work was very impressive. Evidently, he'd worked with Dr. Li and they were hoping to clone endangered animals like white tigers and pandas. Unfortunately, the success rate had been very low. It took over two hundred and seventy-five tries to create "Dolly," the first cloned sheep. More bad news.

Before his work with Dr. Li, he'd specialized in therapeutic cloning: the cloning of body tissues and organs to aid people with medical maladies such as bad skin or faulty kidneys.

I did a search on "sex change" and after sifting through some porn that Claude had stored in his D: drive, I found an important-looking document written by Dr. Rara Li discussing a procedure for something called "interstitial injection of clone embryos."

The clone embryo was grown in a Petri dish and the sex was determined by interstitial injection of the X or Y chromosome at the earliest stage of its development. The procedure was first tested by a Chinese doctor Zhu in Shenzhen in 2004. Then it was practiced and perfected in Pusan by W.H.S. It didn't take me long to figure out Wi Hua Soong's initials.

I did a word search on WHS and W.H.S. Bingo! I stared at papers that had been penned by the good doctor Soong herself, then translated to English for Tourneau. She outlined procedures for basic cloning of animals. Though very careful in her wording, she made it very clear that all procedures would work with humans.

So it was a reality. Not only could we possibly clone things, but we could change their sex to whatever we wanted. If I could learn advanced biology and cloning science, then I might find a way to make a female clone with an alternate host. I needed to learn more.

Everything in the lab with the exception of Tourneau's area was written in Korean. I would have to learn Korean to decipher it. Soong's journals might be written in English as she was working with other scientists from other countries. If we didn't find her home, we'd come a long way for very little. If I'd had a magic lamp in my hands then, I would've been rubbing it and wishing. *Help me find the home of Dr. Wi Hua Soong.* Maybe another shout-out was in order.

Day 47 – November 14th

9:15 am

Beau and I went to the Genetic Research Center again and checked for more learning materials. I checked the Korean tech's desks on higher floors for English-written materials. If they'd had contact with Tourneau, they probably had to communicate and write things in English.

11:15 am

I brought a bag full of books and journals back with me to the boat. Some had English written in them. I would check them more closely later. I also went back to the clean water area and cleaned up. I refilled some of our jugs. Beau and I were off to the northeast mountain now.

9:30 pm

I still had not found Dr. Soong's house. It stood to reason she'd probably been hassled a lot for her work and as a result was probably a recluse. I might have passed her house on the first day and never realized it. This whole project from the very start was "ambitious" to say the least. I was disheartened by the amount of work I had put forth with very little to show for it. Tools, food, and boats I could get in Georgia. Beau and I would give it one more shot tomorrow, but I felt I was beating a dead horse here.

Day 48 – November 15th

9:00 am

I read some more of the journals and computer files last night. I started to understand the process of cloning better. And finding Dr. Rara Li's notes yesterday (didn't realize it until late last night) helped a lot. Much of her work was detailed and written in Korean and English. The scanned pages were all in her handwriting.

I was too tired to write about it last night. In reality, I fell asleep reading the journals and did not wake up until now. Beau and I would continue the search of the northeast mountain today. If we didn't find anything, well so be it. We would shove off soon and head for home.

3:15 pm

While walking along a road on the westside of the northeast mountain, I saw a name out of the corner of my eye and I literally did a double-take. On a mailbox below some Korean characters was the name RARA LI. I turned and walked up the overgrown driveway. The drive was long and wound up to a nice house covered from view by trees and shrubbery. I broke in and was shocked to see not only pictures of Dr. Rara Li, but also Wi Hua Soong, both of whom I recognized from photos in the news articles and in pictures from the research center.

The pictures showed the two Asian women holding each other like spouses. I chuckled to myself. Obviously, these two girls had been closer than they both ever let on. Even in the early twenty-first century homosexuality was highly frowned upon by Asian cultures. In China, people were institutionalized for it.

I was elated because I had found what I was looking for, but furious that it was in the last damned place I had looked. "You rolls yer dice... you takes yer chances."

I found several books on cloning written in English. "Fan-Fucking-Tastic!" as my old college chum Paul used to say. It had always made me laugh when he said it. I found journals written in Korean with English notes. I packed them hastily. I searched the house bottom to top.

While in the upstairs bathroom, I stopped when I saw two dusty hairbrushes laying on the counter and two toothbrushes in a moldy cup by the sink. I packed them along with the photos of the women. They had given me so much hope, I wanted mementos.

Something told me to check the cellar. I went down into the cold underbelly of the mountain home and shivered. At the bottom of the stairs was what appeared to be a mini-lab. I packed beakers and boxes and whatever I thought would help me with my own experiments and I ran across a metal box. Inside it were DNA samples on slides.

Though they were obviously dried up, I thought to myself: "Could I still glean some actual DNA from these?" I carefully packed it in my bag.

I gave the house another once over, wondering if there was any important thing I missed. The thought hit me that the remains of Wi Hua Soong and Rara Li were conspicuously missing. They would've certainly wanted to be together in the end. Maybe they had abandoned their home and went to a shelter.

I got a ghost-like feeling that caused the hair on my arms to stand straight up. I saw an entrance to the attic in the ceiling of the upstairs hallway. I pulled down the doorway hatch and a ladder folded down for me invitingly. I made my way up the ladder and it was there I found what was left of Dr. Wi Hua Soong and Dr. Rara Li. I wasn't sure which was which but one lay in the lap of the other. They sat together in an overstuffed, high-backed chair pulled up to the only window in the room. The view from this vantage point was of the setting sun. Their last moment together was probably a painful but touching one. I actually teared up thinking about it.

I felt bad now about ransacking their resting place but desperate times called for desperate measures and I gave the room a once over (respectfully). I didn't find anything special. I was just meant to come here and meet my hosts. I nodded to them (respectfully) and made my exit.

5:45 pm

I found some wild vegetables near the house: lots of peppers, onions, new potatoes, and tomatoes: The last gift for me from these special ladies. "Thank you," I said aloud before Beau and I made our way back to the yacht. I thought to myself on the cycle ride back that I should name my new boats. My Pacific beast of a boat would be called "The Lovely Soong," and my boat back in Panama would become "The Rara Li."

7:30 pm

If you hadn't guessed, I generalized on the time here. Rounding forward or backward to the nearest convenient time: typical lazy American. Also, I didn't want anyone who read this to think I was some nerd nut-ball who had to mark down every correct minute, to the second. Putting the time down probably came from the old TV shows I used to watch, where the time was always displayed before the action. This was common in the TV shows of my youth in the early twenty first century.

We would leave Pusan tomorrow and head for home. We would check the Japanese coastline as we went, but I was not expecting much. In any worldwide apocalypse, I was sure Japan would be a target. Most cultures were still holding grudges against Japan for past war atrocities like Nanjing and Pearl Harbor. And, no doubt, after centuries, tradition and pride forbade them to ever say they were sorry.

Day 49 - November 16th

8:30 am

I pulled up our shrimp traps and we had more shrimp than usual today. I put the little critters in a plastic bucket I found on the Lovely Soong. One of those big white industrial buckets like painters used. You could turn them upside-down and actually stand on them. I put some saltwater in the bucket to keep them alive. Fresh shrimp made better bait (And boiled shrimp cocktail! We still have lemons aboard.) I packed lots of fire kindling and reminded myself to find a barbecue grill. We would have "shrimp on the barby" or barbecued eggplant for dinner.

We hoisted anchor and were off to new territory. I wouldn't say I would miss Pusan. It was a nice place to visit, but I certainly wouldn't want to spend my post-apocalyptic time there. As we set sail that morning and watched Pusan get smaller at our stern, my mind went strangely back to the roaches. I wondered if I would have trouble with such things in Atlanta. I'd been there for over a week and nothing invaded. I could put mosquito nets around my bed. Let's hope that would be enough.

Beau seemed happy to be back on the open sea. I laughed to myself as I watched him at the bow of the yacht. I was happy to be yachting again myself. I was an old salt and Beau was my old, salty dog.

2:00 pm

We had been making our way quickly southward down the western coast of Japan. As expected, the whole coast was devoid of any structures: No buildings, no houses, and no sizable trees. It was a barren paradise like its big neighbor China. The compass said we were heading east now, so we would turn the wheel soon and head straight for Mexico. If we hit Hawaii again on the way, so be it.

2:45 pm

I started to doze at the wheel when I spotted some knocked-over houses just now. I just hoped I was not hallucinating. I thought I saw a city in the distance. Amazing! If the city was like Pusan, Beau and I might have to stay in Asia another day or two. Write more later.

3:20 pm

We docked at what I felt was the remnant city of Kyoto. It looked like Godzilla, Rodan, and Mothra had all rampaged through here. I saw a fallen tower which I recognized from photos I'd seen when I was a child. Kyoto Tower was as distinctive as the Space Satellite Tower in Seattle, Washington. Like Pusan, the city had been rocked, but it was still standing (for the most part). Beau and I would take a quick look around before nightfall and scout around to see if we found anything interesting.

9:20 pm

We went into Kyoto this afternoon. Signs with English sub-writing confirmed that Kyoto was where we were. We raided a store called "Jusco," which was like a Japanese version of Walmart, and I grabbed myself a Hibachi barbecue grill and several bags of charcoal. Nobody had looted it before us: must be an American thing. Beau and I had barbecued fish and shrimp for dinner. It was delicious.

I was kicking myself because I hadn't brought a lot of reading material on Japan. While glossing through a Science magazine, I did find an article about nuclear warfare and EMPs which interested me. I remembered Dr. Swail's comment on electronics not working: EMP: Electromagnetic Pulses from detonated nuclear devices had fried all electronic circuitry. Obviously, some things might still work, like the MP3 player and magnetic-electrical engines with no computer chips in them, while the other ninety-nine percent wouldn't. If something were shielded, such as the laptop being down in a laboratory with thick iron and concrete walls, it might survive the shockwave EMP.

I had a marvelous idea. Tomorrow, I would check local banks to see what might be in their vaults. I might find more laptops or gadgetry that worked there. I found the robot bride article again. How desperate do you have to be to marry a robot bride? I laughed to myself again because I was the guy with a valid excuse. I was the last man on Earth.

Day 50 - November 17th

7:15 am

I was up early and excited about raiding Japan today. Beau would stay on board and I would take the folding bike to the local banks and see what I could find. This side trip may have turned out to be very beneficial indeed. I fried up some home-fries made from the new potatoes with onion. I would've killed for a couple of eggs right then. I would make a nice omelet with the green peppers and tomatoes.

11:45 am

I was already back from my first trip. I'd hit two banks already. I didn't find anything in the first bank except Japanese yen which was totally useless to me. The second bank was larger, and the safety deposit box area was massive. A short search of the lobby desks yielded keys to the boxes and I spent most of the morning emptying them. I found all sorts of crazy things including a woman's husband's ashes in a decorative urn and a large vibrator. More importantly, I found a couple of computer back-up drives.

I found a door which had a similar number plate on it. I smiled and thought to myself: "A safety deposit closet?" It obviously belonged to a very rich customer. When I went in, I shined my candle in the room and got quite a shock.

The room was decorated like a small apartment, with a nice-sized bed, a dining table set for two, and a window with a large picture of the city in it, just like a real view.

Standing in the corner was a mannequin of a beautiful Japanese girl of about 20 or so. On closer inspection, I realized she was not a mannequin, but one of the robot girls I had read about. Her mouth was slightly open, revealing a full set of teeth, a tongue, and a normal-sized airway. Her eyes looked real though the expression was blank at the moment. She had short, red hair and was dressed in a red and white kimono mini-dress. Her feet were bare, and her toes looked very lifelike. Someone had actually taken the time to even paint her dainty toenails red to match her outfit.

A trunk next to her had a name on it, but it was in Japanese. I found a key to the trunk on a string around her neck. I opened it and found a full wardrobe of fancy dinner clothes and naughty street girl-type outfits. There were also colorful wigs of all lengths and styles, some in neon colors. Obviously her master was one sick puppy.

I stood looking at her for several minutes debating on whether I should take her with me. Obviously, her batteries were long dead. This little robot geisha girl would be of little use to me: now just a pretty statue to look at. I inspected her closer. Though made of rubber, her skin was surprisingly soft. I checked her neck and back for any clue as to where her power supply was. At the small of her back was a plastic flap. I checked under the flap and she had different connection slots. One felt like USB and the others...

"Oh my God!" I said aloud. "She's rechargeable."

I smiled as I searched the cozy love nest and found a box under the bed which contained her connection cables, along with various electric plug adaptors, some computer disks, and two oblong back-up batteries, still wrapped in plastic. They looked to be in good shape, too. No split seams or discoloration from acid leakage.

Even though there was no instruction manual (it would have been in Japanese anyway), on pure impulse, I packed her up along with her accessories and comically lugged her back to The Lovely Soong. If I could find a way to power her, I would have someone to talk to or maybe even play games with. It would be nice to be able to communicate with someone, at least until I could create a clone or defrost another human. Sorry if I sound like I was trying to justify this decision a little too much,... but she was damned impressive.

I also grabbed a sweet Bose music system from this safety deposit box fantasy room. I prayed to the heavens it worked. It would've been so nice to have tunes in this day and age. I wanted to hear The Beatles, Elvis Presley, Queen, Roy Orbison, Pink Floyd, and all of my other favorites. I grabbed a table lamp and a power strip, too. I couldn't complain. If even half of this shit worked, I had scored huge today. I chuckled to my looting, no-good self.

10:15 pm

I raided another Kyoto bank in the middle of the afternoon and found a small laptop with accessories. That and a lot of jewelry which really had no value to me at all, but I stowed some of it anyway. If I did get a proper mate, it would be nice to give her some nice jewelry to wear.

I actually found a store that had digital movies and music in the window. I went in and tried and found some drives to test in my new stereo. I found "best of" drive collections for most of the afore-mentioned favorites as well as Ray Charles, Johnny Cash, and Jerry Lee Lewis. What could I say? I loved classic rock-and-roll.

I thought we'd found all that we were going to find here. Beau and I shoved off just before sundown and I had set the rudder toward the East. We were going home.

I checked the laptop, drive, and sound system. My hunch was correct again. All the bank vault items were working. I listened to Freddie Mercury belt out "We Will Rock You" and soon got my favorite: "We Are the Champions."

I checked my new female partner and she was not only anatomically correct. She was just amazing. Without clothes on, she looked like a young college girl. Her smooth nubile body did not have a blemish on it. I was embarrassed to admit I was aroused by her. Her previous master had even shaved her pubic region so the tuft of hair there was small and manageable. I harkened back to a time when I used to look up Japanese porn on the internet. Japanese girls had usually been very hairy (bushy) in the pubic region. They usually didn't trim their genital muff. I could only assume this little trimmed fantasy girl had cost a fortune.

I pulled her battery before we left and cleaned her battery compartment thoroughly. I unwrapped one of the spare batteries and popped it in. She was connected to the generator and recharging. At least, I thought she was. We would know tomorrow if she was still…functional.

Beau didn't quite know what to think of her. He kept his distance and his tail went under his body when he inched around her. He even growled once when I pulled her old battery out. It surprised me because he had never done that before.

At sundown, I pulled the traps and we scored more shrimp, which I bucketed in fresh seawater like before. We would use them for bait tomorrow.

It had been a long productive day full of surprises, but we needed to make some headway so I navigated and steered The Lovely Soong until I got tired and started to fall asleep. Only then, would I drop the anchor. The next several days, we would be on the open sea, so I am signing off for now.

Day 52 - November 19th

9:45 am

Ugh! I felt like absolute total shit this morning. I'd slept most of yesterday and I felt rough today: Achy, tired, and nauseous as hell. The sun shined hot and the sea was calm. I'd never suffered from motion sickness before. I had to ask myself, after a month at sea, why now?

I stumbled about the boat and Beau was out on the back deck. He was happy to see me, but he looked scared. I turn around and my naked robot girl stood in the doorway of the cabin, staring at us blankly. I actually did a comical double take à la Three Stooges / Lou Costello as the sight was unexpected and quite unnerving. She said something in Japanese, which I did not understand. I didn't know what bothered me more—the fact she spoke Japanese or that her voice, although very lifelike, did have a definite robotic twang to it.

I spoke to her in English, saying, "I am going to rest now." She remained motionless, probably because she did not comprehend me. "I am going to sleep now in my bed." Her head tilted slightly, indicating again that she did not understand what I had said. I pushed past her and went to my bed. As she turned, I pointed to the king-sized mattress, and rolled my eyes, realizing I was trying to communicate with a foreign robot.

When she moved, I could hear motors and gears moving ever so slightly. Her movements were kind of jerky, not exactly graceful or quick. The thought "What have I done to myself here?" popped into my head. I shook it off.

I crawled onto my bed and my Japanese robo-girl slowly sauntered over to the side of my bed. "I am not feeling well!" I shouted. She looked at me blankly and blinked. She smiled, actually smiled, and it surprised me. Her hand moved down to my crotch and she began rubbing. I almost jumped off of the bed. "No!" I said forcefully. "I need to sleep." She continued her assault and, despite my aches and pains, I began to get an erection.

I remembered the fantasy room at the bank: the specially decorated safety deposit room. She was built for this kind of thing. Or maybe I should say that she was *programmed* for this kind of thing: a sex-bot. Even though I felt lousy, what she was doing felt good and I relaxed and let her caress me. Her smile was comforting. She didn't make me feel like I was "just another trick." Soon, she had my member out of my pants and she skillfully relieved the pressure of this past week's adventure. I drifted off to strong, sound slumber. Typical man: I got mine, I'm going to sleep. She was okay with that, I supposed. She didn't need to "get hers" or be loved. She felt no emotion or disgust at my quick lapse into forty winks. I dreamed deeply, and in that dream saw this robo-girl as a real female whom I could take a shower with.

7:00 pm

I awoke to the sound of Beau barking. I'd slept all day for two days and hadn't feed him. When my eyes adjusted, my robo-girl stood by my bed exactly as I'd left her when I fell asleep. I zipped myself up, ignoring the mess I made which had dried there. I rolled out of bed being careful not to knock her over. I still grabbed her arm to brace myself as I stood and my feet hit the floor. She was soft, but sturdy. I didn't know how to better explain it. She was a very solid piece of machinery, but her skin was soft and her demeanor was very demure. It was kind of weird and awkward. I pushed past her.

I prepared Beau a meal and she walked over to me and watched me. I cut up the last of the eggplant and heated it up. I sautéd a couple of diced shrimp with it, let it cool a bit, then gave it to Beau. He scarfed it up hungrily. I turned to the robo-girl. She looked at me in wonder. She said something in Japanese and I caught the word "arigato," which I remembered from an old song, meaning "thank you." She'd thanked me for something. When she blinked, it looked like a camera shutter closing and opening slowly.

I felt better than earlier today, but I was not hungry at all. I looked around the dimly-lit cabin, then I looked at my robo-girl again. I grabbed one of my shirts and put it on her. She watched me intently through the whole process. She said something and again, she thanked me.

"You're welcome," I replied as I pushed past her again.

I grabbed the box with her cables and parts. I put a computer disk marked 1 (of 6) into the laptop. Of course, it was in Japanese, but after navigating around the open window a bit, I saw the word "English." I clicked on it and a program began running. I saw a welcome message from the Shinto corporation, and it introduced the robotic woman, showing a 3D computer graphic of a robot girl that looked pretty much like the one that I had, only their hair was black.

I ran and got the long USB cable from her box, then pulled her over to where I was looking at the computer. She seemed confused but allowed me to manipulate her without much struggle. With some effort, I sat her on the bed next to the computer and I attached the cable to the connector on her back.

I navigated the screens until I found languages. Again, I chose English and waited for a pop-up window. A few seconds later, I saw another pop-up window which asked if I wanted to upload now. I clicked yes and watched a blue bar load up my companion's new language. I watched excitedly for about ten minutes, having to change the computer disks during the process until it was done.

There was a long pause. I looked at my robo-girl who had sat patiently on the crate the entire time. "Hello?" I asked, feeling a little stupid. She turned her head to look at me and answered flatly, "Hello, my name is Komaki. I am a fully functional robot companion." Her name was Komaki.

"What can you do, Komaki?" I said, genuinely interested in her full capabilities beyond giving me a decent hand-job. She blinked as if she were thinking for a second and replied, "I can clean house, cook meals, make drinks, have conversations, and fulfill all of your sexual needs." I listened patiently as she continued. Her voice was smooth and even but still had a tiny tinge of robotic cadence to it. "I am programmed to play most board games, card games, and party games."

The computer told me she was a learning robot, which explained why she was watching me so intently when I was cooking. It also said she was a voice recognition model, which meant I could just tell her what I wanted, and she could do it. She was an impressive toy and I was growing fonder of her as I realized her assets and capabilities.

In a very crazy, bizarre way, I started to understand now why these Japanese men would invest in such a thing: A young girl who had no regrets and no emotional baggage who would never age and never care if you got old or fat. She would wait on you hand and foot all day and all night long without complaining or getting tired and never expected any payment for her services.

During the twentieth century, the Japanese culture had the women following the men and obeying their every command, "but the times they were-a-changin'." Women over the entire world had become more independent and many women were becoming top executives, doctors, lawyers, and politicians. The days of men ruling over women were coming to an end. In fact, the whole ball of wax was about to come to an abrupt end, they (the men and the women) just didn't know it.

I navigated around her program some more and I found she was registered to a Yutaka Ito.

I asked her, "Do you know who Yutaka is?"

She registered for a second and answered, "Yutaka Ito is my owner."

I nodded and went back to the computer. I erased Yutaka's name and re-registered Komaki in my name. Luckily, there was no password involved. He'd been either too lazy or he figured no one would ever find his robotic mistress in her bank vault Barbie Doll apartment. After a few seconds, a pop-up window explained the procedure was successful.

I asked Komaki who she was registered to. She blinked and said without hesitation, "Brandon Hoffman is my owner."

Upon checking, I realized I had spelled my name wrong when I registered. "Close enough," I said.

She queried, "Would you like me to call you, Brandon, Mr. Hoffman, or Master?"

The last title threw me a bit. I answered, "Brandon will be fine."

She smiled and nodded. "Thank you, Brandon," she said. "You may call me Komaki, if you like."

I laughed. "Okay," I said. "Komaki." I had to know, so I asked: "What did Yutaka have you call him?"

She looked up at me and said, "He liked me to call him 'Master.'"

"It figures," I said. "The chauvinist swine."

She corrected me. "No," she said. "Yutaka was a middle-aged, Japanese man."

I laughed, realizing I had to be careful what I said around her.

That night I told Komaki about myself and what had happened to mankind. She seemed to understand, but being a machine, she registered little (okay, no) emotion over it. I told her we were now a mismatched Adam and Eve in this post-apocalyptic world. She recited the story of Adam and Eve from the bible to let me know she'd understood my weak analogy. I stopped her, telling her I had read and knew the story.

"When were you purchased by Yutaka?" I asked.

She hesitated for a second, gathering the appropriate data to answer my question. "I was registered to Yutaka Ito from June 11, 2020 until this date."

I teased her. "You look great for a sixty-two-year-old lady."

She retorted, "I am fashioned to look like a girl of twenty years-old."

I smiled and conceded. "I stand corrected."

Then she said something that struck me hard: "My batteries, if maintained properly, have a life expectancy of sixty-five years."

I looked at her grimly. "Yutaka had her for roughly fourteen years," I thought to myself. If what she said was a fact (and robots rarely lied), then I would probably have her for less than that. A couple of years if I was lucky. Whatever I was going to do to find a proper mate, I had Komaki's help for two or three years to do it successfully.

We played card games for a while, continuing our talk and learning more about each other. They had said computers were only as smart as the people who programed them: All I could say to that was, "My hat goes off to Komaki's inventor." He had infused her with a personality and a sense of humor. I grew to like her more and more.

She knew my favorite games: blackjack and poker and had a knack for playing both. I stumped her when I'd told her I wanted to play "Go Fish." She looked toward the outside of the cabin and I pulled her focus back to the table and explained the game to her. She learned it quickly. Every time I beat Komaki at a game, she would say, "Ah, you beat me, Brandon." Every time she won, she would say "I beat you again, Brandon." I had a wonderful time with her that night.

I took her out on the deck under the stars and showed her how to steer the boat, set the rudder, and keep us on target by checking our compass. It was so nice having someone to talk to after weeks of solitude.

She looked up at me and asked me, "Brandon, do you want to fuck me now?"

The moment was so perfect and tender that I lost myself. I pulled her to me and kissed her. This was not-so-great as I was aware there were no feeling on her end, but the sex was good. Her vagina was soft and snug around me. She was skilled (programmed well.) She matched my rhythms and she moaned appropriately during the process. Afterward, I went back to bed, leaving her to pilot the boat.

Day 53 - November 20th

9:10 am

I woke up and felt rough again this morning. I started to worry because if there was something wrong with me medically, I had no doctor to go to, which meant I wouldn't get the proper treatment or meds. This realization made my bad morning worse.

Komaki had been at the wheel steering us toward Panama. What a bonus. Having a robot ship pilot who did not have to sleep would cut our return time in half. We didn't have to drop anchor. This made me happy again, though physically, I still felt like shit in a warm spoon.

Komaki saw me and said, "Good morning, Brandon. Did you sleep well?"

I told her, "Not exactly. I am feeling sick again today."

Komaki hesitated for a second and said, "I'm sorry to hear that, Brandon." Despite her robotic tone, she sounded sincere enough to me. I checked the compass and we were still heading southeast.

"By my calculations, based on the position of the stars last night, we should reach the Panama Canal by day after tomorrow — morning — Brandon."

My heart leapt. "That's wonderful," I said to her. "That means we will be in Savannah, Georgia in about six days."

After a pause, Komaki smiled and said, "You are correct, Brandon."

10:30 am

We had brunch together. Beau was near us. He seemed to be accepting Komaki now. She pet him and said, "Good dog" to him, which he liked. I stir-fried some vegetables for us, wishing I had some cooking oil so the veggies wouldn't scorch. Back home we had peanut oil, but here it was just the hot pan and ingredients. Komaki watched me cook. I was sure I would soon turn the cooking over to her as well. Maybe when we got back home. I was not a good cook. Hopefully she would learn to be better at it than me. I was excited about getting to The Rara Li.

Over our meal, I told Komaki about Atlanta. She told me a few things about it I hadn't known. I kept forgetting she had an encyclopedia brain.

I wrote in my journal as we listened to music. Komaki had been checking the wheel and the compass from time to time. She was an excellent navigator. She had a trunk full of slutty clothes, but I just let her wear one of my button-down shirts. She looked great wearing just that. When the Rolling Stones' "I Can't Get No Satisfaction" came on, she asked me, "Brandon, do you want to see me dance?"

"Sure," I replied.

Komaki did a very sexy dance, and though her movements were slightly robotic, I was impressed with her robo-boogie.

I hollered, "You got the moves, girl!" and "Shake that thang!"

Like most girls, she was unfazed by my comments; she was only into the dance.

4:30 pm

I felt a little better after a short nap. I tried to teach Komaki how to fish but she needed practice. She didn't have a good grip on one of the rods and it fell into the drink. I caught another nice yellowtail with my gear. I hadn't been hungry since we left Japan. I was probably coming down with something. I had to hang in there until we got home. Sleeping seemed to help. Most illnesses would go away if you drank lots of fluids and got plenty of sleep. I had no noticeable fever, so whatever I had was not a virus. I had one filter left for our water. That would probably give us enough good water until we could get to Key West.

My mind went back to Key West. A short side trip to Key West would be very nice with Komaki. We could sleep in Hemingway's bed and maybe I could scavenge some filters from someplace there. I could also replace my lost rod and reel. I made up my mind we would do it.

10:00 pm

I made dinner for Beau and ate a little myself, but I didn't enjoy it. I played more games with Komaki this evening. She kept my spirits up, but I turned in early due to my illness. It was true most men were big babies when it came to sickness. I was no exception. I made a note here: "Get a book on herbal medicine when you get back to the United States."

Day 54 - November 21st

11:00 am

Again, I was under the weather, but I got up to check our bearings. Komaki showed me on the map that the shortest distance between two points was a straight line. It was amazing but the straight line from Kyoto to the Panama Canal bypassed all the Pacific islands completely. I had taken the Hawaii route a few weeks ago, because I was not sure of my own skills as a navigator. I just went with what I knew.

It was a shame we wouldn't be seeing Hawaii or my other Island again. I could have refilled with fresh spring water at those places, but…we would be at the Canal tomorrow with Cuba and Key West soon after.

10:45 pm

Slept most of today and let Komaki handle the skippering. She tried to cheer me up with her usual services, but (and I never in my wildest dreams would think I would ever say this) I just was not in the mood for sex. What was funny was, when I told her "no," she matter-of-factly turned and went to find something else to do. No weeping or insecurity. No "You don't love me anymore!" She just turned and left. Side note: This nautical shit was wearin' thin on me here. It was fun and exciting to a point, but after six weeks...it got old.

Day 55 - November 22nd

8:45 am

I felt okay today. I still felt tired, but I was not feeling the usual aches and pains, this morning. I thought now that maybe it was just fatigue from this last month's adventure. Komaki piloted the boat and we were still on course. I did not see land yet, but Komaki's calculations had us close to the Panama Canal.

Soon we would be on the smaller Rara Lee again. I would certainly miss my yacht, but The Rara Li was a fine cruiser. I thought Komaki would like it. It was clean, moved faster and also had a soft bed. This may sound crazy, but I wanted Komaki to sleep with me — or pretend to sleep with me. A long time ago, I had a wonderful girlfriend named "Annie." She was very funny and very sexy, and I loved when she slept over because it was just nice waking up next to someone. A baseball player's schedule was very hectic, so you didn't get to cultivate meaningful relationships. Annie was nice. She was "the one that got away."

1:05 pm

We still hadn't seen land. I always thought computers were supposed to be damned near infallible when it came to calculations. Komaki claimed since she had been in hibernation for well over fifty-five years, she'd obviously miscalculated on the position of the stars. We must have been close though.

7:00 pm

The sun set behind us and, though it looked nice, there was no sign of land. Komaki had gotten my hopes up. I really couldn't fault her for her mistake, but I was disappointed. I would probably turn in early tonight.

11:40 pm

I awoke by falling out of my bed onto the floor, scraping up my right arm. The boat lurched suddenly, and the inside cabin was now a shambles. All our belongings lay scattered everywhere. Beau was okay, but he was shaking and looking around, confused.

I went outside and found out Komaki had run the yacht into the oil tanker ship blocking the Panama Canal. I yelled out, "Komaki, what the fuck is going on?"

She turned to me and said very matter-of-factly, "Brandon, it appears I have run into an oil tanker."

Now I was fuming. "Oh," I said angrily. "You figured that out all by yourself, did you?"

Komaki blinked and said coolly, "Yes, Brandon. I did."

I slapped my good hand over my face in exasperation. "Why didn't you wake me when we got to the Panama Canal?"

Her answer was simple. "You did not tell me to wake you, Brandon." She was correct, of course. The last few nights she had been piloting the ship as I slept, and I'd never told her to wake me. "Brandon," she continued. "You also neglected to tell me there was an oil tanker blocking our path through the Panama Canal."

I stopped for a moment and exhaled. I couldn't argue with logic like that. I had forgotten to mention that very important thing the other night when telling her stories about myself and my adventures. "You're right, Komaki," I said sincerely. "I apologize. I shouldn't have faulted you for it."

She looked at me for a moment. "Apology accepted, Brandon." Though I knew she had no true feeling or pride to speak of, the moment was a touching one on my end. She continued by saying, "And I am sorry I piloted your yacht into an oil tanker." How could I be angry?

We spent a couple of hours putting everything on The Lovely Soong back in its proper place. I checked below to make sure the hull hadn't split. We didn't appear to be taking on any water.

I went back to the cabin. Komaki opened her shirt and said "Brandon, do you want to fuck me now?"

I paused and I smiled. "No," I said gently. "I am tired, Komaki." I laid down on the bed and covered myself with the blanket. I could have walked around the tanker and went to The Rara Li to sleep, but I felt lazy. We would start fresh tomorrow morning. Komaki stood by the bed.

Day 56 - November 23rd

8:45 am

I woke up with my head pounding. Beau barked when he saw me rise slowly. Komaki stood next to me exactly the way she was when I'd gone to sleep. When she saw me move, her head tilted downward slightly so her eyes focused on me. "Good morning, Brandon."

I grunted something akin to: "Yeah... right...," and I struggled my way back to my feet.

Outside, it was another beautiful day. I looked over the bow to inspect the damage to the junk and it was minimal. We weren't going very fast when we'd hit the tanker, so we'd just bounced off her hard hull. The top of the bow was splintered, but she was far from being sunk. If I ever did come in contact with anyone else, and they asked me about it, I would just tell them the truth: "My Japanese robot girlfriend ran it into an oil tanker."

The funny thing was that Komaki was smart enough to drop anchor during all of the confusion, so we didn't drift all over the now open canal. We had left our special loading ramp down and I helped Komaki and Beau onto the dock. Beau ran around happily. He was probably feeling "cooped up" having been stuck on the yacht for so long. I worked hard to get the last of our belongings off The Lovely Soong and ready to transport to The Rara Li at the backside of the Tanker.

2:30 pm

We were on The Rara Li and heading back toward the Atlantic. We had lunch and put everything in its proper place. We didn't leave much back on The Lovely Soong. Komaki carried a lot of our stuff to the new boat quickly. I thought to myself that I wanted to grab some more coffee beans in Cuba. Not because I was out, but because I just wanted an ample supply. We would be in Key West by tomorrow evening.

9:20 pm

We pulled out of the canal and into the Caribbean just after sundown. Tonight, Komaki and I read whatever we could on cloning while she piloted. The programming disks that came with her included Korean language. If I could load the language into her brain tonight, she might translate the Korean books and notes for me. This would obviously help me a great deal. I was so glad I'd decided to bring her with me. She might've proved to be the answer to many of my current problems. She was my little Japanese Swiss Army Knife.

12:30 am

Komaki was amazing. She was now programmed in three languages with her main language being English. She read three Korean books on cloning and translated them for me this very second. Now, robots didn't read in the traditional sense. Komaki scanned the pages by looking at them for a second, then moved on to the next page, averaging about three to four seconds per page. She got through well over nine hundred pages in just over an hour. She explained a lot of it to me and it actually made more sense now.

She confirmed my fears that the success rate of cloning was very low as it still had not been perfected at the time of mankind's demise. The lack of a female egg to work from and a female host to complete the cloning process had also been big problems we would have to face and overcome.

I looked at her seriously and said, "So, in your opinion, do you think this cloning idea is a waste of time?" I wanted her opinion. She thought in a purely analytical way, without emotion.

She thought for a second and said, "No, Brandon." The answer came swift and sure. "This research is still experimental and possibly useful. We should not abandon it altogether."

I sighed in relief. It was what I needed to hear. Komaki said she would also retype the material in the laptop in English while I slept tonight. I thanked her. She said, "No need to thank me, Brandon. I am here to serve you." I smiled. I'd really hit the jackpot when I stepped into that bank vault. She continued by saying, "I want you to be happy, Brandon."

We dropped anchor and the shrimp traps to see what we could pull in. Komaki pulled everything up after she had translated the Korean books, then, she would pilot the boat towards Cuba. She actually made a joke about it, saying, "I hope there are no more oil tankers in the way, Brandon." Her sense of humor definitely made her seem more human than machine. Her character kept my spirits lifted on this tedious journey back to our oasis in Atlanta.

"Brandon?" I turned my head to see her. She unbuttoned my shirt and it was open now, revealing her firm smooth body. In soft lighting it was amazing how lifelike she looked. "Do you want to fuck me now?"

It was truly astonishing how fast a man could get aroused. In a single second, the human brain could send dozens of flashing images through our mind, then blood went rushing in a torrent to our penis.

I simply smiled and said, "Come here," and she did. I pushed the shirt over her shoulders and let it drop to the deck, then I pulled her tiny frame close to me. What transpired then was not just a carnal delight but also the perfect ending to a very productive day.

Day 57 - November 24th

8:20 am

Komaki did everything requested of her perfectly. I woke up at sunrise as she pulled up the anchor, and I helped move the shrimp from the cages into the bucket. After that, I went back to sleep for another hour and a half. We would be at Cuba by midafternoon.

3:30 pm

We landed at Cuba again, but I'd forgotten to make a marker for the spot where I found the coffee. Luckily, I spotted my footprints on the top end of the beach by the trees (after about an hour of searching). I found some nice, big bananas along with the coffee beans. I tied one of my blue shirts high around a tree on the beach to mark the spot so I could find it again later.

8:30 pm

We just finished dinner in Key West. We barbecued on the boat again. We got to the Keys around five-ish and watched the sunset from the dock near the southernmost point. I don't know why, but sunsets were always best from there and many people would gather to watch it every evening. It was just so incredibly peaceful and relaxing.

We found another electric bike, the kind you could peddle. Today I peddled it, but we would try and get its batteries running when we get back to Atlanta. I took Komaki to Hemingway's house. I didn't mention this before, but you could imagine what the yard was like around the yellow and green plantation-style home after not being tended for over sixty years. It was like a jungle. However, I had already cleared the path from the front gate up through the front door on my previous trip.

I showed her around the museum house by candlelight, stopping along the way to show her famous photographs of the celebrity author at various stages in his exciting life. There were pictures of him as a young man in his military uniform, pictures of him in his midlife with various big game trophies, and pictures of him in his later years when boredom and depression set in, including the most famous picture of him, the one most associated with him because it was used in all advertisements for a bar he frequented called Sloppy Joe's. I always thought he looked distant and sad in that photo. Of course, he would end up at the business end of a shotgun in his last suicidal moments.

I was excited because Komaki and I would sleep in Hemingway's soft bed tonight. I'd asked her to pretend to sleep, so I could wake up next to her. She seemed amused by the request because it meant she would have to act, something she hadn't done before. This only made the moment that much more special and memorable.

Day 58 - November 25th

8:00 am

Komaki was sleeping next to me when I got up. I made no sudden movements because I wanted to watch her for a while as she pretended to sleep. She lay on her back very stiff with her hands by her side, but she was still cute. I moved slightly and her eyes snapped open. Her head turned so she could look at me.

She smiled and said, "Good morning, Brandon. I hope you slept well."

I told her I did sleep well and I had many dreams.

"What are dreams, Brandon?" It was a legitimate question from a humanoid automaton.

"Well," I started, "dreams are like movies that play in our head while we are sleeping." It was the best explanation I could come up with on short notice. "Oh, I like movies." She continued by saying, "Yutaka used to show me movies to teach me how to have proper sexual intercourse with him."

"Really?" I said sarcastically, getting up into a sitting position with my feet now touching the floor.

"Yes," she said, rising herself. "He showed me one movie where the girls flicked their tongues like this." She stuck out her tongue and it vibrated fast, moving up and down. I actually heard a sound like a sex vibrator toy.

I nodded to show her I had seen it, but the action was ill-timed. I made my way to the bathroom. I called over my shoulder. "You can show me that again when I am more in the mood."

Now, in this crazy world I was in, I had to keep telling myself I was going to see strange shit all along the way. I opened the door and was greeted by several cat skeletons. Hemingway was renowned for his Key West collection of six-toed felines. Yep. A closer inspection of what was left of the critters confirmed they had six digits on each foot. The window was open and long vines now grew in the bathroom. These cats had obviously chosen this room to be their final resting place.

I had a breakfast of coffee and bananas. Komaki and I spent the morning looking for food in the less populated areas. If we shoved off by noon, we might make Savannah by tomorrow morning.

8:40 pm

Komaki and I found avocadoes, coconuts, grapefruits, key limes, and mangoes. With the new electric bike, we did well. We pulled up anchor early and passed Key Largo by lunchtime. Beau enjoyed mangoes (when I peeled the skin for him—spoiled fucker!) He lapped up a lot of coconut milk, too.

We caught a large Jewfish on the way back around Boca Raton, Florida. I showed Komaki how to scale, cut open, and properly clean a fish. She watched intently because I told her she would have to do this particular job from now on.

After dinner, I had Komaki look at the Korean scientist's cloning journals. She also looked at the French scientist's notes and logs. She claimed she could rewrite all the information in English and re-organize it for me, so it made better sense, kind of like "ADVANCED CLONING SCIENCE FOR DUMMIES." She was a wonder.

I piloted the boat and kept an eye out for the dock where my scooter was parked. The coastline looked more like southern Georgia now, so we would see it soon.

12 Midnight

We got to the dock in Savannah. We were almost home. Though I was tired, it was just a couple of hours to Atlanta and I missed my home. But I only had a small electric car that needed recharging and I now had a dog, a robot companion, and a ton of stuff to carry. I left Beau on the boat and Komaki and I searched for an electric car dealership.

4:00 am

Just before sunrise, we found a car dealership which had some electric cars. My robo-girl held the solar generator against her back as we rode because she didn't get tired. After we pulled up, Komaki calmly got off of the scooter, never losing her balance, and gently put the generator on the pavement. When I pointed at the fence with the giant padlock, she easily broke it apart.

Day 59 – November 26th

Dawn

We went from car-to-car trying to charge one to see if it would go. No luck. Komaki turned to me and said, "These vehicles are all damaged, Brandon. Their computer chips were destroyed by an electromagnetic pulse."

I nodded as I listened to her state the obvious. "So we keep looking until we find one that is not damaged," I replied.

"Like your electric scooter," she said.

I nodded again. "Might I suggest that we look under flyovers as they often times are built with iron, which might shield a vehicle from EMP damage?"

"Flyover" was the British word for "overpass." We hopped aboard the scooter and rode around Savannah looking for electric cars under overpasses.

2:30 pm

After quite a search, we found an electric RV by EcoUno Industries under an overpass. We lost three hours because we had to recharge the generator which took about six hours. So we had to do a lot of searching on foot. But we found a nice RV and Komaki's idea paid off. After charging the battery, it started. I had to fix a flat tire on the right rear end as well, but it was well worth it. We had a large vehicle for getting around. We drove back to the boat dock and had something to eat. Surprisingly, I was not that hungry, and I hadn't eaten in a long while.

5:00 pm

Beau and I ate some of our provisions. I transferred my dog, the food, the bikes, and all the looted gear to the E-RV, and I decide to just tie the boat off there.

"Nobody's gonna mess with it." I said to myself in a silly kind of tone.

With Komaki's help, I tied the scooter to the back of our new vehicle. We could drive home doing 60 mph. I wish I could've done 80 as there was no one out there to give us a ticket, but I was not complaining. I was so happy with my new wheels.

11:00 pm

I sang songs to Beau and Komaki and we made the trip back in good time. Everything was unpacked and where it should've been now.

"Ah, my bed—so soft and clean," I said to myself. I took Komaki up the stairs and asked her "Can you shower?"

She blinked and said, "I think I will be fine, so long as I keep my mouth shut." The statement was so cute that I grabbed her and we made passionate love in the shower. It was good. I was so totally satisfied and spent at the same time. It was so good to be home and where I felt comfortable.

I took Komaki to my bed. "I will see you in the morning, dear." And I laid down for forty winks. Again, she pretended to sleep.

Day 60 - November 27th

10:00 am

Once more, I watched little Komaki as she gave the illusion of sleep... for me. I smiled but didn't move or say a word for over ten minutes. She looked so peaceful and serene. She was my robotic angel. I must've been cracking up to already be this attached to a mechanical imitation of a female. She was everything that I had ever feared, but she was everything I had ever wanted in a girl... except living.

Her eyes snapped open and she smiled. She did not look at me right away. She just said, "Good morning, Brandon."

I reached out and touched her cold, soft cheek. "Good morning." I said it lovingly and I meant it lovingly. She was now my best friend.

She quickly followed with: "Do you want to fuck me now, Brandon?"

I was tempted, but I said, "No, Komaki." Then I continued with, "You shouldn't say, 'fuck,' dear. You should say, 'make love.'"

She looked at me, slightly confused. "Yutaka always liked it when I said, 'do you want to fuck me now.'"

I nodded and said, "I understand, but I would like it more if you said would you like to make love to me now." I stopped, suddenly realizing what I was trying to explain and who I was explaining it to. I also caught myself calling her "dear." This was bad. I really needed to focus on the cloning project more now.

I showed her around the house that morning and I cut up some fruit for breakfast. It was cold today. We would spend the day setting up our own little cloning laboratory in the house next door. First, I would have Komaki remove the furniture and clean the place thoroughly. I went to hospitals nearby and to the hardware stores in the neighborhood (though most had been looted) and procured tables, more generators and whatever else might've been helpful to us. I would be able to make working lights without computer chips. Hell, we'd all done it in junior high school, right?

117

12:40 pm

I made three trips back and forth from the hospitals and transported a lot of medical furniture and laboratory equipment to the house next to ours. Komaki had the entire place cleaned out with the furniture stacked in the shed behind the house before I came back from my first trip. When I arrived the second time, she had completely cleaned the floors and walls of the house. The smell of old phosphate soap filled the air. Laundry powder was what we had to clean with because it was stored in plastic buckets and kept better over the decades.

I made Beau and I a lunch of sautéed vegetables in peanut oil. The thought that winter was coming had me worried. We had better go to the library tonight and pick up books on how to preserve food items. My Aunt Mable used to can goods like peaches and pears, but I would be damned if I could remember what she'd preserved them with.

8:30 pm

We were at the library now. Komaki was in her paradise. It never dawned on me that a robot would want to read. Komaki was eager to learn whatever she could. She zoomed through books and I decided to write an entry now while we were here. I got a couple of books on canning and cooking. I also picked up a couple of chemistry books, including a few "Farmer's Almanacs" and "The Anarchist's How to Book." I wanted to learn how to create the simple things I desired that I could not find anymore, like bar soap, bug repellent (in case we had nuclear cockroaches here in Atlanta), and fertilizer.

I ruminated about the winter problem a lot today, and I thought of finding or building a green house. Then I could grow food year-round for Beau and me. I would not have to heat it most of the year. I had Komaki read-scan a book on hydroponics and indoor gardening. She also found some good books on alternative energy sources like hydro power and wind power.

The key to our comfort in this time was to check out every inch of the area not devastated and log our resources. Find raw materials

118

and turn them into what we needed. I had to become a chemist, a blacksmith, and an inventor.

As the last man on earth I realized I had much responsibility and I had to wear many hats. I was the almighty creator, or at the very least, the almighty clone maker. The repopulation of this planet was in my hands. If I failed, it would take hundreds of thousands of years for beings to crawl out of the sea and evolve into humanoids. Imagine their surprise when they dug up the ruins of Pusan and Kyoto or "Lost Atlanta."

Perhaps that was when this book would be read. Note to self: Keep journal tucked away in plastic. Would this text become the bible for the next race of beings? I haden't walked on water or changed water into wine (yet), but hey… I could handle being someone who was worshipped on Sundays.

11:35 pm

Tomorrow would be another busy day. We gathered more food and tried to find more power sources. Atlanta was a big place with lots of stores, so it shouldn't have been too hard.

Komaki asked me if I would like to "make love to her now." I was definitely in the mood tonight, but I apologize now to you, my reader. I don't feel it is appropriate for me to relay my sexual escapades with my robot girlfriend any more than I already have, not at this stage of our relationship. It is not an important part of this journal and I just don't feel right about it as a Southern Gentleman.

Day 61 - November 28th

6:00 am

We were up at the ass-crack of dawn. My uncle Butch used to use that expression and though I never fully understood it, I always liked the sound of it. It was just a cool way of saying "sun-up." It was very cold again today.

I felt a bit rough again, like I did those couple of days on The Lovely Soong. It was just a general feeling of being tired and achy. I'd been experiencing some sharp pains internally. They were brief, but sometimes very painful. I had moved a lot of heavy shit yesterday from the hospital and I was not getting any younger.

Late last night, I heard a cat yowling. It was Max or Myra. It started Beau barking and it surprised Komaki. She asked what it was, and I relayed my tale of bringing the two cats to life.

She responded to my tale by saying, "So now the planet is populated by one man, one male dog, a male cat, and a female cat." I quickly followed up with "And a shitload of mean cockroaches in Pusan, South Korea."

After that, she only nodded and said, "I see."

2:20 pm

We went out into the fields on the electric scooter. Komaki liked riding on the cycle (Heck, most girls did). We found a wheatfield, a cornfield, and some wild rice. These items would be harvested in bulk over the next few days. We filled several sacks today. I also found some peach trees (though they were not bearing much fruit at this time of the year). The location was noted.

8:00 pm

We didn't get to any stores today. We had a sensational day of gathering food though. We found all kinds of grain and late in the afternoon we found sugarcane and fresh grapes. I was going to attempt to make some wine and store it.

I got Komaki to gather sacks of peanuts as well. Peanuts were protein that could be stored for a long time.

I bypassed the local looted supermarkets and went to the back ends of drug stores where I found some grinding bowls and pestle sets for making my own flour and corn meal. I could make flat breads with flour and water. I rummaged local garages and found some glass mason jars with seal-tight lids for canning and some large, plastic bins (the giant toybox kind) that also sealed up tightly like Tupperware. I stored my grains in those, so the winter would be less of a problem. Komaki didn't eat so the trickiest part, I thought, would be feeding Beau.

Komaki had done an excellent job of setting up the cloning lab in the house next door. It looked professional and would be more than suitable for our experiments. Later, if we cloned animals, we would get cages and place them around the house, but I was getting ahead of myself.

While walking back to our house I heard a low guttural growl. It was one of the cats: Max or Myra. I had revived them over a month ago. It was close, very close but I couldn't get a bearing on its location. The growl sounded savage. When I brought them out of their slumber, I hadn't taken into consideration it would be near impossible for them to find food. Felines needed meat. They usually didn't eat fruits and vegetables. Max and Myra probably hadn't discovered that fish were still around and with no birds or rodents to hunt, they were probably very hungry and very pissed right now. It'd been several weeks.

I looked around carefully and spied it in the tree in front of my house, or I should say I saw its eyes reflecting light. I threw a rock at the tree and yelled, "Get outta here, you stupid cat!" It scurried down the tree trunk quickly and ran off. Its hair was greasy-looking and matted down. It was very emaciated.

As I watched the little beast bolt away, Komaki came out onto the porch. "What are you yelling at, Brandon?"

I continued to watch the pathway the cat ran off to. "Just a stupid cat," I said. And I meant it. Not long ago, I'd given it renewed life, but I was ruing the day I did. I knew now it would be a nuisance to us. Just one more thing to worry about.

Day 62 - November 29st

9:00 am

I slept later than usual this morning. I felt like shit again today but, as the saying goes, a man's got to do what a man's got to do. I needed to hit some malls and stores in my neighborhood. We had power, but it wouldn't last forever, especially the way we were running the generator every morning and every night.

Komaki went to look for raw materials to make special liquid solutions needed for the cloning experiments. Clone cells needed to be grown and harvested in these medicinal solutions until they became fully functional embryos. I kept my fingers crossed, hoping she would find everything she needed.

1:15 pm

Now that I had been out and about, I felt better. It really sucked not having any medicine at all to help me when I felt ill. The stuff at the local hospitals was way past its expiration date. I kept telling myself that I should swing by the library and hijack a couple of books on home remedies, herbal medicine, and the like.

I found another solar generator. I loaded it up and brought it to the house. I would test it tomorrow morning.

10:20 pm

Komaki went to several hospitals, drug stores, and even a pharmaceutical company. Unfortunately, she found very little that we could use—another stumbling block in the road that was my existence. Maybe I was thinking too small. What did they always say in advertising right before I was put under? "ALWAYS THINK OUTSIDE THE BOX." If I wanted materials, I needed to go right to the source. The water was still running (albeit, I wouldn't drink it), so the electric company might've been functional as well. If I wanted power, I would find the power company and try to turn on the juice myself. I was The Boss Man in this world so… no utility bills.

If I wanted raw materials, I could check the factories in the area. Hell, I might even be able to produce products. Atlanta was the biggest city in the South. It had to be full of resources. I just had to go out further on my walk-abouts and "think outside the box." That was what I'd done when I went to Asia and came back with vital cloning information, a working computer, a superior sound system, and a top-of-the-line Japanese robot girlfriend.

12:55 am

That fucking cat wailed again. I was going to catch a big fish and fill it with poison I would make myself. I gave it life and I would take it away just as easily.

Day 63 - November 30th

9:40 am

The cat kept me up for most of the morning. If there were one reason to load my own ammo and get a gun working in this time and age, this feline nuisance would be it. My gut feeling was that even if I feed it, it would probably wail at night. Obviously, one of the cats had died and the other was left all alone. It might have even killed the other one and fed on it. All I knew was that I didn't care if it was the last cat on earth, it was one dead pussy.

I went to look up poisons in the Anarchist book, then I went to Taggart Springs to see if I could catch a freshwater fish. When I'd been out there a while back, swimming about, I hadn't seen any fish, but I wasn't looking for any either. It stood to reason that if fish had survived in the ocean then the freshwater aquatic creatures probably made it through the apocalypse as well. I took my freshwater tackle and lures with me. I also loaded up more of the other foods and brought them back.

Komaki continued her search for medicinal products, things for cloning and things for my personal medicine. I had asked her to try and locate the power station for our neighborhood, as well. When I was a kid, we'd had telephone books to aid us in our quests. No such help was available today. We both had our tasks to do now.

3:30 pm

My hunch was right. I caught three small fish at the springs. I put them into a plastic bag with water and now they were in a bucket here at the house. Now I needed to make some poison.

4:20 pm

Komaki returned. She had a location on the power station for our neighborhood. I got nowhere making poison because the Anarchist book's ingredients were all store-bought items. I would have to find poisonous plants in the wild and grind them into what I needed.

8:00 pm

Komaki and I went to the power station. I cut open the fence around it and we checked it out carefully. Everything seemed to be turned on and working properly, but still no power. The problem must've been at the main station.

We went to the library and found a book on advanced horticulture. In there we found pictures of many varieties of poisonous plants, such as hemlock. Tomorrow, Komaki and I would try and find some in the woods along with some of the medicinal plants that could help us with our home remedies.

11:10 pm

Komaki informed me again there were several problems with our plan to clone things, the main one being the lack of living tissue to clone. I pointed out the French scientist's work on DNA cloning skin and organs, but Komaki shot it down, saying his notes were inconclusive. He studied it, experimented on it, but never finished his work. So, as it stood, if we could find the raw materials we needed to facilitate the process, we could clone Beau, fish (no need for that), the cat (no fucking way), and me.

I told her, "Cloning me is an option, so we continue forward with the plan," but I was disheartened by the news. I wanted a farm with cows that gave milk and chickens that laid eggs. I would have even enjoyed setting a Panda free in the Georgia wild, but without living tissue to clone from, none of that was going to happen. The dried-up sample slides were not going to provide us with what we needed, not to mention, no living host to cultivate with.

I'm embarrassed to admit I had another tantrum on hearing the news with me throwing furniture about. Komaki stared at me in wonder until I calmed down. As I breathed heavily, I heard her voice say, "Would you like to make love to me now, dear?" She was the bearer of bad news, but I couldn't blame the messenger. She had learned to call me "dear." I picked her up in my arms and took her to bed. Luckily, we didn't hear the cat on this night.

Day 64 - December 1st

8:30 am

It was very cold today. There was frost on the ground. The sky was medium-gray. Still, I felt good today. No internal pains, aching joints, or headaches. Komaki and I went into the woods today gathering plant samples.

I haven't mentioned Beau much lately. He usually stayed home when we went on our jaunts. He felt comfortable at the house. He was always happy to see Komaki or I when we come back. He had totally accepted her as his second master, and she was very good to him. She told me she feeds him and pets him when I was not home. I had no reason to doubt her. Robots did what they did, would gladly tell you what they'd done and, like I said before, none of them were programmed to lie (that I knew of.)

10:45 am

We stumbled onto a grisly scene. In the woods just east of our place, we found an overgrown church. Inside, the pews were filled with the remains of the faithful. Many were children. Like the two Korean scientists, most were entwined and/or embracing each other. If there had been a leader to this poor, ill-fated flock, I could not distinguish him from the other skeletal inhabitants. Komaki was more curious than horrified. She looked around carefully, inspecting the carcasses, not worrying about paying final respects or fearing the wrath of God. Robots were atheists.

We left the scene as we'd found it, and not ten minutes later, we found many of the plants we were looking for. Pure luck or divine intervention—you make the call. It was an eerie coincidence.

5:15 pm

I grabbed another bowl and pestle set (which I was calling "my poison pestle set.") The fish in the bucket were all belly up, but no matter. I ground up some hemlock for our little neighborhood nuisance. I mixed in some tap water and, when it got to the right consistency, I cut two small slits on the sides of a fish and packed it good with the toxic paste. I locked Beau in the house and placed the fish in the backyard. "Bon Appetite,... you little bastard," I laughed to myself. "I hope you enjoy your last meal."

10:00 pm

Komaki and I turned off all the lights and used candles to get around. I waited by the back-kitchen window for what seemed like a century. (I've reread some of my notes here. I am a pretty good

126

writer. I mean, I am no Tom Clancy or Michael Crichton, but I feel my notes here are succinct and mildly entertaining.)

I looked up and I was overjoyed to see the irksome little kitty taking the bait. He ripped and chomped viciously too. Like a wild animal that had been gnawing on tree bark for a couple of months. I giggled to myself, satisfied my ploy had been succeeded. After he'd finished everything but the bones, he licked his paws and ran off. Hopefully, that would be the last I ever saw or heard from it.

11:45 pm

We turned the lights back on and I cleaned up the fishbones and my poison pestle. Beau could go outside for a walk and roam about the house freely again.

We heard a couple of cat screeches and they sounded very painful. But the noise had subsided now so we could move on to more important matters.

I abandoned the idea of finding the main power station for the time being. A memory came back to me from an old junior high school lesson. The giant turbine engines creating electricity in most cities were run by coal. Without anyone to load coal into the furnaces of those turbines… well, there just was no power.

Instead, I raided more houses and tried to find materials to make windmills and checked the roofs of said houses for solar panels. Where there were solar panels, there were solar heating units.

Day 65 - December 2nd

8:50 am

It snowed today and I felt lousy again. Komaki told me she could not go out of the house because, as a mechanical apparatus, she would freeze. Genius that I was, I said, "Well, bundle up. Put a coat on, girl." But it just wasn't that simple. Komaki had no body heat to speak of, so if she froze up, it would cause irreparable damage to her.

Even though she could not stay outside in the snow for any length of time, she could study up on herbal medicine for me and if she made a mad dash for the house next door, she could do initial cloning experiments. I had already rigged the lab house with the other working generator. I just had to get some space heaters from my neighbors.

1:00 pm

I got off to a late start on my neighborhood rounds. I checked the roofs of houses for any solar panels. I got Komaki set up with space heaters in both houses. I needed her and her computer brain to help me with everything I must do to survive and get my cloning work done. So I had to take care of her above all else. No luck finding solar equipment so far. There was a hoity-toity, rich neighborhood just north of here. I would check there next. I had my well-stocked tool kit with me in the E-RV.

11:20 pm

I found lots of solar panels and parts in the neighborhood north of here. I dismantled several units that were the same or similar, making notes about how it all went together, and I would try and rig up the two houses tomorrow. I just hoped it was not snowing tomorrow.

I made some flatbread tonight. It needed salt but it was edible. I ground the flour from wheat and mixed it with water. It would get us through the winter. With the aid of one of my canning books, Komaki and I canned some fruit and shelved it. It was fun, like a family activity.

Komaki spent the day scanning our herbal medicine and home remedy books. She made some medicines from plants we had gathered to ease sore muscles and skin irritation. She also found a recipe for a compound that would get our blood flowing like pain killers. That would be handy for me when I woke up feeling bad.

All in all, we were more productive on this snowy day than I'd thought we would be. Of course, I was freezing when I got in, but a quick shower and the space heaters brought me back to normal. Komaki gave me a nice, long back rub tonight as well. She didn't get tired, so she massaged my tired aching muscles for almost two hours. That was nice. Life would've certainly been less bearable without her. Having her here was a real joy.

Day 66 - December 3rd

7:00 am

I had bad nightmares last night. I could not remember much about them, but I did remember I had a loose tooth and it came out when I pulled it, followed quickly by others. Suddenly I was pulling out my teeth by the handfuls. I woke up abruptly. Komaki said, "Good morning, Brandon," as usual, not realizing I was shaken.

I was no Sigmund Freud, but you didn't have to be a lauded Austrian psychiatrist to know that was some serious shit and it meant something was creeping around in my subconscious mind.

There was no doubt my feelings were very scattered right then. Yes, I was surviving and quite comfortably. What was left in this world was basically mine, but it did feel like for every step I took forward, I took three steps back. The cloning idea was fast becoming folly and I knew it. If I cloned myself, I would have to wait at least fifteen years before I could even attempt to try and repopulate the planet. If and when that happened, I would literally fuck myself and the future of mankind because there was a good chance the offspring would look like most mongoloid, humanoid beings created from same family sex with old-aged sperm.

Though I had mixed emotions about that problem, I felt something else was behind the images in my nightmares. After I hooked up the solar panels and heaters, I went to the library to see if

I could find some answers. The key to this lied in the past of Brandon Hoffner, forty-something ex-baseball star, and ex-entrepreneur.

It was funny but I remembered very little about my past before I re-awoke in this situation I was in. Every now and again, if I saw something that looked familiar to me, I got flashes of my past, like when I thought about Annie.

I was grateful for the library. Computers had all but taken over text in my time but when the chips all came crashing down, it was books that withstood the test of time. I didn't know what I would have done without them. (Remember this entry well. If you can find a way to highlight it, you should. The future should still have a place for paper with text printed on it.)

8:15 am

It snowed today, so Komaki had to stay inside again, and I would go straight to the library. She asked me to grab whatever advanced Science and Biology books I could find. If she understood science better, she might make better sense of the notes and logs from the Pusan Institute for Genetic Research. She needed input, so I would "hook her up."

10:45 pm

It was like a blizzard outside now. The weather had really turned nasty. I spent the day at the library. I grabbed several good Science and Biology books for Komaki as well as some Science magazines and professional journals. She was scanning them now.

I found an old, microfilm cabinet and when I got it home, it worked: old machinery – no computer chips. I spent the entire day looking at microfilms of newspapers. The library had the New York Times from the 1860's to 2024 and they had every issue of the Atlanta Herald. Obviously, I looked over the last ten years of man's rule over the planet hoping to find stories about myself.

I was an okay ballplayer, but I was not what you would call a fan draw. I did my job and had fun playing the game. My life away from the field attracted more attention. I was prone to wild parties, drinking and coking it up with celebs, punching a few photographers along the way. The headlines were less than flattering. I was a relatively rugged-looking and handsome guy back in the day, so invariably I would get conned into doing some hair-brained publicity stunt with a female movie-star wannabe. Good God, had that really been my life?

I'd been smart with my money. I invested heavily into real estate and started my own chain of sports gear stores. Marketing was easy if you were slipping greenbacks to the best athletes of the Southern United States. I was in a bad car accident in 2017. I stopped suddenly. There was no need to search any further. I remembered seeing the doctors and them telling me I would be okay. But when they did tests on me, they found something unexpected: cancer. Not just any cancer—bone cancer.

It all came rushing back to me like a flood of images and feelings. I remembered them telling me we had caught it in just the nick of time. The prognosis was optimistic. I remembered chemo treatments that were somewhat successful in the beginning, though they made me very weak and nauseous. I remember them telling me in the end, we had lost the battle. Oh God! How long did they give me to live? Six months. Maybe three to six months?

This was why I'd been frozen. It was the last desperate act of a dying man's family. How could I have forgotten it all? I was so depressed at the time; the doctors had me on all types of anti-depressants: Haldol, Lithium, and Prozac, the cocktail of the stars. I took them all one night, hoping to go to sleep forever and avoid a very painful death.

A further search confirmed the rest of the story with a headline of: "BASEBALL OUTFIELDER BRANDON HOFFNER IN DRUG INDUCED COMA." A few weeks later, my brother Wallace had me frozen. I couldn't say I blamed him. It was hard to let family members go. He would certainly be very surprised to know how I'd ended up—Back at square one with only a dog and a Japanese sex-bot to help me.

I told Komaki what I was now facing. No tears from her, not even a flinch of emotion or: "I'm sorry, Brandon," which kind of pissed me off a bit. She just stared at me, obviously not knowing what to say. I was about to chastise her for her lack of caring, again almost completely forgetting what I was talking to, when she said calmly and coolly, as only she can. "I think we can clone your bone marrow and transplant it into your body slowly, thus removing any danger to you."

I stared at her with my mouth open for almost a full minute. She continued, "It will undoubtedly be very painful, Brandon, and without proper antiseptics it will be risky, but it is a chance for you to live longer."

I harkened back to the time when I'd first seen her and almost left her in that bedroom-sized, safety deposit box in Kyoto. "I can give you herbal medicines which will help with the pain and help fight off infection," she said.

I grabbed her hands and pulled her closer to me. "Thank you," I said in the most meaningful tone I could muster. I was almost in tears. Her head tilted a little to the side to indicate confusion.

"There is no need to thank me, Brandon," she said. "I am your robot companion. It is my duty to serve you." Then she smiled. How I had grown to love her little smile. "Your happiness is my success."

I know by now that you think I am completely off my rocker, but I don't care. You were not there. You were not experiencing what I was experiencing, and I realized at that moment that finding Komaki was truly the best thing that had ever happened to me. I told her that too. I was in love.

At that moment, all of the goals changed. We were going to clone my bone marrow and replace my tainted tissue with it. If I survived the process or not, Komaki would take DNA to clone me and the next task would be to search for a female host whom Komaki could clone so they could repopulate the planet. I could also do everything in my power to recreate her power cell giving her another 65 years to live.

They said behind every great man, there was a good woman. Well, Komaki had certainly helped me to see things more clearly. I had to stop being selfish, stop feeling sorry for myself and get my act together.

I had also read that the best couples always had a dreamer (a child at heart, a slob with imagination) and a partner who was totally grounded (the voice of reason). The Chinese even had a symbol for it. It was called the "Yin and Yang" symbol. It meant living in perfect balance and harmony.

That night, when she cooed, "Brandon, do you want to make love to me," I made love to her as I never had before.

Day 67 - December 4th

9:20 am

Komaki helped me shower again this morning. I felt pretty good today, despite the bad weather outside. After feeding myself and Beau, my robot companion showed me an interesting article in a Foxfire catalog about making your own still, like a moonshine still. If we could build one of these in the lab, then we could create our own disinfectants and alcohols that would help us with the cloning and surgery I would need to replace my bone marrow.

The really crazy thing about this was that this was not an option for me back when I'd been diagnosed because the USA, especially the Southern Bible Belt part of the USA, was thoroughly opposed to cloning research. But the process certainly made sense and sounded like it would work.

Though the drawing of the moonshine still was crude, I was sure we could find better material on how to build a proper still. Again, my girl had come up with a fantastic idea that would aid us immeasurably in our newest tasks.

She continued to study by the warmth of the space heaters and recharge her battery, which she did about every three or four days. I was off to the library and hardware stores again to find information and parts for our medicinal still.

1:30 pm

It was cold as a witch's tit outside—another bizarre saying used by old friends that I'd never fully understood. What was the significance of the tit being a witch's tit and why would a witch's tit be any colder than a regular breast? The expression ranked up there with "shit eatin' grin."

It was cold out, however. It was cold inside as well, despite the space heaters. When would this snowstorm let up?

Beau hurried on his trips outside to defecate and urinate. He was a smart dog and he knew not to dally or dawdle in his duties, otherwise he would become a pooch-sickle (again.)

I too, had to make quick trips from various nearby locations back to the home base lab. I gathered what I thought we needed to make a fully functional distillation device. From one of our many trips to the library, I secured an excellent book on electrical wiring, so I would rig it, so that it would be electrical and hook up a thermostat so that it didn't overheat.

11:00 pm

It was crudely fashioned, but the distillation apparatus worked. Komaki made a mad dash to the lab to inspect my work and she gave it the thumbs up. As a typical man, I was very proud of my work, even though it wouldn't win any prizes for the design. We tested it by distilling water and making some grain alcohol.

Komaki would stay in the lab tonight and try to create and bottle what she needed for our cloning experiments. The generator in the lab was working fine. I filled it before I left to come back home. The snow in the yard was almost up to my knees now. The thought of collecting more "stuff" and trying to find more food in this weather was a sobering one. We hadn't collected enough food for the entire winter. This hard freeze would kill a lot of what we could eat. We could make a trip down to Central or South Florida if necessary and there was always fishing. Ugh! One step forward and three days of snow.

Like a good dog, Beau was waiting for his master's return. Good boy. We would certainly clone him many times. He jumped about friskily and I pet him to calm him down. He lay on the floor next to me as he always did when I wrote in my journal.

As I wrote these notes a heavy feeling came over me. I realized my mortality and my importance again. It was the feeling like when you were in a foreign country where nobody spoke your language and you stopped for a second and said to yourself: "Man, nobody around me speaks my language... and yet... here I am."

I was really very lucky to have two such loyal companions. As you read this, you may think to yourself that I was some domineering maniac who needed people to bow down to my will, but not true. I realized most direly how I needed them and the help they offered. The fact they were subservient and did not complain was cherished because if I were alone and had to do all of this without their support, I would not have succeeded in most of my endeavors. This was a team, not a dictatorship.

Beau was my heart and Komaki was my brains. We were one, the three of us. Beau kept my spirits lifted the same way good pets could keep elderly people alive for decades. You surely know what I mean. A grandparent who spoiled their cat or dog mercilessly, like the animal was their child. It gave them a purpose and a friend when people forgot to call. It kept them out of the nursing home chair where dementia sets in quickly.

I was waxing poetic because my brain was not here. I was missing her now. I wanted to hear her ask me: "Would you like to make love to me now, Brandon." I didn't want to actually do it, but I did love to hear her say it. It made me feel manly and needed. I needed to get a set of walkie-talkies or rig up some kind of phone between the two houses... and not two tin cans connected by a string. I heard the front door bang slightly, then the soft music to my ears: "Do you want to make love to me, Brandon?" I now had a shit eatin' grin on my face. It was midnight.

Day 68 - December 5th

8:15 am

The blizzard had stopped, and the sun was shining. Hallelujah! Komaki and I needed to get going to try and find as much food as we could today and I needed to rig the solar panels.

9:45 pm

We gathered several bags of moist corn, grains, peanuts, and wild rice. We would eat these first and boil or steam them to ensure they were healthy. Though still probably not enough to feed Beau and I over the winter, I felt much more relieved at our assets.

I rigged up our solar panels and heater units according to the crude diagrams I'd made when I pulled them from other houses. Though a bit scratched and dented from the uprooting and re-fix, they looked functional. We would find out tomorrow morning if they worked.

This evening Komaki took blood and skin samples from Beau and me. She said, "Brandon, your cancer is getting worse."

I replied, "Well, I could have told you that." Again… another classic situation of "tell a robot a joke…"

We all had a busy day, so we turned in early.

Day 69 - December 6th

7:00 am

I woke up, and though it was still cold, the sun shone and there was no snow today. Komaki greeted me as usual and I tested the solar heating units. The water in our house was hot and the central

136

heating units in both homes appeared to be working. There was a slight smell of burning dust but that would subside. It happened with all heaters that hadn't been used in a while. So long as we had sun, we had power.

Komaki explained to me that we would need to take samples of my bone marrow from several key points in my body. To do this, we would have to drill holes into me and that meant I would have to get very drunk so the shock of the painful procedure wouldn't kill me.

No one liked going to the doctor or the dentist for just this kind of reason. But I knew it must be done and so... it would be done.

11:30 am

I raided several liquor cabinets in our area. Wine could go for centuries on the shelf and it just got better with age. I used to be quite the drinker in my day and my preference was brown liquor a la Jack Daniels Whiskey and Crown Royal. As I had not had much alcohol in the last sixty-some years, it wouldn't take too much for me to get FUBAR (Fucked UP Beyond All Recognition). Back in the Civil War—some two hundred years ago—they would inebriate soldiers before amputation. If they could do it, then so could I.

4:32 pm - KOMAKI'S MEDICAL NOTES:

Brandon is thoroughly inebriated. I drilled into his left fibula. He is in a lot of pain and he has passed out. I gave him a thick sterile cloth to bite down on and it is clenched tightly in his teeth. I used a special hollow glass rod to gather the marrow sample, and then I disinfected the drilled area and bandaged it. I have labeled and catalogued the glass rods so we know which sample came from which part of Brandon's body. I will let him rest before drilling his right fibula.

5:57 pm

I drilled into Brandon's body again, and he came awake long enough to scream, then he passed out again. I am constantly checking his pulse rate and monitoring his blood pressure. He is in a lot of pain but is pulling through the procedure adequately. Next, I will drill into each tibia. Each sample of Brandon's bone marrow will be tested and the cells which contain no cancer will be cloned for his transplant operation.

7:33 pm

Brandon is still sleeping. His vital signs are stable now. I have waited until now before drilling into his tibias because I wanted the shock from the last procedure to subside.

I woke him to give him another glass of aged whiskey so that he remains anesthetized. He is not happy that I have woken him. Most of his speech is slurred and incoherent. He complained he was "in a lot of pain" and said, "leave me alone." He called me a "bitch," which is very strange because he knows that I am not a female dog. I fear he is hallucinating.

8:10 pm

I have drilled into Brandon's left tibia. He screamed like I have never heard him scream before, so obviously his level of pain has peaked. I worked quickly and got the sample I needed. The samples look good on first sight, but I will need to examine them under a microscope to be sure.

9:22 pm

I hesitate to drill on Brandon again to get a final sample from his right tibia. He appears to be in agony and despite my disinfecting the holes I drilled in his body, he is sweating profusely, and I fear infection may have already set in.

9:41 pm

I have woken Brandon again and explained the situation. He is groggy, irritable and I have to hold him to keep him up. He has instructed me to "just get on with it," which means the procedure. He mumbles something I decipher to mean: "I want to get this over with." I will do one last drilling, then monitor his condition carefully during the night.

10:05 pm

I have drilled the fourth hole into Brandon's body. I have extracted a sample of bone marrow from his right tibia. He stayed asleep for the procedure, only crying out minimally when I first drilled into his epidermis, then again when the drill made its way into his bone. I have everything that I need for now. I will let Brandon rest.

11:47 pm

Brandon is nauseous and regurgitated twice just now. I have cleaned him up and cleaned up the mess on the floor. It is mostly whiskey as he had little to eat before starting the procedure. It is probably best he purges some of the alcohol from his system now. He is still sweating, so I have him wrapped in blankets.

11:56 pm

I am checking the samples of marrow that I have extracted from his body. Three samples contain cancerous cells, which mean that Brandon's cancer is in a relatively advanced stage, but the last sample I extracted from his right tibia appears to be normal. I can clone these cells and use them to save Brandon's life.

This evening I quickly read through Brandon's journal to better understand his purpose and mission. It is clear to me that Brandon Hoffner must live to repopulate the human species on this planet.

I have gathered other interesting facts that will help me to help him complete this mission successfully. There is a woman in cryo-suspension near here, and though she is too old for Brandon to make babies with, I can possibly clone her so he can begin this task in approximately fifteen to sixteen years. That is, if he survives that long.

Also, there is the issue of cockroaches. I have seen a few of them in our houses this past week.

Day 70 - December 7^{th,} 2082

1:44 am

It was cold outside, but not freezing so I ran to the library and retrieved another book on pharmaceutical medicine. There was a chapter on penicillin and how to culture it that I would use to help fight off Brandon's apparent infection. This book in conjunction with what I have learned from our herbal medicine books will aid me immensely with caring for Brandon during his recovery and subsequent bone marrow transplant operations.

5:12 am

I continue to clean Brandon's puncture wounds with sterilized cloth bandages. There is no redness around the openings, so his fever and sweats might have been a result of the excessive alcohol consumption and the shock of the actual procedure itself. He is sleeping very peacefully now.

I found some suitable mold in the refrigerator of the house next door to this one and I will use it to culture some penicillin. I still want to give Brandon the best care and I want to ensure he does not contract an infection. Soon I will gather items to create proper anesthetics for future experiments.

9:35 am

Brandon got up briefly to urinate this morning. I asked him if he wanted anything to eat but he refused. He is still in pain and says he is "hung over" from his drinking last night. Though I am unfamiliar with this phrase, I assume it is associated with a general feeling of fatigue with headache and dizziness. I only surmise this from the way Brandon was moving about slowly and holding his head. His eyes are bloodshot and, though I have cleaned him throughout the night, he still smells of aged whiskey.

When he exited the bathroom and made his way back to his medical bed, I asked him again if there was anything I could get him, as I was due to recharge my battery. He stumbled past me and said, "Fuck off!" I told him that sex this soon after his operation was not advisable. He went back to sleep.

2:42 pm

I have fed Beau some wheat and peanut paste. Brandon is still sleeping peacefully. I am now fully recharged, and it is a cool but sunny day, so I will attempt to go out and gather the raw materials needed to make the medicines and pharmaceutical supplies we need. It might take me a long time as I must walk but I do not get tired, so it will be done.

8:48 pm

It took me longer than expected to gather what I needed, but I feel certain I have all that I require to finish my aforementioned tasks.

Brandon is still sleeping in the laboratory on his sick bed. He has a small fever of 99 degrees, but I have checked his wounds again and there doesn't seem to be any redness from infection.

When I was walking, I came across the remains of one of the Siamese cats Brandon had mentioned. My guess from the cat's very pained expression, as well as some skin discoloration around its mouth, was that it was the cat Brandon had poisoned not long ago. It was a male cat, so it must have been the one called "Max."

Quite disturbing was the fact there were many cockroaches feeding on the carcass. The cockroaches began to scatter and crawl into the grass when I came close to inspect the dead feline. Even stranger was the fact there were bite marks on the cat that were much too big to be from cockroaches. It is my supposition that another animal had fed on Max recently. These two pieces of news will be most distressing to Brandon, so I will wait to tell him.

Day 71 - December 8th

8:30 am - BRANDON HOFFNER'S NOTES:

I was up. I felt rough but it was snowing outside this morning again, so I felt I should be up and doing something. I read Komaki's notes in my journal. I apologized to her even though the gesture was wasted because she wasn't emotional. I only hoped she could whip up some proper anesthetic so we didn't have to go through that kind of nightmare again. Yesterday was Pearl Harbor Day, and I certainly felt like the Japanese had attacked me.

The holes in my body were healing (slowly, but surely), but my thoughts were consumed by visions of cockroaches. It didn't dawn on me until now that by killing Max, I'd killed the one animal that was probably the best help in keeping the pest population down around my house. I just had to feed it regularly to keep it in line. And what animal had fed upon Max? That was the sixty-four-dollar question. I wracked my brain and Komaki and I came to the same conclusion: Myra must've still been alive out there somewhere in our neighborhood.

Even more exciting was Komaki's idea to clone Ms. Constance Giles, residing in the cryo-center not far from here. We wouldn't have to wake the old girl up. We'd just have to re-tuck her pillow and take a small DNA sample from her. Then we could leave her in peace.

I was upset we could not get on this today. It looked like we would have to wait for everything: my tissue samples to develop, finding Myra, and checking on old lady Giles.

11:30 am

Komaki showed me what I need to do at the cryo-center. I would check on the status of Constance Giles and try and get a DNA sample from her without disturbing her hibernation.

It was cold out, but I was bundled up tight. I didn't feel great, but this was important and couldn't wait. Komaki said she should have penicillin for me tomorrow and that meant I could take this chance.

2:15 pm

I went to the cryo-center this afternoon. I found Ms. Constance Giles just as I had left her weeks ago. I checked her LED panel on the cryo-unit and the panel blinked that her battery was down to critical. Her cryo-chamber would malfunction soon. This meant she had days or maybe weeks before the lights went out forever. I was torn in what to do. If I revived her, we could care for her, but she would probably die because she couldn't eat solid foods and we had no way to feed her intravenously. If I left her in the chamber, she would die like all the others. The chamber would malfunction and all her dreams would fade to black.

Should I share my private hell with this woman and become attached to her just in time to let her pass away a few days later? Or do I just plain let her rest in peace? Her living will probably didn't have a clause in it about post-nuclear revival. I carefully opened her chamber and took the DNA samples per Komaki's instructions.

Constance would get a second chance at life, but this one was over. I was so sorry. Like the others, there was no way to know it would all end up like this. An alarm on her cry-chamber sounded. It scared the shit out of me too, as I was not expecting it. I realized I had overstayed my welcome and closed her chamber quickly. After it closed, the alarm stopped. I checked her panel again and it seemed to be back to what it was when I first went in.

I came quickly home, and Komaki seemed happy with the samples I'd collected. I told her about the situation with Ms. Giles and she remarked, "Brandon, if this person is important to you, then we can probably find a way to recharge her battery or make a new one." I was in awe again at her resourcefulness. "You said that you would try to do the same for me…," She paused, then finished, "… in your notes."

She was right again. If I could find a way to manufacture working batteries, then I could rework Constance's cryo-chamber and lengthen her time on this barren paradise. Think outside the box.

Day 72 - December 9th

7:00 am

I went to sleep after dinner last night and slept until now. The holes in my body were sore and my joints got that cancerous feeling I had become so accustomed to. I was nauseous again this morning and I would have to force myself to eat again.

At least the sun was shining. We used the solar panels but I could get some work done by daylight so we could recharge our generators. I searched for a suitable factory for finding raw materials and making batteries.

Komaki says that I will have penicillin this afternoon to help me heal faster and it appeared my bone marrow cells were dividing and reproducing a la normal cloning procedure. That was all good news. I just hoped this procedure worked and did not end up being a big waste of time. Even if it bought me another six months, it would have been worth it. We would just have to wait and see.

8:45 pm

We had a busy day today. I went through the North neighborhood again searching for useful items. So I made numerous trips back and forth to our home base with batteries and another solar generator. It tested positive, so that made three generators now. I also found some outdoor lights on tripods that worked. We could light up the yards, if need be. The way I saw it, the heat from the lamps would help Komaki if she ran from one house to the other in the snow.

I had a map of Atlanta on the inside door of the storage shed. I marked the neighborhoods and shopping plazas we raided. This would help me keep track later when I started going out farther away from base camp.

My mind went back to the phonebook idea. Did libraries have copies of phonebooks in their collections? I was going to find out now.

11:15 pm

I remembered running out of the house and almost falling down the stairs. Komaki yelled after me, "Brandon, where are you going?"

I called back hastily, "To the library! I'll be back shortly."

In the old days, every house was given a phonebook and every outdoor payphone had a phonebook attached to it. But cellphones and the internet made them obsolete in the 20-teens. No more records on paper. Except at the library. "YES!" I said as I found my prize. White pages for individual phone number and yellow pages for the business phone numbers, all together in one book. I kissed its dusty, tasteless, glossy, paper cover.

I did not run back home. I casually walked back with a swagger in my step. I did not need a robot to come up with all of my ideas. Every now and again, I could come up with my own. I was so grateful the libraries had not gone the way of the dodo bird. What an invaluable resource for the last man on earth.

I returned home with my treasure and held it up for Komaki to see. She walked over and I handed to her. She opened it and skimmed the first few pages. She looked up at me. "Brandon, with this book, we can find everything we need in this city that you call 'Atlanta.'"

I nodded with a wicked smile. "Yep!" I said it in a self-satisfied tone. "So I know what you're going to being learning tonight."

She looked at me blankly. "Do you want me to memorize this book, Brandon?" "Just the yellow pages, my dear." I chuckled to myself and said it again, "Just the yellow pages."

She flipped the pages quickly. It wasn't long before she found the pages with the factory listings. There was a factory for making power cells north of town and now we had a physical address we could check. But I was tired so I let my robot nurse give me penicillin and I slept like a good patient while she scanned and memorized the Atlanta yellow pages.

Day 74 - December 11th

8:00 am

I slept through yesterday, but I felt okay today. Mentally I realized the payload I carried and that still made me feel shitty. Though it was cold, the sun shone, and it was not snowing, so Komaki and I took the E-RV over to the north end of town and checked out Georgia PCM (Power Cell Manufacturing.)

I brought along my fishing rod and gear, so if we saw a river or watering hole along the way, we could stop and hook a meal for Myra.

9:45 am

Komaki and I were in the factory. The main door was locked, but Komaki broke the lock easily with a powerful grip and twist of her dainty-looking hand.

It was not as big as I'd expected, just a small factory, but it appeared we had everything we needed to make crude batteries. I checked small storage rooms with wooden pallets loaded with connectors, contacts, and different-sized casings. I brought Komaki's old battery with us, and I found a casing that was a very close match. It was the same kind of re-chargeable cadmium battery they'd used in T.V. production cameras.

The chemicals needed for her battery were probably mercury and/or cadmium, which we would have to find or probably manufacture ourselves.

In the early part of the twenty-first century, the same technology which had given us long lasting mobile phone batteries had allowed all batteries to last a lifetime and they only had to be charged every three or four days, depending on what you used them for.

Komaki actually had a sensor telling her when her battery was getting low and she knew to hook herself up and recharge. She'd probably recharged herself for several weeks in the dark waiting for Yutaka until no power was available in her padded cell. Her battery remained powerless for decades, killing it. I constantly worried about the shelf life of the power cell in her now and that was why I wanted to prepare some back-up batteries for her.

Komaki scanned workers' manuals in the various employees and supervisors' offices. After a while, she came out and we broke into various boxes and packed up battery parts. "I feel certain I can make what we need at our home, Brandon."

I raised an eyebrow. "Don't we need the factory machines to do that for us?"

She looked at me blankly and said, "I am a robot, Brandon." Then, after she continued to search for parts, she further quipped, "I am all the assembly line you will need."

I just smiled, thinking to myself once again, "She is amazing."

12:15 pm

It was warm now. We stopped on a bridge over a small canal and I dropped a line in the water. It only took me a few minutes to get a bite. In less than an hour, I caught Myra's next meal and four other small fish. I told Komaki we would have to remember this spot. She looked around and sid, "It is in my memory bank now."

Though it was another Komaki moment for me, it brought up a serious question. "Komaki," I asked tenderly. "If something should happen to you… will your memory banks still contain everything that you have experienced with me?"

She answered quickly, "Of course, Brandon."

I continued. "So if your memory chips, cards, banks, whatever are not damaged, then I might be able to rebuild you, right?"

Again, she answered with little hesitation. "Yes, Brandon, that is a possibility." It made me feel better about my dependency on her. No. That was not fair. It made me feel better about my love for her.

She continued, "My memory cards are well-shielded with special surge protectors. There are eight cards in all, housed in my upper back, just above my battery compartment. Each card allows me to store up to a thousand terabytes of information." She hesitated for a moment and smiled at me. "So far, I have only used about seventeen percent of my memory capacity."

I laughed and hugged her. "That's wonderful, Komaki."

The hug confused her. She looked at me and said, "Do you want to make love to me now, Brandon?"

God, I loved to hear her say that. I got aroused immediately and took her—right there—on the bridge. It was savage lovemaking with most of our clothes still on. In my head, I sang John Lennon's, "Why Don't We Do It in the Road?" and I laughed to myself at the situation.

When it was over, and we were cleaning up, she smiled.

I said, "Why are you smiling?"

She almost looked embarrassed, but of course that was impossible, so I realized she must have been confused by my question. She finally answered, "Because I know I have made you happy, Brandon." I was surprised by her answer. She continued, "If you are happy because we have just made love, then that means you are happy with me." At this point, I was a little weirded out, because her answer sounded not just very human but also very female to me.

"Yes," I replied. "That is right, Komaki."

There was a pause and she smiled again. "If you are happy with me, then you will continue to protect me as I protect you." She paused. "That is very good." She gave a little nod and walked back to the E-RV, grabbing the bucket of fish along the way. I was left standing there with my mouth wide open.

As I'd written in these pages before, Komaki was supposed to be a learning robot, but I bet her creator never imagined in his wildest fantasies she would learn the all-important lesson of self-preservation. It was a very human quality. She continued to amaze me every day, but I had to, at all costs, keep everything in proper perspective. She was a machine and she did not have the capacity to actually feel. I must never forget this.

8:45 pm

Komaki worked on building back-up batteries in the laboratory and I put a fresh fish on the lawn for Myra. I hoped she enjoyed it. It was not poisoned. I would put another one out for her tomorrow night.

I checked the bug netting around my bed. It seemed very secure. No holes or gaped. I too started seeing roaches around the main house. They were quick though and scattered away before I could kill them, not as aggressive as the Asian cockroaches which were downright creepy. Poor Beau would have to fend for himself.

11:30 pm

Komaki and I were in our home now. She said she would have to go out tomorrow to gather natural elements for the batteries. Tonight, we relaxed on the sofa and listened to light music. I educated her in rock and roll music, but this sitting I played a little jazz, some classical tunes, and easy listening. As we listened to a Rat Pack CD I had picked up (because I liked listening to them when I'd been a misunderstood teen) she told me, "I like the voice of this man Dean Martin." I laughed when she said it. "His voice sounds very smooth." She listened as he crooned the tune "Inamorata," and I could swear I almost saw her swaying a little bit to the rhythm. She got up from the couch as the song ended and played it again. The song began with the words: *"If our lips should meet... Inamorata. Kiss me; kiss me, sweet Inamorata..."*

She looked down at me and her expression was surprisingly wonton for a robot. "Brandon," she said. "Once, you kissed me on the boat. Do you remember?"

I nodded and simply said, "Yeah."

She listened to the music some more and said, "I did not know how to do that properly."

I paused, not knowing what to say to that. I stammered out another: "Yeah?"

Very quickly, she climbed on top of me. I was shocked but in a pleasantly surprised kind of way. Her face was just an inch from

149

mine. "I want you to teach me how to kiss, Brandon." Her request knocked me for a loop. "I want to be a good lover to you." She said it almost aggressively. "I want to make love again like we did today on the road."

Now, let me stop for just a minute reader before I go on and explain that when any attractive woman tells a man this—no matter the time, or the place—it was going to get all of his juices flowing at once.

The moment was so raw I flipped Komaki over on the sofa and kissed her passionately. This time I was getting kissed back, softly at first, then with more

ardor and enthusiasm as she was learning. As a matter of fact, we kissed so passionately at that moment that Komaki split my bottom lip. I could feel it and I could taste it, but like a shark, it just made me wilder. Love on the sofa that night was animalistic. She spun me over and got on top of me. She ripped my clothes off. I mean, literally, and we broke one of the legs on the sofa.

Let's not forget, dear reader, that I was a cancer patient. Though enjoyable, I thought tI was near death when it was over. But Komaki held me. She ran her fingers through my hair and we actually cuddled. This was another first. To say I was stunned by the events would be the understatement of the apocalypse. It happened so fast and so furious I was almost scared by it.

It did feel good to be held by someone, though. Girls didn't realize men liked this a lot too. We enjoyed the closeness of a good cuddle or caress just like you women did. We just had to be men and when we did not get that kind of treatment, we could not complain about it so much, because that was, well, wimpy. Truth be told, I really enjoyed it because I had missed it. All right, maybe I shared just a little too much on this entry.

We went up to bed. I was very tired and would write about this crazy incident later (in case you're wondering how I was able to write about it like this right after it all happened.) I slept deeply with Komaki pressed next to me.

Day 75 - December 12th

9:10 am

I felt absolutely rotten this morning. It wasn't snowing, but it was cold. I took Komaki to see Ms. Giles' cryo-chamber. She needed to grab a battery from a like-chamber for reference. I was getting very thin now. I just didn't feel like eating anything.

Komaki made Beau some breakfast. Then she bundled up in several layers of clothes to keep her machinery from freezing up. I too was bundled up. My drill holes still hurt, but they had scabbed over and were healing nicely.

The fish on the lawn was gone, so Myra must have gotten it. I would put out another one tonight.

12:05 pm

I was back home. I was not feeling at all well. My bone marrow cells were still multiplying rapidly in the lab, but we still did not have enough to replace the marrow in me. I was back in bed and might stay here the rest of the day.

We raided one of the malfunctioned cryo-chambers that was the same model as Mrs. Giles.' Her panel was still flashing critical, so she was okay for now. Komaki brought the battery from the other cryo-chamber home with her. She pulled it apart, studied it, and would hopefully build a new one tonight. Komaki went out to get raw materials to make the batteries. She could drive the scooter now, albeit clumsily. I hoped she could find what she needed, and I hoped she did not wreck our electric bike.

5:20 pm

I was up again, and Komaki was still not back. I was worried. It was cold out and it would be getting dark soon.

5:45 pm

Komaki returned with a big sack filled with rocks and sand. I scolded her for staying out so long. She replied, "I am sorry, Brandon. I have been digging all afternoon for different mineral deposits." She smiled and continued, "As you can see, I have gathered quite a lot."

"I was worried that something might have happened to you."

She tilted her head slightly again. "Do not worry, Brandon. I am a robot. I am very strong and impervious to pain. I cannot get lost, even in the dark, and my thermostat tells me when it is getting too cold."

I had to concede, at least to myself, that I was being just silly. I went back to bed and Komaki went to the lab to work through the night with her new minerals. I hoped she could build back-up batteries for Ms. Giles and herself.

Day 76 - December 13th

10:30 am

I was up at nine sharp, but Komaki was not around. It was snowing again… Oh, shit! I was feeling so bad yesterday, I did not recharge the backup generators. I quickly put on clothes and ran over to the lab.

The heaters were running. Komaki came out and saw me. "Good morning, Brandon."

I smiled. I was glad she was all right. "I thought maybe you ran out of power here last night." I said it lovingly but was a little embarrassed.

She blinked once. "I recharged the back-up generators yesterday afternoon. You did not need to worry." She put her hand out, beckoning me. I slowly came into the room, which was now our laboratory. On the table were four batteries: two different sets. The first set looked like the one for Ms. Giles' cryo-unit. The other two were decent matches for Komaki's rechargeable life cell. Wires from the generator were crudely hooked up to one of the cryo-batteries.

"I have succeeded in duplicating the power cells. I am charging them now." She smiled and nodded at me. "Hopefully, they will retain a charge."

I moved in closer for a better look. I have to admit, I was impressed again with my girl's handy-work. Now you may ask yourself, "How does the cryo-battery hold such a long charge?" It was a fair question, reader. My battery had kept my cryo-chamber functional from almost sixty years without power or recharge. So I asked Komaki the same question.

"Unfortunately, I haven't totally figured that out yet." Not the answer I was expecting from her, but she continued at length. "The battery is also a mini-capacitor, so I believe all of the batteries for all of the cryo-units were feeding off of each other somehow and possibly feeding off of your bodies. Your unit woke you up when all of the power drained from your chamber and obviously, Ms. Giles' chamber was the last one in the line-up. As the animal chambers were smaller, with smaller inhabitants, it would obviously take longer for their power system to de-energize." She paused for a moment, looking at me as if she were wondering if I comprehended anything she had just told me. Then she quickly added. "That is my best guess."

My mind reeled at the concept. "So," I said a little befuddled, "the batteries that were keeping our chambers cooling were actually feeding off of our body energy after the main power shut down?"

Komaki nodded. "That is what I believe," she said coldly. "It is probably what killed many of the other patients who were stored there." Komaki could see the horror in my eyes. She added, "You had no way of knowing that this would happen, Brandon."

All of those other dozens of bodies had kept my cryo-chamber going for fifty-eight years, slowly giving up their life for mine. Had I just been in the right cryo-chamber at the right time?

Komaki put a hand on my shoulder. "You were very lucky. You are alive because your chamber malfunctioned." When she said it, reader, it didn't really give me much comfort at the time. I think my body language or maybe my facial expression might have told her that. She added, "Because you are alive now, I can transplant your marrow for you and you can go on living, Brandon."

Now that I had a short time to think about it, I did realize how fortunate I was. I didn't know why I was the lucky one, but I did know the circumstances leading to this had been amazing. Obviously, I hadn't done everything right, but all of my choices had brought me here, to this moment. And though the future might not have been the brightest, it was a future nonetheless.

7:45 pm

Komaki informed me she had rewired Ms. Giles' battery in her cryo-chamber, so it was a regular, rechargeable battery set-up. We would now have to recharge her battery ourselves about every three days. I felt better about that. Ms. Giles was still sleeping peacefully.

10:00 pm

Tomorrow, we would attempt to extract my bone marrow from my upper body and replace it with freshly cloned clean bone marrow. Then I would recuperate for a couple of days and Komaki would continue to produce the cloned marrow for my legs. Next week, we would finish the process. As I would be anesthetized and sedated most of the time, Komaki, would make notes on the procedure.

It would obviously be painful, and the risk was great, but I could not see any other option. In the plus column, my surgeon was a skilled robot, well-versed in what to do. She had distilled proper anesthetics and antibiotics to aid us in this procedure. She knew how to recharge the generators and recharge herself in my absence. Komaki had proven she could move between the two houses, even during heavy snow by wearing a hot water bottle harness under a long overcoat, thick gloves, multiple stocking caps, etc. And the lights and heaters were all set up for her.

The second fish was eaten again, so I felt Myra was under one of the houses in this neighborhood. Komaki made a crude DDT type bug powder which we sprinkled around the houses to keep the roaches out. The roaches needed to be kept at bay.

I went to bed since tomorrow would undoubtedly be harrowing. As prayers had kept me going until now, I said a little one, hoping it too would be answered.

Day 77 – December 14^{th,} 2092

7:11 am - KOMAKI'S MEDICAL NOTES:

I have just anesthetized Brandon and he appears to be sleeping peacefully. We have a liposuction apparatus we brought home from the hospital, which should adequately extract his bone marrow, but first I must drill each bone in key locations as I did before. For these records, the drill we are using was also made especially for this type of operation and was brought home from one of the area hospitals. After reading my previous medical notes, Brandon told me I should clarify that for you, the reader. I am doing so per his wishes.

11:57 am

I have drilled small holes in Brandon's bones in his shoulders and arms. I slowly suctioned out the cancerous marrow and have replaced it with fresh clean marrow that was cloned here in our laboratory over the last few days. I have made a small cap (or plug) out of aluminum, for each bone hole. They screw tightly into place, sealing each bone. I learned to do this from one of the many medical journals I have scanned. Brandon is doing fine. His vital signs have remained normal all morning.

4: 10 pm

I have just finished replacing the bone marrow in Brandon's collar bones and rib cage. His temperature is slightly elevated (99.5 F) and his heart rate increased when I was working on his rib cage, but he seems to be all right.

The effects of the anesthesia should wear off soon. I will give him painkillers and antibiotics through the evening, and I will continue to monitor him and his condition through the night.

Unfortunately, I did not have enough cloned marrow to replace the bad cells in his spinal column and back bone. The aforementioned procedure will have to wait until next time when I purge his legs. It is probably better that way.

I am also giving him mild doses of herbal medicines that are close to chemical therapy medicines regularly prescribed for patients with his kind of bone marrow cancer. Although they may weaken him in his current state, I feel it will help him to fight off any new cancer cells that may try to develop and possibly spread to the areas we have just cleansed. If his condition changes drastically, I have drugs and back-up hospital machinery on standby to aid me in an emergency.

6:34 pm

Brandon awoke at 6:20 pm. I asked him how he was feeling at this particular time and he responded by saying, "Like shit." An odd verbal expression, but he has so many of them that I do not fully comprehend. When I asked him to clarify, he told me he was feeling a lot of pain in his joints. This is natural as that is where I drilled many of the holes in the bones of his upper body.

Obviously, the local anesthetic I had administered has worn off before my general anesthetic. This was something I did not anticipate, and I have noted it here to remind me to give more local anesthetic next time we operate on his lower body. When I informed him of this, he said, "No shit." Again, I am wondering about his preoccupation with feces. I ask him if he needs me to help him go to the toilet, but he said, "No," just rolling his eyes, then closing them. I do not think he is happy with me. I gave him a shot of pain killer upon his request and he has an intravenous drip of antibiotic, which I will check and change regularly tonight.

He is sleeping again now. I will go to the house and make some vegetable and barley soup for him. It is snowing again, so I must dress in thick layers of clothes.

Day 78 – December 15th

6:00 am - BRANDON SHEFFLER'S NOTES:

Komaki was down and in danger.

At about 8:00 pm my IV bag drained, and I had to pull out the needle myself. Komaki was nowhere in the laboratory. I called several times and felt that maybe she was busy, so I went back to sleep.

At just after 2 am (my best estimtion,) the lights went out. I woke up and fumbled around until I got to the front door. I could see Komaki fallen over in the snow near the steps of the house. Her battery must have given out and she had probably been lying in the snow for most of the night. Fuck!

Despite my present condition, I dug her out and pulled her inside the house. Beau barked up a storm as I did so. I collapsed next to her on the kitchen floor.

I woke up at dawn with my head spinning, my ears ringing, and my shoulders bleeding. Again, the house was cold, and the generator had shut down. I breathed cold mist from my hot breath. Amazingly, I staggered over to the other side of the house where Generator 1 was located and hoped to God it had juice. I flipped the switch, the space heaters fired up, and warmth began to permeate the room.

This I challenge anybody to do when they've just had holes drilled in their shoulders, arms, and ribcage. The pain in my joints was like being shot multiple times with low caliber firearms (my best guess as to how it probably felt.) It hurt like all-fucking-hell, okay?

I slipped around and staggered back to the kitchen. Bleeding and sweating, I dragged Komaki's limp body up and placed it on the dining room table. I didn't know why, but I placed her face down with her shoulder and head hanging over the side. Her mouth was slightly open, and it looked like she was drooling. Again, something inside told me I should not hook her up or connect her to any power.

A voice in my head seemed guide my actions. It told me: "Get back to the sterilized lab!" And: "Set up the generators. You need to sleep." It sounded like my voice, so it might have been my subconscious or the voice of reason… Actually, it sounded a lot like my father.

It was funny that at a crisis like this, I harkened back to memories of my Dad. As I slipped and fell in the snow just outside the house, I remembered how my Dad used to fall asleep on the couch watching the news after dinner. If I ever tried to change the channel, he would wake up and mutter out something like, "Hey, I was watching that!" I would have to change the channel back. He worked so hard—two jobs.

I made it to the generator in the lab and placed it in the sun. Again, major pain, then blackness.

Day 79 – December 16th

3:00 am

I sweated profusely. I woke up on the floor by my hospital bed. The room was spinning. Komaki was dead in the kitchen next door and the sound of the wind that woke me up told me it was probably snowing up a storm outside. Situation: not good.

I looked around the room. Of course, nothing was labeled. I saw syringes, bottles of prepared fluids that looked like good drugs, but nothing had a name on it. . . "Ya rolls yer dice, ya takes yer chance." I filled two syringes with medicinal liquid I found, and I administered my own cocktail (whatever the hell it was.)

11:00 am

I blacked out again. At least this time, I had the sense to get in the bed. Well, kind of. I had been laying lengthwise over the middle of the bed with my feet touching the floor on one side and the blood rushing to my head for God knows how long, then I remembered waking up for just long enough to correct my sleeping position. I didn't know what time that was.

Beau barked and yelped. That was what woke me up this time. I probably would have woken up sooner, but I thought I injected myself with one of the anesthetic solutions. It was a miracle I did not overdose. Yeah, here was the future of humanity—right here. Deal with it.

Again, I trudged over to the house as the snow came down sideways. The lights and heaters were off, and Komaki was just as I'd left her. No surprise there. Beau was flipping out because he was hungry. I saw dead roaches on the kitchen floor. Our homemade DDT mix was working.

I made some quick food for my animal companion and grabbed a chair and sat next to lifeless Komaki on the kitchen table. The room was starting to swirl around again, and I was out of breath, shivering from cold (and probably fever). My arms were a mass of drilled holes and intravenous needle marks. This was officially a mess.

As I looked at my robotic female askew as she was on the table, I wished I could say I did not feel any emotion about her being in her situation. She was just a machine, right? But we had too much history now. Too many good moments.

I remembered her saying it was not good for her to get water down her airway. I hoped if I just let her dry out today, then I could hook her up to power tonight and there would not be too much damage to her. If she'd shorted out from condensation inside, she was done for. If she just ran out of juice, then there was a chance she would be all right.

4:00 pm

I passed out again. If you were wondering how I was writing all of this, I think the answer is obvious. I wrote these log entries well after everything had happened. So you know I survived, but it was a hell in a hand basket when it happened.

I switched the generators so there was warmth in the houses again. I still couldn't believe I functioned at all during this crisis much less, lugging generators about, but I was half-delirious, and I had to do it. I staggered to the bathroom and pissed. I grabbed an old hair blow dryer that I remembered seeing there. I hooked it up and it still worked. I blew warm air in Komaki's airway for a long time, maybe an hour or two. I removed her battery and checked and cleaned her battery compartment. She seemed okay. I re-plugged in her battery and hooked her up to her power adaptor. Then... I waited. I was in such pain. The place spun about me.

Now usually Komaki perked up just minutes after hookup, kind of like when you recharged your mobile phone. But I waited a long time, and nothing happened. I was sure I had lost her. Weak and sore, I broke down completely and cried. Without her, I would surely die. I could not finish my cancer treatment alone, but I didn't cry for myself. I sobbed at the loss of my good friend... my lover... my companion of unquestionable faith and loyalty.

I had one last thing I had to try. I replaced her old battery with the new one she had skillfully made for herself, then re-plugged her into her power adaptor. I cursed her for not recharging herself, which she was so good about doing. I cursed myself because I knew deep down all of her attention on me and my surgery was probably what had caused her to wait until it was too late to recharge.

Then she snapped up and jerked around, repositioning herself so she was sitting up. If a robot ever woke up from sleep, I saw it at that moment. She blinked and actually looked around, confused. I yelled out a pitiful "yahoo" of some kind. Her first words were: "Brandon, my power cell has died." I should have known that was what had happened. She always knew when her own power was getting low and she was so good about recharging herself. I wanted to get up and hug her, but I was too weak. I was so happy to have her back.

She looked at me. "We need to get you back to the laboratory, Brandon." The words were music to my ears. "You should not be here now. The house isn't sterile." She re-clothed herself in her winter snow protection gear and put a clean comforter around me. She ushered me back to the hospital room in our other house. She reset up my intravenous drip and gave me some injections.

"I thank you for coming to my rescue, Brandon." She brushed my hair off my forehead gently, like a good lover. "But you have put yourself in jeopardy." She re-attached me up to the vital signs box. "You have a fever of 103." She said it like a mother hen, and it made me smile all the more. "That is bad. That means infection has set in."

It was amazing I didn't die. I endured freezing snow, over medicating myself, and deadly infection by the sheer determination and drive to make sure my companion survived. I was sure that when the world was still spinning with us still on it that millions of people on this globe had done similar miraculous death-defying feats for the sake of other loved ones,...but this moment was mine.

10:42 pm - KOMAKI'S MEDICAL NOTES:

Upon his insistence, I let Brandon dictate his ordeal over the last two days to me and I recorded it here. He is sleeping peacefully now and has handed the log duties back to me. His vital signs are stabilizing but his body temperature is 101 degrees Fahrenheit. I have cleaned and redressed his wounds and I occasionally wash him with cool water.

I read Brandon's notes and he did exactly what was required to save me, even though he did not know exactly what had caused my power failure. I am very gratified he was able to restore my power and keep me alive.

Day 80 – December 17, 2092

12:12 am

I have made some soup for Brandon. He has not eaten in over two days. He ate two bowls full and went back to sleep. I feel I should mention he also kissed my cheek when he thanked me for the soup. I am not sure why he did this; perhaps it is an American cultural ritual I have not learned yet. I will query him on it later when he is feeling better.

3:42 am

Brandon's fever is coming down. He is back to 99.6 degrees Fahrenheit now. His shoulder wounds are bleeding slightly. I have kept him on a constant antibiotic drip and will continue to do so until his temperature stabilizes. He is sleeping peacefully.

7:20 am

I am in the main house now and must report that the dog Beau is not well. He has vomited several times and seems less active than usual. He is whimpering and lies in his bed not wanting to come out. I have cleaned up the vomit and I have prepared food for him, but he has not eaten it as of this writing. I fear he is seriously ill.

10:17 am

Brandon is doing well. He has eaten a prepared breakfast of flatbread and peanut paste and his temperature is 99 degrees Fahrenheit.

The dog Beau's situation has not changed. He refuses to eat or move from his bed. I have made more food for him, but he does not seem to want to eat anything. He makes strange motions like he is trying to vomit or spit something out, but nothing comes out. I believe Brandon called this action in humans "the dry heaves." My feeling is that despite all of my efforts to try and save him, the dog Beau is going to die very soon.

3:45 pm

Brandon is stable and says he is tired of sleeping. I have brought him clean clothes and have told him of the situation with the dog Beau. He has said he will go to the house and see the dog Beau himself.

5:28 pm

Brandon is back in his hospital bed and seems very depressed. He has concurred that our animal companion, the dog Beau, is dying. Brandon says the situation is irreversible. His exact words are: "There is nothing that we can do." I feel the dog Beau is suffering from possible DDT poisoning, but Brandon mentioned "Beau is just old." I will continue to monitor the animal, but Brandon feels the dog Beau will probably not survive the night.

8:05 pm

I fed Brandon again and have also attempted to feed the dog Beau. Beau's situation is the same. I petted him for a long time, which he seemed to like but he is clearly suffering, and he is ready to die. The way the animal looks at me, I feel he wants me to leave him alone, but I know Brandon wants me to check on him, so I have made several trips between the houses to monitor both of my sick companions.

10:22 pm

I have told Brandon about this evening's rounds and my time with the dog Beau. He looked very somber and did not say anything for a long time. Then he told me I should stay in the laboratory for the rest of the night. As Brandon is my master and he has given me a direct order, I must abide by it, though I am confused as to why he would not want me to continue to check on the dog Beau. Brandon said ,"Animals usually want to be alone at this time."

Day 81 – December 18, 2092

7:52 am

The snowstorm has passed, and the dog Beau has died. I was told we will bury the dog Beau in a couple of days when Brandon is feeling better and the weather permits. This is evidently an American death ritual where a large hole is dug and the body of the person, or in this case, the animal is placed into the hole and covered up. A marker is set to reveal to others where the burial site actually is.

He has not instructed me to do so, but I will fashion a sensible marker for the dog Beau's burial site. I believe he will be buried in what Brandon calls the backyard of the house.

9:05 am

I have taken DNA samples of the dog Beau in the off chance we may find a way to clone him. Brandon has not asked me to do this, but per our previous discussions in this matter, I decided there would be no harm in doing so. Brandon has asked me to put the dog's remains in a sealed plastic bag, which I have done as instructed. This is actually a wise thing to do for many reasons, the most important of which is proper sanitation.

11:15 pm - BRANDON SHEFFLER'S NOTES:

I was depressed. The only other living thing that shared this Godforsaken planet with me was gone. The roaches and the stupid fucking cat didn't count. Beau was a good dog. Don't worry—I'm not going to get all "Old Yeller" on you here. It just really sucked after everything we'd been through these last few months. I'd fucking jumped off a boat in tempest tossed waters to save him and we'd fought audacious Asian cockroaches side by side.

I couldn't go down to the local pet store and replace him. I had to hope there was another frozen pooch somewhere I could re-animate and hopefully he would have the same temperament and smarts as my dog. The odds were pretty much against us on that, weren't they?

Komaki was fantastic in so many ways, but she had no emotions at all which made her pretty much the last thing I needed to talk to when my only canine companion died. She just blinked and tried to think of the best way to dig the hole so we could bury him.

So maybe my mission changed again. Maybe when the spring came, Komaki and I would go to find other cities. If we found them, we'd look for other cryo-centers. If I'd made it this far, maybe there were others. Maybe this should have been my mission from the start. Sometimes the simplest plan was the best. Until that time came, we just stayed alive.

Day 82 – December 19th

9:20 am

I felt much better this morning and though it was cold, there was not much wind and no snow today. It was a good time to bury Beau. Komaki dug a nice three foot by three foot by three feet-deep hole in the back yard. She placed Beau in it. She watched as I came up to the fresh grave and said my few words. I knew this was alien to her, but I didn't care. He deserved a decent burial like any living thing. It was not that I was overly religious. I was not. It just made me feel better to do it that way.

"Beau," I started, "I am thankful for the short time we had together." I looked down at the lifeless bag in the hole and began to tear up. Komaki stood motionless nearby. I continued, "I brought you back because I didn't want to do this alone." I stopped, choking up a bit. "I brought you back because a short time in the fresh air is better for a dog than a long time in a frozen box."

I had never done a eulogy at anyone's funeral, much less a dog's. It seemed like the right thing to say. I kept it short and sweet by ending with: "You were a good dog." I nodded quickly, turned, and walked back to the house.

On cue, Komaki walked over to the grave, then shoveled dirt into the hole. When all was said and done, the site was covered and packed so flawlessly with the ground being perfectly level that I would bet money that in a few months' time, after the grass had grown over it, you would never know anything was buried there. Luckily for Beau, Komaki had designed a nice, thick, plastic head marker with his name on it. It read: "THE DOG – BEAU."

12:05 pm

I hadn't talked much to Komaki. I probably should've to taken my mind off of this morning's grim affair. I was just not in a talkative mood. I was "in a funk" as my old friend Greg Horseman used to say. Komaki continued to work as usual. She never let up. She had her main job to do, which was cloning Brandon Hoffner bone marrow for my cancerous hips and legs. She also cooked lunch for me. She was getting better at cooking and I told her so. It helped break the ice.

She said, "Brandon" and the way she said it sounded sincere. "I am not familiar with what you are experiencing now." She actually reached out and touched my hand. It surprised me and I jumped a little. She continued, "But I do know from what I have seen and read that I should tell you that I am sorry we have lost Beau."

The gesture was surprisingly tender, and it did help. As she walked to the door, she turned back to me, smiled a little, and said, "I am here for you, Brandon," then exited.

4:20 pm

Komaki had come back to the main house after a day of cloning. She came over to me. "Would you like for me to play some of your music for you?"

I shook my head.

"Would you like to play a game? Maybe a card game?"

Again, I indicated: "No."

She walked out of the room, not disgusted or angry at my ambivalence.

For the longest time she did not appear, then she came in wearing a white leather top, red miniskirt, black fishnet stockings, and a white-silver pageboy wig. She stood over me as I slumped on the broken sofa. I looked up slowly.

"Yutaka used to like this outfit. It was one of his favorites." I had to admit, she was eye-catching in it, though there were no other eyes around. "What do you think of it?" She said it coyly with a tinge of naughtiness.

I stammered out a soft, "Um,… it looks nice."

She smiled and exited. In a mere fraction of a moment, a fashion show had begun as she came out in outfit after garish outfit and I had to admit, it was bringing my spirit back because I knew she was doing it for me. She knew I was down and needed a pick-me-up of some kind.

Obviously, I was in no condition to have sex, and she knew that too, but I made mental notes of the outfits and wigs I liked for the future.

Komaki could see I was getting aroused. She stopped posing and knelt down between my legs. She wore a black, plastic dress and a purple, shoulder-length wig. She unzipped my member and said, "Don't move, Brandon. Just relax."

What she did next was amazing. The Asian's called it "Ants climbing up a tree," and I assumed it was another one of Yutaka's favorites. I don't feel right elaborating here on what happened other than to say it was gentle and pleasing and I did not have to move at all, not one muscle. All I knew was, thanks to Komaki, the stress of the entire past week went away immediately, and it was a better sleep inducer than her home-made anesthetics.

I thanked her as I fell asleep and she climbed up onto the sofa and held me. My mind went back to finding her in the snow a few days ago. Images of her lying over the kitchen table flashed in my mind. I'd almost lost both of my loyal companions this week.

As she rocked with me, I thought to myself how I must protect her as best as I could. She was all I had left now. If I lost Komaki too, I didn't know what I would do. I might not keep it all together. In a couple of days, my cancer treatment would be completed, but I relied on my Japanese robot girlfriend for so much more now. I dreamed of having a little house in the country with my wife Komaki and two kids. Real kids: a boy and a girl.

11:00 pm

At this moment, I was catching up on the last few day's worth of journal writing. I rested long and my mind was fairly clear now. Komaki went to check on Ms. Giles earlier and was now working in the laboratory in the house next door. It was chilly tonight but not snowing. She said the lab was where I should be and as usual, she was right. I went and slept there in my antiseptic bed for safety.

It seemed like I had lived a long time here, but it had just been under three months. In that time, I had conquered and failed, loved and lost. I had seen unspeakable horrors these past few months and equally stunning beauty.

The question of the moment was what did tomorrow hold for Komaki and me? What the next few weeks would be like, I could not say. You certainly understand by now I was a "jump into it head-on" kind of guy. I never was overly cautious. Should I have been? I was the last man on Earth and my partner relied on me for safety. Right now, I had to focus on getting myself well. Then and only then could I set my sites on new ventures. Lately, my projects had been finding me; I hadn't exactly been picking them.

Christmas was just around the corner. I didn't know if I could get Komaki excited about the holiday season, but it would be nice to concentrate our efforts on something positive.

Day 83 – December 20th

7:45 am

Komaki prepared to operate on me again. This time, she would replace the bone marrow in my hips and legs. Tonight, she would work on my backbone as well. We moved most of what we needed into the med house, including food, cooking utensils, and two of the generators. This would keep Komaki from having to run back and forth through the snow so much. Yes, it snowed again.

I was a bit apprehensive as expected, but Komaki had done a great job so far and I survived the first half of the procedure despite our winter perils. I was sure the worst was over now.

9:27 am - KOMAKI'S MEDICAL NOTES:

Brandon is under sedation now. He is sleeping soundly. I have made the necessary incisions on his left hip area, and I am now drilling into his bone to extract the marrow from inside. Everything is progressing well. I am becoming more skillful with using the drill and the vacuum apparatus. There is a little more blood this time, but that is to be expected. I have to be careful as Brandon cannot lose too much blood. Though I have cloned some spare blood cells, we do not have too much for a normal transfusion.

12:42 pm

Brandon appears to be doing well. His vital signs have been stable all morning. I have just finished the procedure on his left hip and will start preparing his right hip for the same operation.

4:51 pm

I have finished the extraction and replacement of marrow in his right hip. I will let him rest. This time we replaced more marrow than before, so I am hoping I still have enough cloned marrow to do his back this time. As the procedure took longer this time, it is probably better that we wait to do his back. When Brandon wakes up, I will feed him. Depending on how he feels, I may wait until tomorrow to do the marrow transfer to his legs.

6:13 pm

Brandon is awake. I have fed him some soup and flat bread. I explained the situation to him, and he understands. His reaction was typical for Brandon. He said, "Do what you can tonight. Jesus Fucking Christ! Let's get this over with!" He is usually ill-tempered when he is groggy from being anesthetized. I will continue the marrow transfer on his legs per his instructions as soon as I get him back to sleep.

10:40 pm

I have replaced the marrow in Brandon's legs. Obviously, the extraction and marrow replacement went faster with his leg bones. I am not sure if it was because the bones are smaller, thereby making it quicker, or maybe it is because I am becoming more skilled at the procedure. Logically, the latter choice makes better sense. It could be both reasons.

As I did not get a sample of marrow from his back to test, I took the liberty of drilling at the base of his backbone this evening and extracting a small sample of marrow as he is still anesthetized. I will check it for cancer, and if any is clean, I will clone it for the final operation, which I hoped we would do in about four to five days.

Though all of the procedures went smoothly today, I knew they were still traumatic to Brandon's body. I will let him rest now.

As with the first bone marrow transfer on December 14, 2092, I injected him post-operation with antibiotics and mild pain killers for his comfort. I will monitor his vital signs regularly through the night. Brandon could not ask for a more vigilant nurse. This is not boasting or bragging on my part. It is just fact. I am a robot. I do not sleep.

Day 84 – December 21, 2092

1:33 am

Brandon is doing very well. His vital signs are normal, and he has no fever. I am glad he had the forethought to move the generators and all the important items we need to this house. I can hear the sound of the wind from outside, so I know the weather is not good.

He is sleeping peacefully now. He did wake up briefly thirteen minutes ago, but he just asked me, "What time is it?" When I told him 1:20 am, he grunted (I am fairly certain it was an affirmative grunt acknowledging he understood what I had just told him) and laid back down properly in his bed. He muttered, "Give me more pain killer," and went back to sleep.

2:45 am

I have tested the cells from Brandon's back and though it does contain minimal cancer, I have sectioned off a clean cluster of cells and will begin cloning this marrow for the operation I will perform on Brandon's back a few days from now. Theoretically, French doctor Claude Tourneau's procedure should cure Brandon's cancer.

4:42 am

I have several projects going on in the Petri dishes in front of me in the lab. Brandon's marrow cells are set to multiply now. I have taken a blood sample from the dog Beau and tested it. Nothing appears to be wrong with it so evidently Brandon was correct in his assessment. The dog Beau died of natural causes. That information will make Brandon feel better, I think.

Human beings have an emotion called "guilt" which constantly preys on their minds and emotions. It causes them to worry excessively and it also causes them to think irrationally. According to all books and articles I have read, the emotion called guilt is generally considered a positive thing because in the opinion of experts it "keeps people doing good." People without guilt sometimes do terrible things and do not feel bad about doing those terrible things. Psychologists call them "sociopaths."

You could certainly argue that a robot is a sociopath and that would be close to true if a robot were programmed to do bad things. Luckily, most robots are not programmed to do bad things...at least none that I have read about. This is surprising considering the number of bad people who used to be in this world. The scientific laws of averages would dictate that there should have been more bad robots.

7:05 am

I wake Brandon and feed him some flat bread for breakfast. He seems to be less cantankerous this morning though I know from his body language that he is feeling a lot of pain. I have increased the dosage of painkiller slightly in his intravenous drip and he is sleeping again.

8:47 am

I have checked outside and though the snow cover on the ground is thick, it is sunny out and it is not snowing at the moment. If the good weather continues, I may venture out for supplies this afternoon.

11:21 am

Brandon is awake again and tells me he does not want to sleep anymore. Per his request, I will bring the Bose stereo sound system to this house and we will listen to music today. He has also asked me to bring him some books to read.

1:06 pm

I have just fed Brandon a lunch of fresh fruit and steamed vegetables. This will aid him in fighting off infection.

We are listening to a singer named Peter Gabriel. His songs are varied in their sound and presentation. Brandon obviously likes him a lot. He has sung along with many of the louder faster-paced tunes titled "Sledgehammer," "Shock the Monkey" and "Kiss the Frog." Brandon is also reading some books I have brought for him. He is currently reading *Road Atlas of America*. This is one he specifically requested.

4:40 pm - BRANDON RESUMES THE NOTE TAKING:

Komaki was listening to Dean Martin again. Why a robot would go for an old crooner like that, I don't know, but I was happy to watch her sway to his rhythms. She liked fellow Rat Packer Frank Sinatra too, but Dino was her favorite. She really seemed to go for the soft ballads like "You Belong to Me" and "Arrivederci Roma." I thought I would make "I've Got My Love to Keep Me Warm" her theme song. It started with the words: *"Well, the snow is snowin' and the wind is blowin' but I can weather the storm..."* She certainly did.

I felt surprisingly good, considering what I'd just been through. I had some pain in my joints, but it was much more bearable this time. The worst pain was at my lower back, probably because I was directly lying on it.

I hoped I would be through with all of this mess and well on the road to recovery in a week's time. Then we could concentrate on finding other oasis places in this barren country that was once the mighty U.S. of A.

I checked some geography earlier and realized there was a road at the top end of Florida running along the lower U.S. coast from the Atlantic Ocean at Jacksonville all the way to the Pacific Ocean at Los Angeles. Interstate 10 would be our path to California. Obviously, it would be torn up in places, but we would take a compass with us and make our way from east to west in the E-RV. With a little luck, we would find havens and supplies along the way.

Then we could make our way north up the western coast from California up to Washington State and over the border into

Vancouver. If any country was spared from total nuclear destruction, it would have been the peaceful nation of Canada. The lower fringes would undoubtedly be scorched, but I banked that there were a lot of resources to glean from up there. It was worth a shot. After my cancer was cured, we would have lots of time on our hands to explore. I was excited about our newest mission.

6:30 pm

Komaki just fed me dinner. I told her about my plan to navigate across the country, then up to Canada. She agreed it was a good proposal. She felt we would see very little on our jaunt across America (though it was a good idea to check around,) but she thought my suggestion about Canada was very logical.

"The only way to know for sure, is to follow your plan, Brandon."

Komaki's loyalty and support were just what I needed right now. It warmed my heart after several, heart-wrenching days of misery and disappointments. "There is one problem, however," she said grimly, "...the safety of Ms. Giles."

Damn! She was right (as usual). If we left Ms. Giles for more than four days, her battery would juice, and she would perish. This predicament needed some serious thought. Perhaps we would rig a battery or maybe several batteries to last longer than two weeks. If anyone could create such an apparatus, it would be my talented Japanese robot girlfriend. We had time to work on it.

11:00 pm

The weather outside was not to windy or cold tonight. I heard the cat Myra howling outside. I'd told Komaki to keep an eye out for her which got me a befuddled Komaki look, so I had to explain the expression "keep an eye out," meant "watch for." I thought she understood now.

I was tired, so I went to sleep with the assistance of my ever-faithful, robot nurse and her effective painkillers.

Day 85 – December 22nd

9:45 am

I felt very little soreness today. Actually, I felt better than I had in a long time. The new marrow was good. As it was cloned marrow of my own, I never had any fear that my body might reject it. Komaki had taken me off intravenous drip and gave my derrière a shot of antibiotic instead. I was actually up and about this morning.

There was frost outside but no snow, so we could actually do things today as well. I didn't want to overexert myself, so I suggested light things like Christmas shopping. I would like to get a tree for the house. As the world went nuke in February, we probably wouldn't find a Christmas tree in the store stockrooms, but we might find one in storage by raiding people's houses. Hell, I could have Komaki check the attics of these houses first. It would save us some time.

11:15 am

The solar panels worked great. I had a late breakfast and Komaki found boxes with sectional Christmas trees along with some ornaments in the attics of our houses. She found a silver tree in this house, but we went with the traditional-looking, plastic, green tree from the other house. The ornaments from this house were fancier, but we picked and choose what we liked to decorate our holiday tree.

7:40 pm

We rode around town in the E-RV today. We went to a department store. They said that CDs and DVDs began to oxidize at about twenty-five years, so stores had begun selling drives with music collections on them. Some people called them "memory sticks" back in the day. I wanted Christmas music. I didn't find much up front, but I did hit the jackpot in a back storeroom. A box way overdue to be sent back to its distributor was filled with holiday memory sticks that just hadn't sold.

174

Komaki was excited when I found a Dean Martin / Frank Sinatra Christmas drive. It had her theme song on it. I also found a Divas Christmas drive (Celine, Cher, Mariah, Whitney) and—holy shit! I scored a Burl Ives Christmas drive! What was a Christmas without fucking Burl Ives? I remembered that guy from my youth, singing "Holly Jolly Christmas" and "Silver Bells" in kid's animated specials. The only man jollier and fatter than yellow-whiskered, banjo playin' Burl was old Chris Kringle himself.

We found other traditional and contemporary Xmas music, so it was going to be a very merry Christmas at our houses this year.

We drove all over town, breaking into rich homes, looting and grabbing what we needed or wanted. Most of the good stuff was boxed or sealed in plastic. Komaki got some new outfits. She did another fashion show for me. It was a fun day of playing and pillaging.

11:40 pm

I got back into my sick bed like a good patient. I didn't know how she did it, but Komaki found a pink nurse's uniform and hat. She looked so incredibly hot in it; I can't begin to tell you. She bent over to get something from a cabinet drawer in one of those rolling medical tables and I caught a flash of black lace and garter under her tight skirt. What was it about girls in uniform that drove men crazy? I got an obvious erection.

"Brandon," she asked. "Do you like this outfit?" At that point I knew she was teasing me on purpose.

"Yeah, it's nice," I said it nonchalantly. "Most guys have a thing for nurses in uniform."

She smiled. "So, I have been told."

"Yutaka," I thought to myself, wondering if I should curse his name or thank him for being such a pervert.

Komaki sashayed over to my bed and looked down at my erection. "Oh, poor baby," she cooed as I rolled my eyes a bit. The candy striper routine was smooth but obviously rehearsed. I would have been a fool to stop it at that point. "You have some swelling. Let me make it feel better."

175

The patient did not have to move a muscle—just lie there and enjoy his nurse's attention. When it was over, she smiled, cleaned me up with a warm washcloth, and let me go to sleep. Ah, how I loved "ants up a tree."

Day 86 – December 23rd

8:30 am

I was up and Komaki fed me some of our canned fruit for breakfast. The naughty little robo-bitch was still in her nurse's outfit. If it was a normal day in a normal world, I would probably be reading a newspaper now.

The weather was still nominal with cold wind but no visible snow. Komaki made a strange request. She asked me if I would teach her to drive the truck. I agreed to do that today as her learning to drive would benefit both of us. She could drive without sleep for upwards of three days. The E-RV had an automatic transmission, so it would be easy. If she wrecked it, we could just steal another one.

5:00 pm

We had an interesting day today. We checked on Ms. Giles this morning. She was fine. This afternoon I gave Komaki a driving lesson. I took her to an open parking lot for safety sake. After she got a feel for the peddles and how to use them for speeding up and slowing down, she then began to master how to steer. She did bang into a few things (shopping cart rack, light pole, neon sign) and as a result, the bumpers of the truck were mildly scratched, but all in all she did a decent job and I felt she could drive the RV now with little or no assistance from me.

10:30 pm

Komaki and I decorated our Christmas tree this evening. It looked great. It had an array of ornaments, tinsel strings, and a big star on top. Komaki asked me a slew of questions about Christmas. I tried to explain the religious significance of the holiday which seemed to confuse her a great deal. Robots, as you were probably aware, had no religious or mystical understanding or faith. Their minds were computerized and therefore more analytical in nature. They understood science but could not comprehend things like magic, myths, religion, or superstition. Robots would always look for the answer to problems or situations. You could not tell a robot, "Just have a little faith, okay?"

Then I explained the holiday spirit of Christmas and giving. This seemed to make better sense to her because she herself could experience it step-by-step… sort of…

The discussion led us here and there—through Easter with the Easter Bunny and Santa Claus. It was fun discussing it, but I felt Komaki did not fully comprehend everything I told her. She said she would try to read up more on holidays and their origins.

I took my antibiotic and we decided to sleep in the regular bed under the bug net tonight. I hoped we would have enough cloned marrow to do the last operation on my back soon.

Day 87 – December 24th

10:00 am

We slept in later than usual today. It felt good to be back in my old bed. At breakfast, I looked over to the spot where Beau's bed used to be. It made me a bit melancholy. I missed him.

2:20 pm

We had a new dilemma on our hands. There was no water coming out of the faucets. It looked like whatever luck we had in that respect had run out. Komaki and I would drive out to the water treatment plant and see if we could get things going again. I could see the water tower for this neighborhood from my house, so it would be no problem locating the source of our water.

7:30 pm

We went to the water treatment plant and, with the aid of some office manuals, Komaki and I figured out that we had used all of the water in the tank. We had to bring a generator out to this site to get the floodgates working and refill the tank. We would have to do this about once every few months. In a normal neighborhood full of people, they probably had to re-prime the tanks a few times every day. Anyway, we had water again.

9:00 pm

Unfortunately, Komaki was not sure if we had enough cloned marrow for my last operation. She said tomorrow evening would be a better time. I was glad she was being so cautious and, to be honest, who wanted to have surgery on Christmas Eve?

I healed up nicely and felt absolutely no pain at all. The scars would be very small and of course, I was already feeling the result. I felt better this week than I had in the entire three months I'd been out of the freezer. If I had a time machine, I would've gone back to my time and tell Rara Li, Wi Hua Soong, and Claude Tourneau: "You guys rock! Your cloning procedure works." I would also tell the rest of the world: "You screwed the pooch, you dumb shits! It all comes to a nice screeching halt in 2034. Nice-fuckin'-goin'."

Though a time machine did not exist, I toyed with the idea of placing a copy of this journal into a plastic airtight container and setting it adrift off the coast of South Florida. When I was a kid, we used to read stories about the Bermuda Triangle being a time portal of sorts: planes and boats disappearing there and coming out again decades later. Scientists often pooh-poohed such nonsensical theories and I was sure Komaki would as well. But there were many strange things in our world never been explained. If I thought it could save mankind, I'd do it.

10:20 pm

I went out and did a little Christmas Eve shopping. Tomorrow was Christmas, so I wanted to get some nice things for Komaki. It was so like me to wait until the last second. I'd been racking my brain trying to figure out what to give her. Seriously, what did you get a Japanese robot companion? This was my latest dilemma.

She had been such a good companion, so helpful and talented. She'd saved my life in more ways than I wanted to admit. She kept me sane above all else. I thought I

might get her some nice dresses and wigs, so she didn't have to wear the trashy stuff (though I was partial to some of the trashy stuff). I would get out there and see what I found. I checked her shoe bottoms and the tags of her clothes, so I knew her sizes.

1:30 am

I got quite a few fashionable things for Komaki, which I put in a box and wrapped in a red-colored, plastic shower curtain. Paper today didn't hold together very well. It was the best I could come up with. On my way back to the homestead, I saw a jewelry store (still intact) so broke into it. I grabbed the biggest diamond necklace in the place: $35,000.00 price tag. It would look great around my little girl's neck.

I made Komaki go to the back of the house while I wrapped everything up. She was curious but obeyed my order not to come back into the living room until I said it was okay.

When she saw the big package by the tree, she smiled. "Ah," she said matter-of-factly. "You have gotten me a Christmas present."

I nodded self-assuredly and said "Yep." I then kidded her by saying, "You don't have x-ray vision do you?"

She stole the wind out of my sails by responding with a flat "No." Then she turned to me and said, "Brandon, what would you like me to get you for your annual Christmas ritual?"

I laughed and told her, "A cheeseburger. But that is pretty much impossible, isn't it?"

She smiled and said, "You are correct, Brandon. Without natural beef and milk to make cheese that would be damned near impossible, as you would say."

I laughed at her joke. It still amazed me that my robot could possess such a sense of humor. I felt for the first time like it was Christmas.

She added, "If the weather permits tomorrow, I will go out and try to gather presents for you, Brandon."

If I had told her, "Nah, don't bother," she would have taken my message at face value and I would never know what kind of gift she would have gotten me. So I kept my smiling mouth shut and just nodded. I was feeling better physically and emotionally than I had felt in a long time.

2:00 am

Just now, we heard Myra yowling outside not far away. How this cat had managed to survive the cold weather and without food? The last time we'd left out fish for her was, like, two weeks ago. I just went back and checked that fact, so you wouldn't have to) was an absolute mystery. Though we had no fish for her, we put out a bowl of bean paste and another bowl of peanut butter on the back lawn. If she was as hungry as I thought she was, both bowls would be empty when we checked them tomorrow.

5:15 am

I got up to go pee. Sometimes you just got up in the middle of the morning to go pee. I used to do that regularly (like clockwork) back in my heyday. Evidently, that habit had returned. I decided to go outside. I checked the bowls and as expected both looked like they had been cleaned by a dishwasher and I could not see any evidence of roach activity. Myra had her Christmas breakfast early. I bet she'd been ravenous.

I went back to bed with no sugar plums dancing in my head. No thoughts of Santa Claus making his great ride around the globe. Santa had been nuked along with all the children that would have been on his lists. Sobering thought, wasn't it. What a legacy. Then I looked to my robot girl, pretending to sleep for me. This was my world now.

Day 88 – December 25th

8:00 am

I didn't know what it was about Christmas that got us up early. When we were kids it was the whole excitement of ripping into the gifts at first day light. When we were older, the excitement was still there, maybe for other reasons. I was certainly a big kid at heart. I felt perky.

It was only snowing ever so lightly today, so Komaki bundled up, headed for the RV, and said she would be back around lunch time. If she didn't show by high noon, I was going out to go and look for her.

11:55 am

Komaki was back. I was waiting on the front porch at eleven forty-five. The snow had started coming down heavier, so I was getting a bit worried. But she came trudging back with her little Santa bag and she bypassed me altogether and went to the lab house. A few minutes later she came back to the porch and said, "Hello, Brandon. I am back from getting you Christmas ritual presents."

I just gaped as she walked past me into the warm house. I was curious to know what she had gotten me. Should I be worried? Her feelings wouldn't be hurt if I didn't like it.

12:30 pm

I gave Komaki her presents (which she seemed to like,) but she wouldn't let me have my present. She said I would get it soon when she was finished with it and went to the med house. I was going crazy trying to figure out what she could have gotten me. What would take so long to prepare and wrap? Now I knew. For lunch, Komaki had made me a cheeseburger with French fries. I hated to admit it, but it was such a miracle that I fought back tears. The fact it tasted great only made it harder on me.

She went out and found whey, which she'd mixed with fresh corn oil and salt to make cheese. The bread actually rose and was soft because she'd found a recipe for making buns and she processed some yeast. The beef patty was a vegetarian beef patty she fashioned with rice, wheat, corn oil, and different seasonings. She barbecued it over charcoal on a small Hibachi she'd smuggled into the back of lab house and topped the thing with tomato, lettuce, and chopped onion. She deep the fresh cut French fries in corn oil and salted them just right. Again, I was amazed at her resourcefulness. She'd given me exactly what I asked for and it moved me deeply. It was the best (most thoughtful) Christmas gift I had ever gotten. To celebrate further, we got out a couple of bottles of "Great Wall" wine we had brought back with us from Asia. I had what professional winers would call a "sweet pallet." After not drinking for almost a century, I was a lightweight drinker.

I knew very little about wine beyond the consumption for "getting myself smashed" phase, so this wine tasted good enough to me. Komaki and I mocked toasted to the holidays and I drank both glasses. She seemed amused by the custom.

6:15 pm

I had cheeseburgers again for dinner. They were even better the second time. I told Komaki we should take her veggie-beef mix and make some spaghetti Bolognese. She said she would look into it. I finished the bottle of wine over our dinner conversation, re-explaining the whole concept of Santa Claus and The Easter Bunny being brought into religious holidays for kids.

I moved to the couch, insisting we do the dishes tomorrow. Komaki did them (saying some shit about the roaches again,) and after a few minutes joined me on the sofa. I played the Sinatra and Dean Martin Christmas CDs for her because I knew she liked them. She allowed me some Burl Ives and I played "Jingle Dogs" in remembrance of Beau and "Jingle Cats" in case Myra was listening somewhere close by.

"How are you feeling, Brandon?" she asked softly, not like my medical companion but more like my lover companion.

"I'm good," I said through the dumbass grin I always get when I am buzzed. And we made tender love without her having to ask me. It was a great Christmas.

Day 89 – December 26

11:30 am

Komaki cooked me stir fried vegetables in peanut oil with garlic and ginger. It was great. She wore a black maid's outfit with lots of lace and a blue page boy wig. She definitely spoiled me.

There was lots of snow on the ground outside from last night, but it was not snowing today. There was no sun out today. After changing into something more suitable, Komaki went over to the lab house to do some work. I put out some more bean paste and peanut butter for Myra. I was still not certain why I was feeding this stupid cat. I was allergic to cats; their dander made my eyes burn. But it was

Christmas. Side note: The DDT did a good job of keeping the bugs out.

5:00 pm

I checked on Mrs. Giles. She was still the same. Komaki had been cloning my cleansed marrow. She told me for the umpteenth time that it would take some time for me to have ample clean marrow to complete my surgical treatment. My busy robo-girl was also working on making a special battery set-up for Ms. Giles' cryo-chamber. If she succeeded, then we were one step closer to our trip across America (the once so beautiful) and up north to Canada.

I read up on coastal towns in the southern parts of the U.S. If we shot down Interstate 75 to Interstate 10 in North Florida, we would make a right and hit Destin in about three hours. We would pass through Pensacola and out of the panhandle of Florida in about five hours. Then we could continue on past Mobile in Alabama, Biloxi in Mississippi, and New Orleans in Louisiana. Then a long dry stretch across Texas and New Mexico before we got to California.

The weather in these southern states on the water would be better than what we were getting here. With Komaki driving at night, we could undoubtedly get to the west coast in just under three days.

6:30 pm

Over dinner, Komaki told me she could not rig a battery to last more than four days with Ms. Giles' cryo-chamber—another set-back. If we left and "go walkabout" as the Aussies said, then we either had to take the old lady with us or we had to let her go peacefully like the others. She wouldn't wake up and she wouldn't feel any pain.

"What if we used a faster mode of transportation?" Komaki's question made me spin on my heels.

I mimicked her question as part of my answer. "Another mode of transport? What do you mean?"

Komaki explained how we could get to these other places faster and search more area if we flew. Oh my God! Why hadn't I thought of that? I was not being a smart-ass. Take that at face value. Neither one of us knew how to pilot a plane, but I bet a helicopter would be easy enough to fly. Stick forward meant "descent," stick backward meant "go up." And Komaki would do some research on mechanics, inspect the engines in the electric vehicles we had, and probably rig a copter to run on electricity with one of our generators. What a great idea.

If we could find the local TV station, I bet there was a news chopper parked out back. There might've also been joyride helicopter places on the outskirts of town. I was so totally stoked about this plan of action.

We planned to load the copter with enough food and water to cover a long journey of two days each way. We could follow maps and mark territory as we went. We would touch down using the scooter for ground transport and, after we checked things out, we would fly back to home base. Fuckin-A, yeah, we fly!

11:30 pm

I was a bit depressed about having to wait for my marrow to clone. It would probably be days. It was snowing again, so we were stuck in the main house. I hoped Myra was somewhere warm…Okay. I really didn't care. Yep, it was the After Christmas Blues.

Day 92 – December 29

9:15 am

No, the heading was not a typographical error. There are no missing pages. It was snowing heavily these last couple days, so we stayed home and did absolutely nothing. We both spent most of the time reading up, listening to music, and I personally slept a lot.

Komaki told me a few days ago that our log entries were becoming redundant, so I decided it was time to skip the boring stuff and only log things of major importance. I know, I know... Too late! The last two days were boring and really did not advance us much. So they are a short opening note to today's entry.

Day 93 – December 30

8:15 am

I did absolutely nothing yesterday. I slept most of the day and read up on helicopter piloting and repair. Komaki cleaned up the two houses. It was cold but not freezing today. I hoped the solar panels would help us more, but the sun hadn't been shining a lot since we installed them.

Day 95 – January 1, 2093

10:00 am

Komaki and I celebrated New Year's Eve last night at midnight. I told her about the annual ritual, and we used a wind-up clock to help us do the countdown together. We didn't have champagne, but we did have another bottle of "Great Wall" wine, so we toasted to the New Year properly.

I told Komaki about New Year's resolutions.

She said, "Is it like a wish?"

I said "No, it's like a promise that you make to yourself."

I continued, "A promise that you intend to keep."

She thought for a second, then said, "But I am your robot servant, Brandon. Can I just make a promise to you?"

After thinking for a bit, I said "Yes. I suppose you could, if you wanted."

She said, "Brandon, my New Year's resolution is to save you from cancer."

It was a sweet and noble promise. I thought to myself that I was literally and figuratively, the luckiest man on Earth at that moment.

"What is your New Year's resolution, Brandon?"

I thought long and hard. Repopulating the planet was a good one, but that goal was far off. Though I did not need to say it to her, I stated firmly, "I promise to protect you, Komaki, and keep you from harm."

She smiled–She liked that.

Day 97 – January 3, 2093

8:15 pm

KOMAKI'S MEDICAL NOTES:

Brandon has been anesthetized and I am now extracting the cancerous marrow from his backbone. I am taking extra care in suctioning out this particular area as I don't want to injure his spinal column.

11:07 pm

Brandon appears to be fine. His heart rate and blood pressure are slightly elevated. I have carefully cleaned out the marrow from his backbone and now I am replacing it with clean cloned marrow cells.

The operation appears to have been successful. I have finished the replacement and I have carefully repositioned Brandon so that he is lying on his right side. He should sleep comfortably for the next couple of hours. I have set up a new antibiotic drip for him in his I.V. bag.

With luck, he will be feeling back to normal in a couple of days. We will check his blood periodically to make sure his cancer does not reoccur. If that happens, we can always repeat the procedure.

Day 98 – January 4, 2093

4:12 am

Something is seriously wrong with Brandon. He has awakened from the anesthesia, but he claims he cannot feel anything. He cannot move anything below his neck. I have done sensory touch checks on his fingers and toes and he in fact does not appear to feel anything. I have made a serious error in the operation on his spinal column.

5:07 am

Brandon is furious with me. His blood pressure is elevated, and he has been shouting for the last twenty minutes. He has called me many terrible expletives that I will not share in these notes as I feel that is unimportant. It has been a terrible, emotional realization to him to find out he is now paralyzed from the neck down. I have just given him a sedative to calm him, but he is very distraught. He is crying.

5:43 am

I am trying to decipher what I must have done wrong during the procedure. I was very careful not to puncture or injure his spinal cord. I drilled in the key points of his backbone as instructed by the notes of Dr. Claude Tourneau. I did everything that I had programmed myself to do and yet, for some strange unknown reason, Brandon is in a state of paralysis.

Tourneau had not done any trial operations on humans. Perhaps this is an unforeseen side effect of the procedure: an unfortunate negative result not anticipated by Tourneau or myself.

One thing Brandon said repeatedly when he was upset just now was: "I don't want to live like this." If his paralysis is permanent, he has made it clear to me that he does not want to go on living. I am programmed not to harm people so I would not carry out his direct request for euthanasia.

If I refuse to recharge my own battery, I will cease to function and Brandon will starve to death, thereby fulfilling his request, but before I even consider this option I must make every possible effort and find a way to restore his sensory feelings.

7:35 am

All blood tests show Brandon to be normal with only a slightly elevated white blood cell count, which was expected during this operation. All of the sensory touch checks I performed are still negative.

9:20 am

Brandon is still emotionally disturbed. He woke up and began yelling and shrieking again. I re-sedated him and tried to explain that I was just as surprised about this outcome as he was. I told him that I was doing everything I could to find out what went wrong and assured him I was trying to correct it.

His reaction at hearing that was silence. He turned his head away from me angrily, which was understandable. I have read that people who experience such maladies go through stages of anger, depression, and denial. I will continue my tests.

11:47 am

I am still baffled. By all intents and purposes, Brandon Hoffner should not be paralyzed. His body could not be rejecting the marrow because it is cloned marrow made from his own marrow. I put exactly the same amount of marrow back into the backbone as was extracted. It defies all logic.

It is possible this is some type of shock to his system that did not occur when I performed the operations before. The backbone and spinal column would be more sensitive to such a change.

2:27 pm

Brandon will not eat. He has stopped talking as well. It is dangerous for me to keep sedating him, and I need him awake for my tests. He is still not responding to sensory touch checks in his fingers and toes. Reflex checks in his knees and elbows also show no response.

I am considering doing another marrow transfer operation on his backbone. It will take me a few days to re-clone enough of his backbone marrow, but it seems the only logical step I can take to cure him of his paralysis.

7:37 pm

Brandon refuses food again. I have explained to him that he should not give up so easily because of this situation. He has faced many obstacles since he was revived from his cryogenic sleep. He does not acknowledge my presence.

11:25 pm

I have continued my tests, but he is still not responding to any treatment. I have bathed him and massaged all of his muscles by hand. His vital signs have been normal all day. He just has no feeling.

Day 99 – January 5, 2093

9:12 am

I feel my log entries are becoming redundant, so I have decided to space them out farther. He is still unresponsive to treatment and he refuses to eat or talk to me. I will go to the hospital today and procure an electro-stimulation unit. This treatment will keep his muscles working even though he is unable to move them at present.

7:30 pm

Brandon's electro-stim therapy is encouraging. His muscles respond to the mild electric current.

Unfortunately, Brandon has not eaten or drank any fluid in almost two days, so I have hooked him up to an I.V. bag. He yelled at me as I did so, saying again he did not want to live anymore. I told him I must do everything I could to keep him alive until we found out what was wrong with him and he screamed at me very loudly. His shouts were so loud that he had damaged his own vocal cords. He told me, "Just get the fuck away from me and let me die, Komaki! I am a vegetable now and I don't want that kind of life!" I told him I was not going to give up so easily and he responded by saying, "I am no longer your boss or your master or whatever, so you can go now, okay? Just leave me in peace. Let me fucking die!"

I then reminded him of his duty to the human race and to the future of mankind. His retort was, "Well, obviously I can't do much for mankind like this now, can I?" I explained that he could advise me on how to search other areas and look for other humans, but he shook his head, saying hoarsely, "It's over for me, Komaki. I am done. Someone else will have to save mankind." He paused for a second and added softly, "Some other poor shmoe who wakes up to this fucking nightmare."

Obviously, I am not going to abandon him as he suggests and telling him that made him angry again. I am not giving up until I am certain there is no way to fix his problem and then—and only then—will I allow him to starve himself to death. If that time comes, then we will die together. I will not let him die alone.

10:35 pm

I have changed Brandon's I.V. bags and now I am recharging myself as scheduled. I will continue to monitor him and will resume my tests again in the morning. I actually saw one of his fingers twitch, but it might have been an involuntary reflex action.

Day 100 – January 6, 2093

6:18 am

Brandon has feeling in fingers again. He responded to touch tests and even said, "Ow!" in response to my sticking his finger with a needle. He is elated, of course, and has apologized for the way he has been acting for the last few days. I told him he did not have to make any apology as I am a robot and it did not bother me to hear him complain about his situation. It was understood but he said, "When I get up and around, I promise I will make it up to you."

8:42 am

Brandon is now feeling sensations in his toes on his left foot. He says he is incredibly hungry, so I will make him something to eat.

10:00 am

Brandon is getting feeling in all of his limbs again. He has eaten breakfast and has asked me to make him more flat bread with peanut paste. Hopefully, he will sit up by himself soon and perhaps be walking again by this evening. He still feels bad emotionally for what he calls "losing faith." I do not care about such things. I just know it is good for both of us that he is not paralyzed. We can focus on what we were discussing before we began the last operation. We can search for other cities and search for other survivors. This is good.

3:27 pm

Brandon is recovering quickly. He is sitting up in his bed now and I have given him some bean and vegetable soup just now. He looks very thin and his face is gaunt and tired-looking. He is smiling a lot though. He is very happy that he is regaining control of his muscles.

The question as to why he was paralyzed for almost two days will continue to be a mystery. Perhaps his backbone needed to adjust to the cloned marrow or maybe I bruised his spinal column by accident during the extraction and it took two days to heal itself. I was very careful during the procedure, knowing how dangerous it was to be drilling in this ultra-sensitive area of his body.

7:48 pm

I just fed Brandon his dinner. He walked to the bathroom with me helping him. His motor skills are returning. I turned on the Bose sound system, which I moved to the medical station. I prefer this term to Brandon's moniker of "lab house." We listen to music again, enjoying "The Beatles Greatest Hits." The sound of the English singers is different than what we have listened to before. Their accent is strange to me and they are very good at mixing their voices in musical harmonies. The style and sound of their songs varies dramatically from track to track.

Brandon sits in his bed reading up on piloting a helicopter. I had to go to the library late in the afternoon to find him books and training manuals on flying. His head bobs up and down slightly to the rhythm of the songs. I think this means he is content.

11:47 pm

Brandon sleeps peacefully. He got up and went to the bathroom again, this time insisting he do it by himself. Though he braced himself on things along the way, he navigated with little trouble on his own.

When he returned to his sick bed, I teased him by telling him I wanted to do one more sensory touch test and I rubbed his penis through his hospital gown. He responded well and I performed the Asian massage technique called "ants going up a tree" on him, which he seems to like very much.

Day 101 – January 7th

8:00 am

BRANDON RESUMES THE NOTE TAKING:

I was relatively back to normal, although I was very embarrassed about how I'd handled myself during our little scare of the last few days. When you felt a shock like that, it was devastating. It didn't excuse my behavior though. I felt like the guy who accused everybody of stealing his hundred dollars, then found the hundred dollars later in his coat pocket. Luckily for me, Komaki "didn't give a rat's ass" about my childish rants. They just rolled off her well-sculpted robot back and she kept moving forward analytically.

Speaking of moving forward, the weather was so nice, we were going to take the truck out today to find a helicopter and maybe do some shopping if we had time.

11:30 am

We found the building for WATL Channel 7 of Atlanta and there was a news helicopter on a helipad out back. Luckily, the helicopter had been covered with a canvas-like tarp which was now worn and falling apart. Komaki would rework the engine today to convert it to electric power. I would have to find a new tarp to put over her, but she appeared to be a fully functional flying machine and would serve our purpose well. The controls were state-of-the-art and I found an owner's manual behind the pilot's seat, which I would begin reading tonight to learn exactly what she could do.

7:30 pm

I'd just finished a late dinner and now I listened to music and read the owner's manual for my new helicopter. Komaki came back from working on the copter. She said it should now fly with the electric power of the solar generator. We would certainly test that in the next few days. With the generator, we could fly for up to four hours at a time. Komaki said she might be able to rewire the generators so they charged with sunlight all the time, but she would need to test her theory further before she was certain.

The thought has also occurred to me: "What do we do if the helicopter breaks down?" Komaki and I would find back-up helicopters and I would pack a moped scooter with back-up batteries when we went on long trips. If we got stuck far from home, Ms. Giles might be lost, so we had to think ahead and take every precaution. If we found a city we wanted to ride around on the scooter anyway; it was just better transport for scavenging.

Komaki worried that I was pushing myself too hard so soon after my latest surgery. I promised her I would finish my notes now and go to bed. We did have a big day ahead tomorrow, testing the helicopter.

Day 102 – January 8th

10:20 am

After breakfast, we drove back out to the helipad. I did not feel that it was a good idea to practice piloting in the actual city and decided it would be best to attempt to fly it to an open field somewhere. Per my flight manual, I flipped switches to the controls and used the joystick to hover and climb. It took some getting used to, but eventually I did a fair job of working the pedals to control the tail rotor and using the joy stick to control my altitude. I flew the copter to a baseball field just a couple of blocks from our houses. Then I walked home and waited for Komaki to return in the E-RV.

4:20 pm

We found another two helicopters just off of I-75 at the northend of town. I decided to let Komaki do a little highway driving and, low and behold, we spotted a helicopter ride place, right by the interstate. One copter was too old and weather-beaten, so I was not too keen on it. The second one was covered with a ratty tarp like the news chopper. It seemed to be in much better shape.

11:15 pm

It was an eventful day. While Komaki tore up the good helicopter we found today, I scavenged some department stores looking for more solar generators. We couln't afford to lose the two we had in our houses. We need those to supply our power there.

After several hours, I could not find a single generator that worked. It was incredibly frustrating. I decided to check people's shed and garages. While doing this, I stumbled across an actual shelter a guy had built in his back yard. The door was shut and locked tight from the inside, so I could've only guessed what I would've found below.

After dinner, I took Komaki to the place. She inspected the door carefully. There was a touchpad to the right I didn't even see. If it was a snake, it would have bitten me. She typed number codes into the pad with lightning speed and precision. After about twenty or so minutes, we heard a loud metal clunk. She had breached the security code. The door could be opened now.

We went down some stairs to a room with my candle lantern. As expected, we found four dead, desiccated bodies on four beds. There were old rusty cans of food on the shelves. The smell was musty but bearable. I noticed plugs and power strips and a generator that looked similar to ours. We went back outside and saw an enclosure above the door. Komaki hoisted me up and sure enough there was the missing solar panel. When we got it home, and tested it, the generator cranked up like it was brand new.

Day 103 – January 9th

9:00 am

Komaki took the new generator out to where the helicopter was just off of the highway. She'd already prepped it for conversion. It would not take her long to adapt the engine on this one. We left the other older one there and could use it for spare parts later if needed be.

I went to the playing field to practice my flying. It was a bit scary, getting my wings, but a hell of a lot of fun. I practiced my hovering and landing mostly. I had to be real good at those. I was elated this idea had come to amazing fruition. I learned that word from Komaki. It was hardly a word that an old baseball goon would use. She made me a better man.

3:30 pm

I skipped lunch and was reminded of the time when Komaki drove up to the field. She took me to where the second chopper was. I cranked it up and flew it back to the baseball field and set it down several yards from copter number 1. I was a novice pilot still clumsy at landing, but it was such a rush of adrenaline when I took off and flew them. It was a great feeling to be up there gliding.

These copters we'd just found were slightly larger than the news chopper we snagged from WATL. These heftier models were the size of the Huey helicopters you saw in all the Vietnam War movies. They accommodated up to eight passengers comfortably in the back section. Of course, we would rip out some of those seats to make room for our electric scooter, a rescue cot, and other supplies.

9:45 pm

I had a light salad for dinner tonight. Komaki brought back the helicopter spare parts just before sundown and stowed them in the backyard shed. She even removed the rotor blades and brought them. She said she had stopped off at the cryo-center and checked on Ms. Giles. The old gal was recharging.

I set the wind-up alarm clock to get us up early in the morning, so Komaki could pack the chopper and I could run out and grab another moped scooter with several back-up batteries. If they didn't hold a charge, Komaki would have to make new ones which would slow us down. It wouldn't stop us though.

What we were planning was ambitious but necessary. My feeling was that we would not have gotten far in the E-RV. Most highways were probably gone now or in pieces, making it near impossible to navigate through. We would see for ourselves very soon.

Day 104 – January 10th

10:00 am

The sun was out melting the snow, and everything went like clockwork this morning. I grabbed another sleeker electric bike from a garage under a mall. The batteries were not holding a charge, but when Komaki tested the bike by rewiring one of our good batteries, the scooter worked. It had a long seat to accommodate myself and my robot companion. I could easily rig a cargo saddlebag of some kind for carrying extra provisions. Komaki carried that over her lap. Her framework did not tire. It just seemed like a better choice. It would fit easily in the back of either of our copters, unlike the unwieldy (but much more fun) beast of a scooter we had been using.

2:30 pm

Komaki ripped the backseats out of both the big copter and the news copter. She said Ms. Giles was recharged for another four days, so we were ready for our test run. We would leave within the hour.

7:45 pm

We were at the French Quarter in Louisiana. I was amazed at how fast you could fly somewhere in a helicopter. You could cover so much ground in a few hours. If we had taken the truck as originally planned, it would have been a very rough ride. Ninety percent of Georgia was just rock and green grass now with an occasional small shrub or tree. This was mostly what we saw today. Florida – nuked! Alabama – nuked! Mississippi – nuked!

By some miracle, the French Quarter had been shaken, but I was happy to report that it was still standing. What was once a party haven with jazz clubs and naughty all night reviews was now an eerie, quiet ghost town. I got a slight chill as we walked up the now empty Bourbon street. I decided not to go into the big church at the front end of the Quarter. I knew if we went in there, we would find wall-to-wall human carcasses and I was not in the mood.

Komaki and I checked into the Statler Hotel for the night. Komaki packed some freshly made candles and clean bed linens so we would be comfortable. Even under the circumstances it was kind of romantic to be there. When couples go on trips together, there was bound to be a spark of passion, an excitement of getting away together. Komaki seemed fascinated and enthusiastic about the new change of local.

As we looked over the now dark street below from the terrace of our room, I grabbed her without warning and kissed her. When the kiss was done, she looked up at me as only Komaki could and said, "Brandon, you want to make love to me now." It was not a question and, yes, I did.

Day 105 – January 11th

6:00 pm

We were back home in Atlanta. To say I was rattled would've been accurate but mildly understated. I will start at the beginning of what happened this morning and get to the weird stuff soon.

Komaki and I got up around eight-ish and had some flatbread we had packed for breakfast. Then we decided to check the local bank safety deposit boxes for anything useful. The search killed time and brought us nothing new.

We took a hiking trip down to the river. I remembered coming here when I was younger (I think it was a trip with my high school choir,) and I'd ridden one of those big paddle riverboats. A river boat was there, lying sideways in the water. Komaki noticed there were no fish in the river. It was odd, but I didn't remember seeing any fish at Taggart Springs back in Georgia either. We had a discussion about freshwater as opposed to saltwater and I noticed several dark patches at the bottom of the river had moved, albeit very slowly. More disturbing was the fact they were moving toward the river bank near us.

I pointed it out to Komaki and, like idiots, we stood there and waited to see what they were. They moved very slowly so, I figured they were not small alligators, plus the shape was all wrong. Finally, after what seemed like a century of waiting, I saw a slimy green-brown tip make its way out of the water. As it inched higher, terror shot through me and I yelled, "They're fucking leeches!" I watched dozens of them, all about the size of my forearm, make their way to the shore, then looked out into the river again and saw hundreds more. Like the other aquatic lifeforms, leeches had survived the fallout and obviously it had caused them to quickly evolve. They ruled the swamps now and somehow, they had detected our presence.

Okay, granted, if I had my choice of anything I would want to run from in a post-nuked world, it would be giant, slow-moving leeches, but I was still freaked out by the whole general concept of what I was experiencing. I imagined what would happen if just one of these grotesque fuckers ever got attached to me. I grabbed Komaki and dragged her back up to the street.

"Let's get the hell out of here, like now!" I said it dramatically and I meant it.

We walked briskly back to where the copter was and made our escape from New Orleans.

My mind swam at this world devoid of human life but teeming with vermin: a world where roaches and giant leeches dominated. What would things be like in another hundred years? Would we have bigger roaches and leeches to deal with? It was the stuff nightmares were made of.

Day 106 – January 12th

7:30 pm

We flew north up to the Canadian border today. Everything had been obliterated on the American east coast. The Carolinas—gone. Ohio—gone.   Massachusetts—gone.   Pennsylvania—gone. Washington D.C.—gone. New York—definitely gone. As far west as we could see, there was nothing but green open land. It was a real estate developer's dream.

Niagara Falls was just as beautiful as it used to be in pictures I'd seen, but everything else being gone, though expected, was a hard pill to swallow. Thoroughly depressed and emotionally drained, I decided to come home before we officially hit Canada. We would do it at another time.

Toronto would be our next target on our next trip, and after we plundered its resources, we might take a trip to the west coast. We've had better luck on the U.S. coastlines. Again, I thanked my lucky stars for being in Atlanta. If I had been anywhere else, I would have been incinerated or sucked dry by giant leeches, like a raisin in the sun.

Komaki cooked dinner wearing fishnet stockings, a black and red satin kimono, and a long black wig, so I will sign off for now.

Day 107 – January 13th

9:00 am

It snowed heavily outside so Komaki and I "are not" (pronounced "ain't" in Georgia) going anywhere today. It was probably for the best. I still had "the heebie-jeebies" from watching those large slugs slither their way up out of the water the other day.

201

Also, we'd earned a little quiet R & R (rest & relaxation) day. It would most likely be good for us.

Komaki made real bread last night and margarine by whipping some of the corn oil with some salt. I enjoyed my unhealthy, buttered toast this morning, but it made me long for several strips of crispy, fried bacon and two eggs sunny side up, with nice, runny yolks to dip this toast into. But Hell, post-apocalyptic looters couldn't be choosy though, right?

Physically, I felt fantastic. I had my doctor to thank for that. The holes around my joints looked like chickenpox scars now. I felt absolutely no soreness despite my strained recovery. Again, my body felt renewed, so now I wanted to use it to its fullest potential.

Komaki wore the large, diamond necklace I'd given her for Christmas. She was probably wearing it all along under her clothes. I could just see it today because she wore a loose robe. She wore it out of loyalty.

If she'd told me she liked it, I would've been surprised (though she had said she "liked" Dean Martin's smooth voice). Robots usually didn't have personal likes or dislikes. They were very loyal to their owners, however. They did what they were programmed to do. I'd noticed she seemed to have one other driving emotion... self-preservation. That one worried me just a little, but she'd made it clear that if I continued to look out for her, she would continue to be loyal to me, and wasn't that what many relationships were built on?

7:45 pm

We went to the liquor store today and grabbed lots of hooch. We raided their wine racks and brought back the most expensive stuff. I could barely read what was left of the price tags on the shelves, but everything I snagged had a four-figured number below it. Perhaps I would be a connoisseur of the vineyards before too long. I was certainly going to drink my share tonight. If I don't write an entry later tonight it's because I got totally smashed. Komaki was not only my doctor; she was my designated driver tonight. She made sure I didn't go anywhere or do anything stupid tonight, though it really didn't matter because if there was no one around to witness your stupidity then you experience no embarrassment, right?

I would explain that tonight was a night I felt like drinking heavily and I intended to do just that. I asked her to make sure I didn't hurt myself in the process.

Day 108 – January 14th

11:00 am

I got trashed last night, like some mid-life crisis dweeb trying to be like a teenager. I'd shown Komaki a few drinking games. I didn't remember much after that. I was naked when I woke up this morning.

Komaki claimed I'd gone outside naked while it was snowing and sang incoherently to the neighborhood. That did sound like me and I had no reason to doubt her. She had always told the truth before.

I used to always think people were feeding me a line when they drank heavily, made asses of themselves, then said, "Really? I did that? I don't remember?" But now I knew from experiences I was not proud of, that you could in fact, lose hours, days, and even weeks of your life through substance and alcohol abuse.

Anyway, I felt a little nausea from mixing my alcohols (beer, wine, and tequila,) but I actually felt better than I'd thought I would. Komaki would take good care of me here in our little safe domain on this snowy day. She fed me, brought me drinks (hair of the dog that bit me!) and saw to my comforts. Why? Because robots knew how to take care of their masters and they did not imbibe or get hangovers.

Day 109 – January 15th

8:00 am

I was up and around at a decent hour. The weather had been good: cool but not freezing. I should post the full date including the year on these January log entries. When I was younger, I used to hate the first two weeks of the year because that was the time when most people wrote down the wrong year on the date because they just were not used to it yet. It was a fact, that more checks got crumpled up and thrown out at that time of the year. Did I just say "checks?"

I felt good so we decided to actually go somewhere today. Toronto? Florida's west coast? California's west coast? We would probably have the best luck in Canada—all the more reason to look in the other places first. California was calling me. It would be a longer trip, but it would tell us the situation of the property west of Louisiana.

I packed up The Fatboy (my new name for the big copter) with plenty of food. Komaki loaded the moped into Fatboy for me and she was recharging Ms. Giles now. I also packed a backpack with a change of clothes for the trip that might take us up to three days. If we headed due west without any deviation, we would hit San Francisco before nightfall. It was another coastal town, not a direct target for nuclear devastation. It had potential.

8:00 pm

We made it to the Bellagio Hotel on the Las Vegas strip. Nevada was the west coast now. California had broken off at the San Andreas Fault line and was now underwater. Komaki said she had no record of this happening before the nuclear holocaust, so it must've happened between the time of the 2034 Armageddon and the time when I woke up. The most logical theory would be that the huge nuclear blasts caused the fault to finally split. If that was true, then Californians got one hell of a ride in the last few moments. It was probably more horrifying than being incinerated in a split second, but in retrospect, it beat a slow, painful death by radiation poisoning.

Vegas still stood for the most part, but it was visibly disheveled. It had taken a serious shock wave. I found it ironic that the three of the biggest party towns in America had survived along with Atlanta when most everything else was wiped away. Just dumb luck. There were weirder coincidences (though none came to mind.)

Komaki and I toured the darkened casinos with our lights. When we were in the French Quarter, I found another old-style lantern you put candles in. They'd proven to be quite effective. I grabbed some old poker chips for souvenirs: old habits die hard. I also had Komaki load a slot machine onto our copter. Tomorrow we would check the local bank vaults.

Day 110 – January 16, 2093

8:00 pm

We were home again. We got up about 6:30 am this morning and biked up and down the Vegas strip. Taylor Swift had made it to Vegas. Her name was on a fallen marquee at the MGM Grand. That made sense. She was probably around fifty or fifty-five when the bombs came down.

We went to two banks and found another mini-laptop. I also found what I thought was a laptop, but it turned out to be a mini-movie player. A guy named Clyde Chancy had left his last will and testament on a digital movie player for his loved ones. I wondered if they'd ever gotten to see it. I watched the intro, then turned it off. It wasn't my place or business to fuck with the last wishes of a man. Call me superstitious, I just didn't like to tempt providence.

I would never cash in big, like I had when I found Komaki. I thought that as I stopped and looked at her shuffling through safety deposit boxes. That had been a lucky day indeed in Kyoto. Today she wore a kind of camouflage, khaki, olive drab, military adventurer ditty.

We didn't find a cryo-center. That made sense in a way. Who would get frozen here? The trip home covered land over central North America. The save-the-planet enthusiast would be happy to know it was all green now.

Day 111 – January 17, 2093

10:45 pm

Spent most of the morning checking the laptop we'd gotten in Vegas. It was a nice one. Though small, it had lots of memory. About 1 terabyte worth. I could use it to play music.

I let Komaki have the mini-movie player so she spent the day watching clips of movies and T.V. shows. She was fascinated by media. It was a fast way for her to learn things about modern life and human behavior. She seemed especially interested in humor. She noticed me laugh at things and that had always puzzled her. She watched television shows and people in the audience laughed. This did not happen in real life and I had to explain that to her. I thought she understood the part about the studio audience and all, but what made us laugh still escaped her.

2:30 pm

We pulled the Christmas Tree down and packed it away. I checked Fatboy and unloaded the slot machine. Tomorrow, we might make the long trip to Canada. I was betting most of Canada was untouched by nuclear warfare. They were an easy-going people that never tried to get into a ruckus with anyone. Being close to psychotic America did not help their situation though. We would just wait and see.

Komaki reminded me that I should gather lumber and other supplies to build our green house. I'd been meaning to do this for some time and kept putting it off, mostly due to the changing weather.

It was amazing that we'd seen so little rain. That was the way autumn was and I had forgotten about the weather. Spring was when you got the most rain, right? It might've been because of the lack of pollutants in the atmosphere. As there had been no cars, aerosol cans, and unclean factories for the last sixty years, the sky was… blue.

I'd never thought about it until now, but when I breathed the air here in the once bustling city of Atlanta, it felt like when you wake up out in the country. It felt good going into your lungs. It made you go: "Ahh!"

6:30 pm

Went to a lumberyard a couple of hours ago and inspected a pile of sixty-year-old two-by-fours. Not exactly what I'd wanted to build with. Wood wasn't supposed to be so gray and warped. I made a snap decision then and there to build the greenhouse frame out of PVC plastic pipes and the walls would be fashioned out of clear, plastic tarps. Yeah, I was sure Komaki could probably chop down trees and cut the boards herself, but the greenhouse would last longer if we made it out of plastic. It would go up much faster too. Sign of the times.

We found PVC pipe and plastic tarps at a do-it-yourself fix-it warehouse store. While we were at it, we stocked up on good tools too. If the Brandon Messiah needed to build an arc, he was ready. Funny, I was just writing about the weather earlier this morning. I had better watch that "mocking God shit." Just when I get my chuckle on him, he'd send a plague of locusts or some shit to put me back in my place.

11:30 pm

Good God, what a day. I hadn't worked this hard in decades. We got most of the framework for the greenhouse together and it definitely took shape. We would finish it tomorrow.

I was not an architect or engineer by any stretch of the imagination, but I sketched out a rough draft of what I wanted on a sheet of paper and, using the PVC pipe lengths as my guide, I pieced together what I wanted, the dimensions being about what I'd envisioned in my head. I was actually a little proud of myself because it was coming together.

The last couple of trips away from Atlanta had been kind of downers for me, so getting around to doing this project was a way of taking my mind off of that unpleasantness. Ruins and families of charred bodies got really depressing if they were experienced on a regular basis. Another sad but honest truth about the initial extinction of the Planet Earth.

Don't get me wrong, loyal reader: I had every intention of continuing my searches of the outside world around me. Komaki and I took the copters out and maybe someday even ventured out on the boats again to find out what had happened to this country or that one. It was a necessary task, regardless of the emotional strain it might've caused me.

Call me a wimp or a pussy if you like, but I planned to make it a rule when we went on these jaunts to send Komaki into buildings first to check on the occupant remains. She was impervious to infection and seeing human bodies didn't faze her one bit. Robots didn't get emotional when facing chaos and carnage.

I was just going to space the trips out more and try and get more things accomplished here in the process. This would keep me motivated and active.

There were many things that needed to be finished here, like the greenhouse, finding other alternate power sources, and better food.

Time to get some shut-eye now, as I have a big day ahead of me tomorrow. It looked like Canada would have to wait again.

Day 112 – January 18, 2093

9:15 am

I just finished a breakfast of fried potatoes with onions. Robot girlfriends didn't care if you have onion breath.

As I could not find PVC glue, we used duct tape to fasten the greenhouse pipes and plastic sheets together. Lots of duct tape. If we got hit by a hurricane, the damn thing would blow away like a giant kite, but we would take that chance until I found a way to secure her to the ground.

How did they keep mobile homes from flying off during typhoons? I needed to take a close look underneath one soon.

12:30 pm

Whoa! I just took a ride across our overgrown lawn just now. I bent one of the big white PVC pipes over and it catapulted me several yards. I landed on my back and it knocked the wind straight out of me. After I realized I was okay, I laughed but it was pretty scary when it happened.

Komaki made me a veggie sandwich with lettuce, tomato, onion, and mayonnaise. She whipped up some oil with salt and lemon. It was good mayo despite the lack of

milk or egg. Her whole wheat bread was good too. Little by little, things become more comfortable. Life was more livable. I missed Beau though.

3:45 pm

The frame was finished. Now we will stretch the plastic over it and seal it up tight. The frame took longer than I had anticipated, but we would still finish this bastard by tonight.

I'd been saving seeds from citrus fruits and we would experiment with planting peanuts, rice, and wheat to see what grew.

10:00 pm

The greenhouse was done. Now we began planting to test what we could grow during this cold time of the year. We went to find good soil from our neighbors' yards. We obtained watering cans and gardening tools for working in what I'd dubbed: "The Plastic Pentagon." We also grabbed some space heaters and put them in there to warm every corner. I needed another solar power source.

When it was finished, Komaki looked at me, and said, "It is a very functional greenhouse, Brandon." That was as good a compliment as I could expect for it—We had one now. Another amenity added to our survival camp.

Day 113 – January 19, 2093

7:30 am

I was up early today. I dug up the earth on the left side of the greenhouse to prepare for our garden. A good farmer always rotated his crop. I read that in the Farmer's Almanac when I was creating some human fertilizer.

As this was an indoor affair, Komaki and I probably had to transport some fresh soil into the greenhouse next year and every year after but we were good for now.

Ate some canned fruit for breakfast—peaches and pears. I needed to get Komaki on finding some cinnamon. That would complement the apples and pears nicely when we put them in the glass jars. Next year, we may process a little sugar from sugar cane as well.

11:00 am

The land had been "tilled" or "turned" if you preferred. I sprinkled it at one end with some wheat and rice grains. I planted a section of peanuts in the middle and citrus seeds at the other end. I saved one little space for the dried-up seeds I'd gotten from the hospital. Hey, you never knew when a little green relaxant might come in handy, especially in this mixed-up scenario. I took the second generator from the med house to keep it warm in there.

2:15 pm

We finished the greenhouse just in time. It started to snow again. Lightly, but kind of weird timing, almost like a divine "Mind your P's and Q's, Hoffner, Because I'm Still in Charge" kind of message. I gave a knowing nod to the clouds.

Komaki cleaned house today. I didn't have to tell her to do it. A robot with initiative: I liked that.

For shits and giggles, I asked her, "What made you clean the house?"

She stared blankly for a minute, almost as if to say, "Brandon, you did not want me to clean house?" But she replied, "Brandon, it has been a week since we last cleaned this house and I had nothing else to do, so I thought it should be done."

As I mentioned before, she was a learning robot. I was so grateful to have her. She kept me together. She was my better half.

10:30 pm

I was tired. I turned in early tonight. I'd spent most of the evening reading about horticulture. Fascinating stuff (being facetious here.)

I admit at this point I was getting a bit stir-crazy. Since I had been re-animated, every day had been an adrenaline rush of sorts. The question was: What would I do tomorrow to get my fix?

Day 114 – January 20, 2093

9:00 am

I decided to raid another bank or two today. I hadn't done that in a while, especially in my own zone. There were many banks in Atlanta. Perhaps I would make a new map-chart and cross them off as I pillaged, just like with the malls and department stores.

6:15 pm

We raided three banks today, but we didn't turn up much of anything. We did score a few back-up drives and an iPad touch computer pad.

Komaki made dinner now. It smelt like soy bean hash or maybe fried rice without the egg. She has become quite the vegetarian chef.

8:00 pm

Komaki informed me that one of the backup drives we'd found contained thousands of digitized movies on it. The eight-terabyte drive contained everything from Rated G to Rated XXX, containing classics and movies made up to 2030. Komaki hooked it into her movie player which had a USB port on it and enjoyed loads of input. It kept her occupied on the bad weather days.

Day 116 – January 22nd

9:00 am

When I woke up, Komaki was still watching movies. She liked musicals but was obviously confused by the people stop everything and start singing. She watched "My Fair Lady," which she said she enjoyed as much as "The Sound of Music." She also watched "West Side Story," which she liked up until the ending. She felt like the two lovers should have run away together, so they could be together always. "The people around them kept them apart when they obviously wanted to be together." Out of the mouths of young machines, came gems.

She really liked "Grease," though she asked me why they'd named the movie this title. I had to explain that, in that time, people who considered themselves cool wore grease in their hair. Her response was, "That is why the boys' hair looked shiny." I nodded. She then asked me, "Why would they put grease in their hair if they were cold? Does it warm their heads?" I had to explain to her that "cool" was also a word for being "hip," "trendy," and "popular." She looked confused for a second, then remembered the song at the beginning of "West Side Story" about being cool. "Now that makes better sense to me, Brandon. Thank you."

It froze out there yesterday and today, so we were cooped up here again. Robots did not get cabin fever, especially when they had movies to watch. I, on the other hand, didn't like to stay in the house for too long. I ventured out in the E-RV later and further inspected what was in the surrounding neighborhoods.

11:00 pm

I slept off my hangover today. My thoughts were back together now because it was actually the next day, but I will relate to you what I can remember. I kept telling myself not to go into churches and see the twisted bodies. I'd been turning a blind eye to it. It was all around me. I knew it wasn't sanitary, but if I tried to bury everyone, it would've taken me the rest of my life, so I just left 'em where they lay. That made me the caretaker.

Anyway, I found a bar in the afternoon at around two-ish and drank a little Jack Daniels—straight up—in a dirty glass. I toasted to the many dead, to the world that might have been and to my success. After toasting a whole bottle's worth, I passed out.

I woke up around eight-thirty and made my way back home. I ran into a few things along the way, denting my front bumper and passenger side fender a bit. Shit happens.

When I got home, I told Komaki I wanted to fuck. Being a good robot companion, she reciprocated. I apologized this morning, which did not make up for it.

Day 117 – January 23rd

10:20 am

Komaki had been watching movies on her media player for days now. She told me she watched them at fast speed so she could watch more movies in a sitting. She said they played in regular speed in her mind. She processed the images and sounds faster than humans could.

She watched several movies last night after our debacle and told me she'd watched "My Fair Lady" again because she really liked the story. She saw me as her Henry Higgins and she was the robot girl who wanted to be a genteel lady. Or maybe she just liked Audrey Hepburn. Hell, I didn't know what went on in that computerized brain of hers.

Speaking of brain matter, my head was surprisingly okay today. My ears rang a bit. I kept telling myself to apologize to Komaki again, but that kind of sentiment was wasted on her. Her heart was filled with gears and rotor wheels. I did feel ashamed of myself for my little bender the other night, but I was more ashamed for the way I'd acted when I came home. I knew it didn't justify it, but the fact that I did feel bad should've accounted for something. Many would've just said, "She's a robot. She doesn't have feelings. She was built for fucking!" But having been through so much with her, she seemed as real to me as any flesh and blood companion I'd ever had. She might have been manufactured, but to me she had a soul and I couldn't deny I owed her a lot. I owed her my life.

The weather was bad again today so I would stay home and watch movies with her. She liked it when I watched them with her, because she could clarify things she might not fully understand. Americans spoke with lots of street lingo and idioms. It was very confusing to robots, like foreign students starting to learn English.

3:00 pm

My guilt got the better of me. In the middle of watching the movie "Titanic" with her (very long at any speed,) I told her I was sorry again for the way I'd behaved. She told me again, as she had done many times, "You do not have to apologize to me, Brandon. I am a robot and I am your servant." I stopped her and took her cold hand, making it warm in mine.

"No," I said. "You are much more to me than that." I looked her straight in her expressionless eyes and confessed to her sincerely, "I would not be where I am now if it wasn't for you. I owe you my life and I owe you my respect." She blinked, not saying anything. "I couldn't ask for a better companion, Komaki. You and I are soulmates now."

She replied, "I am fine, Brandon. As long as you protect me and do not try to hurt me, we will be together."

She never ceased to amaze me with how she answered me when I brought such things up. Again, her response was logical, precise, and surprisingly very human. Like any living creature, the first instinct learned was self-preservation. If I had attempted to hurt her last night in my drunken stupor, she would have not hit back. She was programmed not to harm any living thing.

She probably would have stopped me, then made an exit to avoid more unpleasantness and remove herself from potential danger. I had to always remember this. I could not repeat my mistake from last night.

Without a moment of hesitation, she turned her head and continued watching the movie. She liked movies where there was romance, and the romance was kind of weird or forbidden. What girl didn't like "Romeo and Juliet" (The Zeffirelli / Whiting / Hussey version. No other's come close) or "Splash." A mermaid falls for a tall, young man? Komaki liked it. It was different.

Though not one of my personal favorites, I sought out and found the movie "Mannequin" with Andrew McCarthy and Kim Cattrall. She liked that one, too. After a quick dinner, we watched "Bladerunner" with Harrison Ford, Sean Young, and Rutger Hauer. She was obviously enthralled throughout but made little comment after. She said, "The robot leader, named Batty, was very handsome."

Now I had nothing to be insecure about in my current situation and yet I was a bit jealous. "Is that what you like?" I said it playfully... mockingly...

She looked at me with a curious tilt to her head. "It does not matter what I find attractive, Brandon." I'd been halfway joking when I opened this up for discussion, but this response floored me. "I am programmed to be your companion and do everything that I can to satisfy you." There was a pregnant pause you could have driven a truck through. "So there is no need to worry."

I looked at Komaki for the longest time. If a robot could look uneasy, I saw it at that moment. She broke the long silence by saying, "Brandon, are you okay? You are very quiet."

I spoke up immediately. "What if I were to program you not to belong to anybody?" I wasn't exactly sure where I was going to end up going with this. She looked at me coldly.

"I am not sure, Brandon. I may just serve anyone I come in contact with or I may cease to function as my current programming dictates I must belong to someone."

Not so long ago, we had discussed the possibility of bad robots and my feeling was that was probably how it all started. The robot lost its programming, then started following the decisions of other rogue robots, sort of a mechanized peer pressure kind of thing. Being the confirmed male chauvinist pig that I was, I chose to "let sleeping dogs lie," and keep her registered to me.

11:45 pm

I had to admit, watching old movies all afternoon and night was fun. I picked flicks with robot characters and themes to give us ideas, help us get a bearing on our relationship or just amuse my humanoid counterpart.

We watched Tim Burton's "Edward Scissorhands" with Johnny Depp and Wynona Ryder. I'd always had a thing for Winona Ryder, even after she got caught swiping clothes and went through a dry period in her career. I forgave her early on and was happy when she made her grand comeback in "Stranger Things." There was another young actress who started out playing Goth teens that turned me on: Christina Ricci. Yeah, I'd often fantasized about being with both of them. Ah, sweet puberty.

After "Edward Scissorhands," I noticed another movie on the list was called "Edward Penishands." It was a pornographic knock-off and I decided to plug it in for laughs. Komaki was enthralled by the sex scenes, but the parody of what we had just seen had me in hysterics.

One actress in the film named "Trinity Lauren" was very well-endowed with huge bosoms. Komaki asked me, "How can a woman have such a big chest?"

I told her many actresses in porn films bought big synthetic boobs, but that Trinity was just naturally healthy.

"Do you like that?" Komaki asked.

I was amused by my android's titty envy.

Day 118 – January 24th

9:45 am

Lasts night's movie session ended with a nice round of lovemaking. Komaki wasn't excited by watching the porn. Robots didn't get horny. She just wanted to try things she saw them doing in the movie. I was tired but I re-gathered my strength for it. My robot girl excited me. We were like newlyweds. I hoped the sex didn't get stale soon.

Weather was nominal today: cold but not freezing. I couldn't really complain. We would try and do some errands. Komaki foraged for elements and chemicals and I checked more banks or local department stores, looking for hardware or other goodies.

I went over to our greenhouse, which I'd neglected to tell you was located behind the med house and I was very happy to report I saw little sprigs of green in our citrus section and (drum roll, please!) in our medicinal relaxant section. Nothing yet in the grain section. I did remember rice needed to be in a wetter soil, so I watered down that area really good and did so every day. I was just very happy my greenhouse produced.

Komaki cleaned the lab house now. We hadn't been in there in a couple of days and we needed to keep it spic and span for experiments and emergencies.

11:00 am

Whilst roaming the grounds, I decided to pay my respects to Beau. I missed my dog. The lack of animal activity was disturbing. It did play on my mind. No birds fluttering about, no insects buzzing around, no crickets chirping at night. It was just real damn quiet. I would 've even been happy to see Myra the cat at this point. We hadn't even seen or heard from her in quite a while.

Part of me was still afraid of what might've been out there. The roaches and leeches had proven that bad things, dangerous things, could survive, even thrive from the fallout.

7:00 pm

I walked down to the Sam's Club down on John Smoltz Avenue. Smoltz was a hell of a pitcher back in the day. I'd idolized the guy growing up. I actually met him at a couple of card shows. He was very down-to-earth. I never had a street named after me. I wasn't one of those guys who soaked up the limelight and hobnobbed with the socialites. I'd just wanted to play pro ball.

Not schmoozing and Smoltzing really hurt me later when I jumped into the business world with my sports clothing stores. If I'd had a few more socialite friends with influence to help me along, my business would have been stronger and made more money. Not that I did badly—quite the contrary. But I didn't make the profits I had hoped for. I wondered what happened to my business after my brother got ahold of it? Oh, good God!

Don't get me wrong here. I loved my brother very dearly, but he wasn't the brightest bulb on the Christmas tree. He always had some hairbrained scheme for making money, which always ended up costing our family money. We fought often because he hated the fact I'd made a success of my life by playing ball. I was the dreamer, and he was the guy working his ass off all day long and breaking even on good days.

Man, did I digress down memory lane or what? That all started with a nod to Johnny Smoltz. Anyway, once inside Sam Walton's world, I thought it would be a standard dusty and deserted department store like all the others. But I was in for another shock.

All the merchandise had been carefully stacked in a huge pyramid at the center of the store. It was one of the creepiest things I'd seen since my revival and that was saying a lot at this point. The place had a more stale and moldy smell to it than most. I decided (against my better judgment) to try and climb the pyramid to see what was at the top. I wasn't going to turn a blind eye this time.

As I made my way slowly up the pile of Walmart goods with their dollar amount and ninety-seven cent price tags, a horrible dread came over me. I debated with myself about finishing the climb. I slipped a couple of times, sending smaller items tumbling downward. Whoever had orchestrated the pyramid was clever. They layered merchandise boxes and clothes together, making the pyramid more stable. It must have taken days, if not weeks.

When I reached the top, I found dozens of twisted bodies huddled around a central figure. Just from the positioning I could tell that this person (a male based on the size of its skeleton) had rallied

THE BACHELOR'S GUIDE TO POST-APOCALYPTIC SUCCESS

these people around him in the end with some bizarre kind of ritual. Whether he conned them into following him, or maybe he'd been chosen by the group for being the smartest or the strongest. Whatever the reason, he ended up on the thrown of small appliance boxes at the top of the pyramid while the others bowed down around him.

Though the skeletons were covered in that all too familiar beef jerky kind of tissue with purple and black muscles covered in burgundy-colored, dried skin tissue, and they came in all shapes and sizes, there was something about them that made me sadder than the others I had seen. What brought them to here? My bet was the churches and hospitals were all full. They had everything they needed here, or so they thought. They obviously did not have protection from the fallout. Like Dr. Swales said, "Everybody was bound to die." This guru was their last hope, but they should have known it was folly. They didn't have a prayer. The cadaverous leader was sitting there mighty on his thrown. They all looked like they were smiling when no lips to cover the teeth, but this guy really looked like he was smiling. Not just an ordinary skeleton smile, but a Joker from Gotham City kind of smile. He was really proud of himself. Another Jim Jones or David Koresh. Who was that other whack-job that convinced a small group of people that an alien ship was coming for them? I couldn't think of him. That was so long ago.

I couldn't take any merchandise from this final resting place. It was just too icky- feeling. Like grave robbing or desecrating an Indian burial site. I left empty handed—the story of my life.

11:00 pm

I left food out for Myra the cat again. I did not tell Komaki about the little blue-light special shrine I'd found today. There was no point in it. She would've just asked me a lot of questions and I wanted to put it behind me. I wondered what living around all of these unburied cadavers was doing for me health-wise. It was not a good thing.

I thought it might be a better idea to grab a mobile home and move out to the country. The greenery on all sides of us was fertilized by the innocent dead but all disease was scorched away by high intensity radioactive heat in mere seconds. Every time I went into a place with dead bodies, I was probably taking a huge health risk. Even though there were no apparent rodents or insects aiding in the spread of disease, I was most likely inhaling God-knew-what as far as bacteria went. It was a valid concern — a new worry.

People lived in the city with smog and dirt all around them, knowing it was shortening their lives, but I couldn't think that way. I was the goddamn savior of mankind. I was the guy who was going to bring back the human race.

There was something to be said about the amenities of the city. Goods were in the city. Modern conveniences made life easier (and I was lazy). A move of that magnitude, which would include finding or building a ranch out in the country, would be a very strenuous and time consuming project (and, as I keep stating: I am no spring chicken). Even with a robot assistant, it would be a massive task.

I was getting ahead of myself here. My paranoia got the better of me. This was something for later. We needed to stay focused on the latest projects at hand: searching and cloning.

Until that day came, I would try to stay out of creepy unknown places and/or at the very least, wear a protective mask over my mouth and nose when I did have to go around these places. The Coronavirus of 2020 had taught us that.

Day 119 – January 25th

10 pm

We stayed in the Hyatt Regency in Toronto. I don't know why I just told you that. It's not like you would come looking for us. Maybe it was my way of telling you that Toronto was still here...well, some of it. A shockwave from an American blast had devastated a lot of it. We found a phonebook in the hotel and Komaki found a cryo-center which we'd pinpointed on a map we brought with us.

Today, we spent most of the day getting here. We did have time to hit a bank we saw. Not much in the safety deposit boxes: So much money, gold and jewelry — in a world where it meant nothing. Nice to look at (mmm shiny!), but again, no help to us at all in our situation.

Found a weird scene in the vault. Several people evidently had packed food, water, and bottled air in there and tried to survive for a few weeks. A few weeks were undoubtedly all they had bought for themselves. I was sure it was hardly worth the effort, just prolonged the agony. The grim-looking carcasses all but confirmed this.

I had found that bomb shelter not long ago, but seriously, how long could you last in a hole like that? Especially with radiation all around. It just didn't make much sense if you really thought about it.

Day 120 – January 26th

10 pm

We had a situation. Her name was Katherine Meagan Powell. We found her in the Toronto Centre for Cryogenics, and she appeared to be the only human survivor here. We had here almost exactly the same circumstances as my situation in the Atlanta center. The only difference was that Katherine Megan Powell was not just in hibernation, she was in hibernation and a coma. From what I saw, she was a stunningly beautiful woman, a supermodel/actress type who had gone to sleep with a brain tumor and was waiting for someone to thaw her out and successfully remove the unwelcome growth.

Obviously, we were not equipped to deal with Ms. Powell's problem just yet, but her cryo-unit flashed critical like Ms. Giles back home. If we left her, she wouldn't last long. Maybe a few days. Maybe a few weeks.

As I could not in good conscience do that, here was our rescue plan. Komaki and I had flown back to Atlanta and she now fashioned a similar cryo-battery that would keep charged for a day or so, so we could move the Toronto cryo-unit of Ms. Katherine Megan Powell to Atlanta via the helicopter. Here we could rig it up next to Ms. Giles and monitor her regularly. Ms. Giles would appreciate the company and Ms. Powell would remain resting serenely.

Day 122 – January 28th

10:30 pm

Over forty-eight hours after my last entry, I finally got a moment to write. We transferred the frozen body and icebox of Ms. Katherine M. Powell to our cryo-facility here in Atlanta. She was now in the same room with Ms. Constance Giles and Komaki rigged her unit with a renewable power source. Like Ms. Giles, her unit could hold a charge for about three to four days.

But that was not all. We found another robot in Toronto. While Komaki secured the cryo-chamber in the back of Fatboy, I made a side trip to check for supplies and spotted a robotics center. I went inside, looked around a bit, and there he was—the cutest little, half-pint droid you ever saw. He stood on a platform and for a minute I thought he might just be a statue—window dressing for the place. When I got closer and inspected, he proved to have some innards. The name on his chest plate read: "GIL-BOT," but I named him "Gilbert."

Now, as far as design went, Komaki had this boy beat, hands down. He looked like all the robots I remembered from the movies of my childhood. Movies like "Silent Running," "Star Wars," "The Black Hole," and "Runaway." Komaki did her best to get him going again, but his chips were probably fried by EMP.

Day 125 – January 31st

11:00 am

It had been cold out and snowing heavily the last couple of days. I got a little stir crazy. I had trouble sleeping now, so I had Komaki make me some medicine to help me sleep.

Komaki got Gilbert running. She reworked him using a microchip from one of the back-up drives we had confiscated. She had to reprogram him completely, but she was able to do it. As a robot, he was functionally very simplistic compared to Komaki. I said it before, she spoiled me. When he talked, it sounded very slow and digital. His vocabulary phrases were limited ("I am Gil-Bot. How are you today?") He rolled around slowly, but he could grab things, he could play games, and he could clean.

I asked Komaki jokingly, "Can we teach him to recharge and run the generators?"

She said, "I can teach him to do these things, Brandon." I was sure I frowned because the joke was lost. She quickly followed up with, "We desperately need to find other rechargeable generators because we need one for Ms. Powell and for Gil-Bot."

I was embarrassed because, as usual, she was right as rain, and I could have been doing that this past couple of days. Sometimes, I was a little slow on the uptake.

I was sure more were out there somewhere, and this was the Deep South where men liked their machines (tractors! trucks! turbo back-up generators!) so I would try to find them, preferably today. Again, I liked my castle here, but I got cabin fever. What started as a joke was now my newest quest. I would bypass the usual spots we raided close by us and see what else I saw out there.

10:30 pm

I brought back some dandy, new efficient solar back-up generators. They were bigger than our older models with bigger panels. The enclosed literature said they could run lights and heat for up to six days on a single charge. Why that was just amazing.

Komaki continued to work with Gilbert to get him to do things around the house. They were playing dress up when I finished checking the generators. She now wore a particularly sexy, red, prostitute number held together with brass rings on the side. This with black fishnets, garter belts, and a blond wig were just the ticket to get master aroused. I took her to my room. Gilbert tried to follow (as Komaki was like his mother now), but I told him to stay. I locked our bedroom door.

In the midst of a fantastic lovemaking session, Gilbert (the little fucker) picked the lock on my door and barged in on us. We would teach him not to do that in the future.

Day 126 – February 1st

11:30 pm

Komaki made me a paste I could eat that would help me sleep. I just had to be careful not to eat too much at once. She made quite a bit and filled two mason jars with the stuff and kept it in the lab house. The taste was horrible, but I hoped it would put me out good tonight.

Some nights I just lied awake thinking about things. It was like I couldn't slow down and stop thinking, you know? A couple of nights, I heard Myra fucking wailing out in the cold. I sometimes wished the last cat on earth was a grease spot on my back lawn. I was not embarrassed to admit the thought of greeting the little freeze-dried bastard by whacking her with a large shovel had popped into my head many times and I welcomed it, even relished it.

While we were in the lab, Komaki brought up an interesting point. If we could revive Katherine Powell, we could clone her by using her as her own host. She would be the perfect host for her clone actually. The thought threw me a bit at first, but it made damned good sense.

Komaki began the preparations for the cloning. According to her, we should have an excellent chance of a success with the combined research notes of our scientists from Korea.

Day 127 – February 2nd

10:00 pm

Komaki's herbal sleep aid worked very well. I didn't get up until after 10 this morning. No snow today, so we decided to take Gilbert to the cryo-center to meet Ms. Giles and Ms. Powell. When we got inside the building, I realized Gilbert was not equipped to handle stairs,… or so I thought. Gilbert's tire treads actually allowed him to ascend stairs, albeit slowly, one step at a time, but he could do it, going up like a reverse slinky.

Komaki showed him how to recharge the generators. Their rewired panels were outside the building, thanks to some robot ingenuity by my girl. She also showed him how to recharge himself and how to recharge the cryo-chamber battery units. He would recharge the two generators by day and recharge himself and the batteries by night. Gilbert was now security and maintenance for Ms. Giles and Ms. Powell. Komaki, and I did not have to come here every three days. This also meant we could leave the girls for longer stretches of time. Gilbert understood and did the job as directed. With Gilbert on duty, we could go off for weeks instead of days at a time.

I wondered how long it would take us to cross the Atlantic to Europe. But I was getting ahead of myself again. We had lots of ground to still cover right here in the USA.

Komaki opened Ms. Katherine Megan Powell's chamber. There was the familiar hiss of the expelling air when the windowed doorway opened upward. Then the cold blast of air as the ice steam dissipated, then we could clearly see the body of Katherine Powell. Even in her current frozen state, she was stunning. I was taken aback at how beautiful she was. I could well understand why her lover had wanted her frozen. I thought to myself, "Katherine, our kids are going to be beautiful."

As Komaki took samples of skin tissue along with some frozen blood for tests, I had to admit I was very excited. Like a child promised a special toy, and now I was about to get it. We were now one step closer to our goal of cloning a human to help repopulate the planet.

Though I knew she was frozen, it still looked like her skin got goose bumps when Komaki clipped some icy, epidermis tissue from her upper left arm.

The samples were taken fast and her chamber re-sealed to prevent any damage to her. I watched the door close over her again, wishing there was some way to revive her: make her my apocalyptic bride.

In a normal world, we would ask, "Why clone? Why not just procreate?" But this situation was unique. It was weird, but it was what it was.

Now, before you get all panty-twisted here and start judging me for my fickleness, let me remind you that Komaki was a loyal and lovely woman who happened to be made of plastic, rubber, and steel.

I had all but sworn my undying love to my Japanese robot companion for saving my life and aiding me in reshaping the modern world, but she could never love me back. She could not produce children either and that was two big strikes against her.

Call me a chauvinist if you like. Call me what you will, but remember you were not there in my situation, so you could not possibly understand the shit I was going through. On one hand I had a totally loyal and hardworking companion, skilled and talented but with no capacity to feel.

On the other hand, I had a beautiful flesh and blood maiden who could possibly help me to breed and repopulate the planet, thus saving the species of man from extinction. It was a no brainer in my opinion, and I thought Komaki would agree with me. If a living female was found, she must help me procreate for the sake of mankind. And, yes, some would say, "Now that is convenient, isn't it?"

This did not mean I would shun my robot companion or cease to take care of her. Why am I explaining this to you? Christ! I'm talking to myself here.

Day 128 – February 3rd

9:00 am

I was a little embarrassed with my last entry. I contemplated ripping that page out of the journal. Maybe this one too. It was obvious I was having guilty feelings about two-timing Komaki for the sake of spawning humankind.

That was ludicrous, I knew but we had been through a lot together. I could not deny that. She had always been there for me, even saved my life. In bad times, she always came through with a good idea or plan.

Katherine was in a coma and in cryo-freeze as well. Chances were we would only use her to clone anyway. So for the time being, Komaki and I were still lovers and close friends.

But you must understand that I did have to think about saving mankind. My main mission since I'd been reanimated had always been to procreate here. That had to come first.

Komaki did not have an ego to bruise. Her pride did not get the better of her. She wouldn't cry and rust if I told her I had another girlfriend. Robots didn't get jealous.

11:00 pm

Komaki was busy today in the lab, so I took the E-RV out to Taggart Springs to see if there were any freshwater fish out there. You might remember this spot from three months back. It was where I'd found freshwater on my first week here.

I packed my fishing poles and gear and headed out about eleven-thirty in the morning. It didn't take me long to find it again. It was just as I had left it.

I dropped my line in the water and waited a short while. There was nothing for a long moment though the tension built in me, then I saw them. The familiar dark patches coming out from beneath the roots of the trees opposite of where I was stationed, then moving slowly along the clear water towards me. I had seen them in Louisiana and I half- expected to see them here today. My fear was confirmed. I spun my line up quickly as the large leeches moved steadily my way.

I watched them, like a train wreck, not able to turn away immediately. They slowly and systematically crawled their way up the banks and onto the grass near where I was. I turned and grabbed my tackle box, and in doing so, my truck keys fell out of my shirt pocket, bounced forward off my boot, and landed in the water.

"Fuck!" I yelled out loud and purposefully. This was not good. Not good at all. I stepped back because the slimy bastards were getting closer to my feet. I tried to come up with a plan. Maybe I could quickly fish out my keys from the water. Dozens of greenish- brown leeches were centimeters away from my ankles. I actually stomped on one, causing it to turn up at the edges and squeak. This totally grossed me out, causing me to panic and run, not far but putting enough space between me and the bloodsuckers to give me some comfort.

"Shit!" I said, defeated.

I walked up the dirt road back to the paved road about a mile away and waited for a couple of hours. I figured my presence — smell or whatever had attracted them — would be gone by then. They would go off back to where they came from and I could return and retrieve my keys before they could sense me again.

I went back later, and the damn things were still out of the water and had surrounded the truck. There were hundreds of them on the grass. How fucked up was that? There was nothing I could do. I turned and made my second exit of the day from Taggart Springs.

It took me over five hours to walk home. With no keys, what other choice did I have? Next time I went freshwater fishing, I would bring a few big bags of salt and have some fun pouring it on these nuisances and watch them shrivel up and die.

Day 130 – February 5th

After 12:00 midnight

Another fucked up day for me. I seemed to be having a lot of them lately.

I had to go out and find a new (new?) electric truck today because of my little, ill-fated fishing trip and hike yesterday. I still couldn't figure out how those slimy sons-a-bitches could sense when people (or any other creatures/mobile sources of food) got near.

I didn't even see Komaki this morning. The lights in the lab house were on. I didn't bother her. I had not told her about the E-RV yet.

At about ten this morning I took the scooter out. I rode around until I found a suitable truck, then looked around for the keys. It took me a couple of hours to figure out the dumbass had put them in the visor of the unlocked vehicle. So, in the end, who was the real dumbass?

Before I found the keys, I went into the guy's home to search and found my latest wondrous corpse tableau. It smelled musty and I cursed myself for forgetting to bring a mask with me—again.

There were four of them lying on the sofa and chair set in the living room. From their styles of clothes, it looked like two teens and a set of middle-aged parents. The most disturbing thing was they were all missing a substantial portion of their heads. The shotgun on the floor between the sofa and the T.V. told the whole story.

As they froze and suffered from radiation poisoning, the father put them out of their misery with his twelve-gauge Mossberg. When the deed was done, he'd sucked on the barrel himself and the whole nightmare was over in an instant. No more suffering.

Goddamn it all to hell! Was there no end to the bizarre and unjust shit I was going to have to see here? Don't go into houses! Don't go into fucking houses!!! It was like twelve hours later and the vision of the headless family was still very fresh in mind. I would never forget that sight until my dying day.

After that, I understandably skipped getting myself something to eat. I got the truck working and decided to peruse a nearby bank for anything useful. There was a big bank on Foxworthy Avenue I wanted to check out.

I remembered when celebrity Jeff Foxworthy became the Governor of Georgia. It was as surprising as when Arnold Schwarzenegger had won the post in California a few decades earlier. The funniest thing was Foxworthy turned out to be a great governor for Georgia. One of the best they had ever had. He understood the people and was attentive to their needs. He was not crooked like many before him.

The bank in question was locked. I smashed the front door, cutting my arm in the process. After bandaging my small cut with my wife-beater undershirt, I made my way around in an effort to find keys to the deposit box area.

Luckily, there was nobody in the bank. After some time, I found the keys and wasted the day finding nothing. The boxes contained papers, money, jewelry, movie collectibles, and even a gun. Yes, somehow someone got a pistol into the bank and into a safety deposit box. It was an old gun, like the kind of revolver you saw in old Western movies. It was probably a family heirloom. I pocketed it but, like everything else, I really had no use for it... another day older and deeper in emotional debt.

I made my way home. As I drove up to the homestead, I saw Komaki had just come out of the lab house.

Her first comment was, "Brandon, you are driving a truck."

I nodded and mumbled, "Yeah, long story."

As I got out of the truck, she noticed I had cut my arm. "You are injured. You should come to the medical station and let me clean that wound and bandage it properly.

In the lab house, she cleaned my arm up and re-bandaged it. She told me she was moving forward with her experiments, but things were going very slow. It would take some time to clone an actual fetus for our lovely host.

I was disappointed but her bad news was light compared to the day I had just had. I settled down to relax on the sofa at about seven and Komaki made me a dinner of vegetable soup and fried rice.

We were not officially getting low on supplies yet, but I went out again to fish and find whatever other edible food that I could rummage. The winter would make its way into spring within a few months' time. That meant possible showers and nominal weather conditions again. I wondered what summer was going to be like here and shuddered. I needed to find some lighter clothes. Maybe I would make some cut-offs and redneck muscle shirts.

I checked my greenhouse at around 10:30 pm and the greenery had grown a little higher now. That meant I might be getting a little higher soon myself: the only positive thing that had happened this week. After what I had witnessed today, a little weed would certainly take the edge off a bit.

I went to the country and I got huge leeches. I stayed in the city and I got horrific scenes of cadavers. Lord, please, let my luck spin around again. Give me a few good days.

Day 115 – January 20th

10:00 pm

Let me catch you up on what Komaki had been doing for the last few days. She worked day and night, testing and cloning Katherine's blood cells and skin cells. She said Katherine was very healthy - She was just in a coma – and frozen. So tomorrow we would thaw her out and attempt to restore her life functions. She would still be in a coma, which meant we would have to feed her intravenously for nine months while she played host to a clone of herself. When the procedure was over, we could put her back in cryo-suspension and everything would go back to normal. Well… the way it was.

There were a lot of things that could go wrong here. Katherine might not survive her cryo-revival. Do you remember my failure with the cat named Cyril? These cryo-suspension units were constructed to revive the subject through the life support tube, which went down your airway. They actually jolted you with an electric charge to get your heart pumping again and start feeding your lungs oxygen at the same time. This was something I did not know until after my failure with Cyril. We already had hospital machines standing by in her room at the cryo-center. Eventually, we would have to move her to the lab house. She would constantly be at the risk of infection because we had to feed her intravenously. But first thing was first: We needed to get her out of cryo-suspension and breathing again.

Day 116 – January 21st

8:00 am

We were up early today. Komaki said we must wait to revive Katherine. Komaki was still working on creating a clone fetus but evidently that might've taken several days or weeks to incubate before we could place it into our selected host.

The collective notes of the Korean cloning team, along with Claude Tourneau's notes, hadn't given us a definitive time set on this as they had never officially cloned a human being before. They had just cloned animals.

I told Komaki I understood and suggested we embark on another journey to check for other cities. She agreed this would be better than just staying home. It snowed again today, so we would prep everything this afternoon and fly to the west coast of Florida tomorrow, weather permitting. It was nearby, so we could get back sooner.

3:45 pm

I decided Komaki and I would take the news chopper this time out. I loaded her up. I placed the small motorcycle in the back of the cargo area where we ripped out the seats. My robot girlfriend sat up front with me, as usual. We carried enough food and water for two days. I could not see this particular trip taking any longer than that.

5:00 pm

Komaki and I went down to the cryo-center to check on Ms. Giles, Ms. Powell, and Gilbert. Everything seemed to be in order and Gilbert would keep the generators and batteries running.

Amazingly, Gilbert had cleaned the whole facility himself over the past week. He did not want to sit idle for any length of time, so he took some cleaning materials from the janitor's closets and the place looked normal again. He only kept the power on in the room where the two women hibernated. And he told Komaki and I that he did most of his work in the dark. He had turned out to be a very efficient, little guy.

While we were there, I looked in on Katherine. I could definitely get used to being around her. When I turned to exit, Komaki was right behind me. I almost walked right into her.

"You wish that Katherine Megan Powell was not in a coma, don't you, Brandon?" The words were flat—very matter-of-fact—with no hint of malice or jealousy. The suddenness of it still made me backpedal a bit.

I will be honest with you, reader. I could have easily lied here, and Komaki would have accepted it, but I said to her, "Yes, Komaki. I would like to have a living human companion." I didn't actually know where that came from or why I'd said it, but it was honest and sincere.

Komaki paused for what seemed like minutes. "You do realize that the probability of her coming out of her coma is very small."

I nodded and said, "I know."

Komaki did a strange thing then. She turned away from me as if she was trying to hide something. She paced a few steps away from me, closer to Gilbert. The moment was very awkward. Gilbert looked back and forth between the two of us, not knowing what to do. Finally, she turned back to me and her expression was typically expressionless.

"Brandon," she said coolly. "If we do succeed in reviving her, you will keep me and protect me, right?" Again, her instinct of self-preservation showed strongly. It was amazing to behold. Again, I answered sincerely.

"Komaki," I said tenderly, walking over to her so she could see I was telling the truth. "You are my friend. Of course, I will take care of you." And I very well meant it, too. If by some strange miracle, I did find a living breathing spouse, Komaki was too valuable to get rid of. She was too important to me and my survival. I followed up with, "I promise you we'll be together until the end." At hearing that she smiled.

Day 131 – February 6th

7:45 am

The weather outside totally defied the laws of nature today. The sun shone and it felt like spring outside. I was serious. Yesterday it had been frosting, but today there was a warm breeze in the air.

I had every reason to believe that all of Florida was re-cultivated real estate, but I felt we should check the gulf area around Tampa Bay, Clearwater, and St. Petersburg. We might even fly down as far as Sarasota if we did not come across ruins. If I didn't check these places, I would always wonder about it and it would drive me crazy.

9:00 pm

We were in St. Petersburg tonight. Actually, most of St. Petersburg was rubble. They'd caught the edge of a blast and most definitely the full effects of a shockwave. We stayed at the Sherman Inn across from the State Theater.

We raided a bank this afternoon but came up emptyhanded. This had been my luck lately. I couldn't even find a cool handgun this time.

There was a cryo-center here, but unfortunately it looked like it had collapsed. There was no way in that we could see.

Day 132 – February 7th

6:00 pm

There was a terrible storm today in the middle of the day at around one o'clock. Komaki is dead. This might be my last entry. I was injured badly and bleeding.

As the storm closed in, Komaki and I thought we could outrun it and fly the chopper to safety. The winds whipped us about, and we crashed the copter. Komaki was damaged but she could still talk and function. She helped free me from the crash.

The storm engulfed us, and it was bad. There was heavy rain and wind with lots of lightning. This was what did Komaki in. Because there were no tall trees in the area and I was lying low because of my injuries, Komaki attracted the bolts from the heavens like a living lightning rod. I couldn't get near her to save her. I lost count of how many hits she took from the Gods. I screamed and shouted. I cried and spat. She was gone. All of her synthetic skin had been burned away and her limbs were melted. Just a scorched torso and head remained. My companion…

My side was split open and it bled badly. I tied my shirt around the deep cut, but my shirt soaked up a lot of blood. I was still close to St. Pete, so I tried to walk back to there.

Day 133 – February 8th

Best guess – 12 noon

I am in a hotel room back in St. Pete. I've lost a lot of blood. I am very dizzy, cold, and tired. You may be wondering why I am still writing in this situation. If you were here and you had put so much into a journal—if you were at the point when there was no turning back and the fate of mankind was about to go down the toilet, well…

I pretty much resigned myself to the fact that this spot would be my final resting space. Even if I was not cut and bleeding, it would be near impossible for me to cross half of Florida and Georgia on foot to get back to my home.

The death of Komaki weighed heavily on me. She was a piece of machinery. Like wrecking a nice car, it should've just made me upset, but there was more to it than that. She was my companion, my friend, my better half, my lover. We had been through so much together. To lose her now realizing how much I needed her… how much I loved her… it has made me lose all hope.

If the Gods saw fit to take her—and for no good reason… then they could take me too. Fuck the future of man. I was not your champion anymore. You screwed up. Now you pay for it. I am taking this massive weight off my shoulders and I went to sleep like the rest of you. I tried and I failed.

I don't know what time it was. It was still light out.

I am dying. My bedsheet is red.

In time - Constance Giles would probably die.

Katherine Powell would most likely die, too.

Gilbert sustained them only if the sun was shining.

Only Myra the cat would survive.

It is weird - I feel high right now. Like drunk.

The room spinning - trying to write pages moving.

I heard an angel's voice calling out: "Are you there?"

I opened my mouth, but nothing came out.

I felt a tear roll down my face, finding its way to my ear canal.

This was the end.

Wait a minute.

Angels didn't need bullhorns...

THE
Bachelor's
GUIDE TO
Post-Apocalyptic
Dating

MONA FELTCHER NOTES:

The subjects name is Brandon Hoffner. We heard a crash from our boat and saw black smoke from the wreckage. We found his crashed helicopter and followed his trail to a building in Area 4B.

I have repaired and stitched his wound shut. He has lost a lot of blood, but he seems stable now.

He has written notes in a journal saying he was accidentally revived from cryogenic freeze. Though unbelievable, the notes throughout are succinct and show no overt signs of insanity.

"Brandon? Do you hear me?"

Subject is unresponsive for the time being. I am fascinated by his entries about cloning and notes of famous doctors who have successfully performed cloning tests. This might be what we have been waiting for.

"Komaki!"

Subject just called out the name of his robot companion. We have pulled her chassis from the wreckage area.

"Komaki,... I'm so sorry."

BRANDON HOFFNER NOTES:

"I can't believe he survived what he did." A different voice... softer, more pleasant. Like an angel.

"I say we take his journal and leave him here." The original voice again. Female, but harsh, cynical, demanding..."We can go up to Atlanta and find the cloning materials."

I opened my eyes, letting the light stream in. When I saw her for the first time, I realized she must have been the owner of the first voice. She was no angel. She had "bitch" written all over her face. Make that "ball busting bitch."

"He's coming around," she said. Did she just roll her eyes? "Next, we will have to feed him." Her tone was so full of meanness and dripping with sarcasm, I guessed she had never had a true friend...ever. It had been less than ten seconds and I totally hated this woman.

A gorgeous blond came into sight. Did I hear divine music playing? There was my angel. "Mr. Hoffner, you had a bad accident."

Okay,...she had stated the obvious, but she was still quite lovely. "Mona here stitched you up, but you need to rest. Give your body time to heal."

I bolted upright and felt a huge pain in my right side. "Komaki!" I yelled it out loud, realizing I'd overstepped by bounds. The blonde helped me lie back down on the bed. "Komaki," I said again. She was gone.

Comments? Questions? Found errors?

Please, reach out to me!

lee@palmcirclepress.net

Sign up for our mailing list at **palmcirclepress.net**

LEAVE A REVIEW

I would be extremely grateful if you could take just a minute to write a review on Amazon about this book. Even if the review is brief (2 or 3 sentences) that would be incredibly helpful. Recommending this book to a friend doesn't hurt either :)

Thank you and I love you!!!

Please visit Amazon to leave a review.

THE MOST BEAUTIFUL INSANITY

SOUTH BEACH CRIME THRILLER SERIES
BOOK ONE

HEATHER WILDE

HEATHER WILDE

SWEET DEMON LOVE BABY

SOUTH BEACH CRIME THRILLER SERIES

BOOK TWO

COMING DECEMBER 2020 FROM PALM CIRCLE PRESS

What if the person you loved wasn't who you thought they were?

Trace Strickland is a homicide detective with a sordid past whose career hangs in the balance. When his fiancé turns up dead from a knife wound in a South Miami Beach hotel, he becomes a suspect. Though he's forced to take a leave, he investigates her death to clear his name. In the process he discovers her prior involvement in an underworld of violence, sex trafficking, and other illicit dealings he knew nothing about. As he struggles to search for her killer and even who she really was, he must also come to terms with who he is himself, why he's a sucker for sinful women, and the lengths he'll go to find answers he would be better off not knowing. When Trace's partner turns up dead, shot down in cold blood with one of Trace's guns, the case turns more dangerous than ever. He begins to suspect the killer is someone he knows. Closely. But who?

To find out more, visit Amazon and PRE-ORDER!

The South Beach Crime Thriller Series is a collection of novels taking place in South Miami Beach, Florida. Exotic locations and luxurious living combine with hard-edged criminals, and even harder-edged good guys to make for some of the most gripping stories in modern crime fiction. Expect the unexpected on every page!

WHAT HAPPENED AT

SISTERS
CREEK

LEE ANDERSON

Made in the USA
Middletown, DE
19 March 2021

35837150R00146